ROBERT B. PARKER'S
HOT PROPERTY

THE SPENSER NOVELS

For a comprehensive title list and a preview of upcoming books,
visit PRH.com/RobertBParker or Facebook.com/RobertBParkerAuthor.

ROBERT B. PARKER'S
HOT PROPERTY

MIKE LUPICA

G. P. PUTNAM'S SONS
NEW YORK

PUTNAM
— EST. 1838 —

G. P. PUTNAM'S SONS
Publishers Since 1838
An imprint of Penguin Random House LLC
penguinrandomhouse.com

Hardcover ISBN: 9780593716137
Ebook ISBN: 9780593716144

Printed in the United States of America
1st Printing

BOOK DESIGN BY KATY RIEGEL

For Taylor McKelvy Lupica.

My one and only.

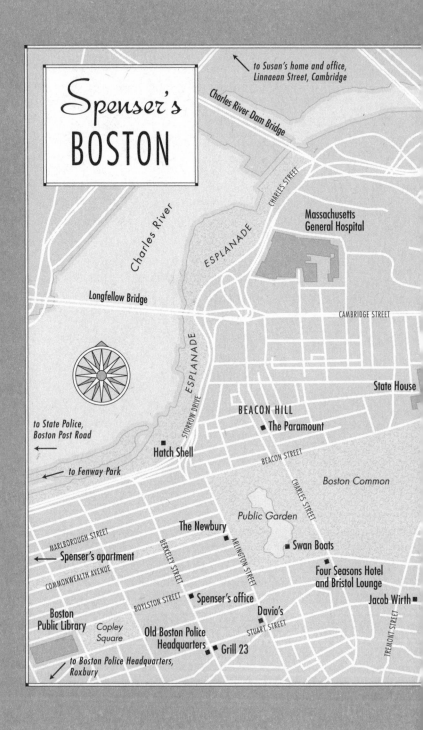

Spenser's BOSTON

to Susan's home and office, Linnaean Street, Cambridge

Charles River Dam Bridge

Charles River

CHARLES STREET

Massachusetts General Hospital

ESPLANADE

Longfellow Bridge

CAMBRIDGE STREET

ESPLANADE

STORROW DRIVE

State House

to State Police, Boston Post Road

BEACON HILL

The Paramount

Hatch Shell

BEACON STREET

Boston Common

to Fenway Park

CHARLES STREET

Public Garden

The Newbury

ARLINGTON STREET

Swan Boats

MARLBOROUGH STREET

BERKELEY STREET

Spenser's apartment

Four Seasons Hotel and Bristol Lounge

COMMONWEALTH AVENUE

Jacob Wirth

BOYLSTON STREET

Spenser's office

Davio's

Boston Public Library

Copley Square

Old Boston Police Headquarters

STUART STREET

Grill 23

TREMONT STREET

to Boston Police Headquarters, Roxbury

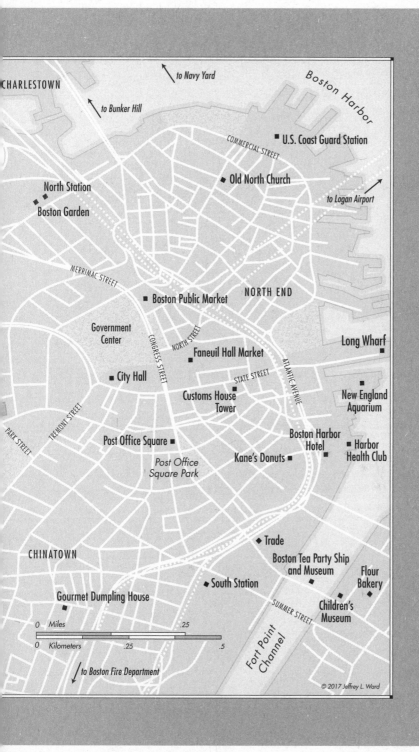

CHARLESTOWN

to Navy Yard

to Bunker Hill

Boston Harbor

COMMERCIAL STREET

■ U.S. Coast Guard Station

◆ Old North Church

North Station

Boston Garden

to Logan Airport

MERRIMAC STREET

■ Boston Public Market

NORTH END

Government
Center

CONGRESS STREET

NORTH STREET

■ Faneuil Hall Market

Long Wharf ■

STATE STREET

ATLANTIC AVENUE

■ City Hall

Customs House
Tower

New England
Aquarium

PARK STREET

TREMONT STREET

Post Office Square ■

Kane's Donuts ■

Boston Harbor
Hotel ■

■ Harbor
Health Club

Post Office
Square Park

◆ Trade

CHINATOWN

Boston Tea Party Ship
and Museum

Flour
Bakery ◆

■ South Station

Gourmet Dumpling House

SUMMER STREET

Children's
Museum

0   Miles   .25

0   Kilometers   .25   .5

*Fort Point
Channel*

to Boston Fire Department

© 2017 Jeffrey L. Ward

ROBERT B. PARKER'S
HOT PROPERTY

ONE

It was early February and snowing again in Boston. I felt as if it had been snowing since Thanksgiving. Or perhaps since the autumn equinox. The TV meteorologists, talking excitedly every night about more record snowfall numbers, and about ten more inches than we'd gotten ten years ago, continued to treat the whole thing like porn.

Hawk, being Hawk, had his own analysis of the city's current weather conditions, void of any statistics about dew points and barometric pressure.

"Climate change," he said, "has now officially worn my ass out."

"It took a winter like this to get you there?" I said.

"Been building up to it for a while," he said. "Feeling like I'm living at the damn North Pole finally took me over the edge."

I stared out my window at the latest storm, the snow blowing sideways across Boylston Street. The morning news shows had already announced another round of school closings. People were being advised to stay off the Pike and the expressway and take public transportation if possible. They were also telling nonessential workers to stay home. I imagined people all over the greater Boston area declaring themselves more essential than the pilot landing a plane at Logan.

I remembered a Carl Sandburg line about fog being on silent haunches over the harbor and the city before moving on. Maybe fog. The snow in Boston wouldn't move on, from the Harbor or anywhere else. They said there hadn't been snowfall like this in ten years in Boston. It had reached the point where just going for donuts had started to feel as if it ought to be one of those cross-country events in the Winter Olympics.

I made myself a second cup of my own coffee and continued reading *The Globe* at my desk. Despite the weather, they were still delivering the paper to my door most mornings, if a couple hours late sometimes. I knew I could just as easily read it online, that it was a generational thing to refuse to do so. But it was a personal choice, as was continuing to use a landline.

"I'm actually surprised that phone on your desk isn't a rotary," Susan Silverman once told me.

"Don't think I didn't consider that," I said. "You can get them for thirty-nine ninety-nine on Amazon. I checked."

"T-Mobile will never take you alive," she said.

"By the way," I said. "You know what never lost messages and texts like my iPhone One Thousand does? My old rotary phone."

Susan had smiled and said, "We really are going to need a much bigger complaints box."

I had the Sports section in front of me now, taking consolation in the fact that even with a new Ice Age upon us, pitchers and catchers would soon be reporting to the Red Sox spring training home in Fort Myers.

It meant that before too very long I would be experiencing the sight and sweet sound of line drives, on radio and TV, coming off the bat of Raffy Devers, our team's young star. It had taken some doing, but I had finally come to grips with the fact that Mookie Betts was never coming back to the Sox from the Dodgers.

I had now given my heart to another.

"They nearly added a fifth level of grief where you and Mookie were concerned," Susan had said the night before at dinner.

Hawk had been with us, at Sorellina on Huntington Ave.

"How many years is it now you been talking about one pint-sized baseball player getting traded like he was your first dog run away from home?" he said.

"It was a very painful breakup," I said.

"Not for him," Hawk said.

I had then broached the idea of Susan perhaps taking a trip with me to the west coast of Florida when the Sox commenced playing spring-training games.

"I'd rather just pay the ransom," she said.

"What if it hasn't stopped snowing by then?" I said.

"I'll just have to risk it," she said.

It had been an extremely slow winter for me professionally, so slow that I'd begun to wonder when the glowing job reports the president kept talking about were going to apply to me again.

The last investigation I'd worked had been for Rita Fiore, work for which I had refused payment.

Rita had ended a relationship with a lawyer from another firm right before Christmas, at which point he had not just been an extremely bad sport about it, but also threatened to release naked pictures of her as a form of retaliation.

"Stop me if you've heard this one," Rita said. "But I once again put my money on the wrong horse's ass."

"Boy," I said. "Who could have ever seen something like *that* coming?"

"Maybe the reason I keep making poor choices is because *you* continue to not choose me," Rita said.

"But I remain devoted to you in other meaningful ways," I said.

"Name one."

"Well, I always tell men who inquire about your availability that while they need to get in line, the good news is that the line moves," I said.

"Don't be mean," she said.

She told me that day that the pictures were just one of her concerns. She also believed the guy had begun stalking her. She'd waited too long, she said, to have the locks changed at her town house on Joy Street, and was certain he'd used his key to get inside on at least one occasion, possibly more than that. I asked if he'd taken anything. She said she didn't think he had; he had rearranged things just enough to let her know he'd been there. And, in the process, make her feel violated.

"Can you get him to stop?" she asked.

"You're in luck," I said. "As convincing men not to behave badly remains one of my specialties."

"I keep thinking that one of these days I might experience some of your other specialties if I catch you in a weak moment."

"I have no weak moments," I said. "Just a stubbornness that can never bear to be frightened at the will of others."

"Which tough guy said that?" she asked.

"Jane Austen," I said.

TWO

The lawyer's name was Donald Harrigan, he of Harrigan and Sons, a white-shoe Boston firm, whiter than the endless snow of the Boston winter, a firm I assumed had started locking in clients around the time when the *Mayflower* landed.

It had taken me only a few days of following him around to realize that he was indeed following Rita. I wasn't certain if he might be moving up on something more dangerous, and how much of a threat he actually posed, but I wasn't going to wait around to find out. Mostly what I wanted to uncover was how and where he had stored these pictures, and to make sure that at some point they didn't end up splashed all over social media from here to Nepal.

Eventually there came the Friday night after Rita had first called me about him, and Hawk and I were waiting for Donald Harrigan inside his own Beacon Hill town house when he arrived home from the office.

"What the fuck," he said.

"Not to make too fine a point of things, Donald," Hawk said, "but the one fucked here appears to be you."

"We are here to collect any and all, ah, compromising photographs of Rita Fiore," I said.

"I have no idea what you're talking about," he said.

There was still snow on the shoulders of his overcoat. He casually hung it on a rack near the front door.

When he turned back to us, Hawk had already moved across the room. He then effortlessly backhanded him across the face, the sound like the crack of a baseball bat, the force of the blow putting Donald Harrigan on his ass.

Hawk knelt next to him.

"Rita's my friend," he said softly. "Been a friend to my trusty sidekick here even longer than me. So what you're going to do, Donald, is go get those pictures of her off your phone or your laptop or your damn iPad or wherever the fuck you stored them away. You're going to get yourself up and do that lippity-lop, or the next time I hit you it will be hard enough to turn you into a Democrat."

Harrigan put his hand to his mouth, took it away, saw the blood on it.

"You can't just come into my house—"

Hawk reached toward him. Harrigan flinched. But all Hawk did was touch a finger to Harrigan's bloody lip.

"Shhhh," Hawk said. "Now, let's start with you handing over your phone."

"I'm not giving you my phone."

Hawk smiled, and shook his head sadly, and backhanded him again, putting him on his back this time.

7

While Harrigan was on the floor, now looking more than a little glassy-eyed, he fumbled inside the jacket of his pin-striped suit and handed Hawk the phone.

"Passcode," Hawk said.

Harrigan told him without hesitation. Hawk sat back down in the chair next to mine and began tapping away.

To me, Hawk said, "You delete pictures from this, dirty or otherwise, you delete it from all his devices."

"And you know this how?"

"Everybody except a Luddite like you knows," Hawk said.

"Yeah, well, at least I know what a Luddite is."

Harrigan was seated on his couch by then. Hawk walked over and handed the phone back to him.

"Where are the printed copies?" Hawk said.

"There aren't any."

"Sho' there are," Hawk said pleasantly.

He turned to me.

"I'm betting Donald here is an old-school perv," Hawk said.

"Agreed," I said.

"Just so you know," Harrigan said. "Rita wanted me to take those pictures of her."

I said, "And now you're going to give them back before I get some swings of my own in, Donald. And you need to know in advance that I hit harder than my friend."

"Do not," Hawk said.

"Do to," I said.

Harrigan looked at me, then back at Hawk. There was still blood on his lip that had spilled down to his chin.

"Wait here," he said.

"I think not," I said.

"Have it your way," he said.

We followed him up the stairs and into his bedroom and watched him take down a Monet print from the wall. There was a safe behind it. Harrigan worked the combination, opened the door, and came out with a manila envelope. Handed it wordlessly to me. Some of the photographs inside were in color, some in black-and-white.

Old-school prints, indeed.

"Is this all of them?" I asked.

"Yes," he said.

I handed the envelope to Hawk and grabbed Harrigan by the lapels of his jacket, pulling him close enough to me that I could smell his cologne.

"You need to understand the consequences of you lying to us about this," I said. "Because if you have lied, your life at that point will become vastly more difficult than it currently is. Are we clear on that? Nod if you understand what I just told you."

He nodded.

"And if you ever go near Rita Fiore or her home again, we will be back," I said.

We left then. When we were inside Hawk's new Jaguar, Hawk said, "Maybe I should hold on to the envelope, just for safekeeping."

"Because there might be something in those pictures you haven't already seen?"

"You got no way of knowing whether Rita and I acted on our mutual attraction or not," he said.

"More like something I intuited," I said.

"So what you gonna do with the pictures?"

"Make a fire when I get home," I said.

I could see him smiling as he noiselessly put the car in motion.

"Your loss," he said.

Rita had once again insisted on paying me when I told her what Hawk and I had done, and once again I refused.

"Just my luck," she said. "You still won't take yes for an answer."

Since then, I had steadfastly remained in the ranks of the unemployed. And like the snow, my winter of discontent showed no signs of ending anytime soon.

"Pretty sure you stole the discontent line," Susan said.

The snow outside came harder. They were predicting six more inches by the end of the day. I was already starting to think about how far I would be willing to walk in these conditions to get lunch when Martin Quirk called.

"Somebody shot Rita Fiore," he said.

THREE

I felt my chest constricting like a fist closing.

"Maybe a hit," Quirk added. "Maybe not. Too early to tell."

"Is she—"

He cut me off.

"No," he said, then told me where to meet him at the Critical Care Center, on Fruit Street.

"I'll be there as soon as I can get to my car," I said. "It's in back of my building and I may need to dig myself out."

"You're at your office?"

He'd called on my cell instead of the landline.

"Yeah."

"One of my cars will pick you up in five minutes," Quirk said.

I told him I'd be waiting downstairs and called Hawk. Then I did go downstairs to stand in the cold, feeling a much tighter fist around my heart as I waited for Quirk and considered the possibility that Rita Fiore might die.

I took great pride, and had from the time I had been raised by my father and my uncles and taught self-reliance almost as soon as they had taught me how to read, to be afraid only of things I could not control.

But I was afraid now.

QUIRK, FRANK BELSON, Hawk, and I were in the waiting area of the Mass General Trauma Center. It was part of Mass General, and part of the hospital's Gun Violence Unit, which helped with that kind of violence only after the fact.

"You know where she lives on Beacon Hill?" Quirk said to me.

"Joy Street."

"What are the odds, Rita ending up with an address like that?"

He said there had been a gym bag found next to her. I nodded.

"She works out at Beacon Hill Athletic," I said. "She was probably on her way there."

"Maybe a half-mile away from her house," Belson said. "On Friend."

"She took me with her there one time. Was a Rita thing, for her own amusement. Taking me. Her way of fucking with the tight asses," Hawk said.

The short trip from my office to the hospital in Quirk's car had felt like a bobsled run, even as slowly as the cop behind the wheel was trying to drive. And there had been a few detours because of some streets that hadn't been plowed. But we had made it, if not as soon as I wanted to.

She was still upstairs in surgery. Quirk, being Quirk, had just come back downstairs, even though he wasn't supposed to be upstairs. But it sounded as if he'd gotten close to the operating room.

Somehow he already knew that the bullet had missed Rita's heart and liver, but that there had been significant damage to her stomach and intestines. A lot of blood loss, almost too much to save her, in the snow. He said she was likely alive because a FedEx driver happened to come around the corner practically before she'd hit the ground, and had decided not to wait to call 911, making the decision to drive her straight to the emergency room himself.

"Turns out the guy is a former EMT," Quirk said, "and knew what he was doing."

The FedEx guy said he'd actually seen the shooter's gun still out the window of some kind of black SUV. As soon as he saw that, and Rita on the ground, he started blowing his horn like a madman, spooking the shooter enough that he didn't get off another shot, just gunned the SUV and headed in the other direction instead, his car nearly sliding into a snowbank.

"Second shot would probably have finished her," Quirk said. "Maybe been a head shot."

"Driver see anybody else in the SUV?" I asked.

Quirk said, "He didn't think so, but it all happened pretty freaking fast."

"Figures," Hawk said. "Pro hitter wouldn't need a second guy. Loose end for him to worry about later."

"I talked to the FedEx guy," Belson said. "He got her into the back of his truck as carefully as he could, did his best to stanch the chest wound with his first-aid kit. Then hauled ass even in these conditions. Says he's pretty sure he got her here in under ten minutes."

"Heroes still walk among us," I said.

"FedEx," Martin Quirk said. "They live to deliver."

"Or deliver to live," I said.

FOUR

Rita was still in surgery four hours later.

Outside, the snow kept falling. The plows kept plowing. The forecast had us getting four to six more inches into the night. Over in Beacon Hill, detectives were still canvassing her neighborhood. Quirk pointed out that on a normal day, there probably would have been more people on the street with Rita at around eight-thirty, which is when it happened, people on their way to work or walking dogs or out for a run, or out for coffee. Just not this morning and not in weather like this.

"Snow day in Beacon Hill," Quirk said. "So far the only one who seemed to see anything useful was that driver. Maybe the shooter had planned to ring her doorbell later and do it that way. But then there was nobody on the street except her, nobody between him and her, shit blowing around like the inside of a snow globe, and he decided to save himself the trouble and get it done right there."

"I know people hate lawyers, including their own some-times," Belson said. "But usually not enough to shoot their ass."

I smiled.

"What's so funny?" Belson said.

"Rita would be thrilled to know we're still discussing her ass," I said. "Even tangentially."

Belson snorted and shook his head. "The shit talk just never stops with you," he said.

"You got a better idea to fill the time while we're waiting?" I said.

"Not even one close," he said.

We sat and drank coffee and waited. We all knew how to do it, the waiting, because of the lives we'd all led. These same men had waited for me in the hospital along with Susan and Hawk, after the Gray Man had shot me and left me for dead in the Charles River. I had waited inside and outside Hawk's hospital room once after he had been ambushed and nearly shot to death, three in the back, by members of the Ukrainian Mob. Both of us had nearly died on those occasions. But it turned out, once again, that we were both hard to kill, or perhaps just too stubborn to die. Now we waited in the hospital to find out if the same would be true of Rita Fiore, whose world did not involve bad men coming for her with guns.

We were tough guys, Hawk and me. Quirk was as hard a cop as I'd ever met, and Frank Belson was right there with him in that particular conversation. But they were as worried about Rita as I was. They were as scared as I was. But it was as if we were all locked in a competition, like one of those Iron Man competitions, to see who could hide it best.

It was tacitly understood that we were not just here out of friendship, our connection to her, or our shared history. There was even something more at work here because of how deeply personal an attack like this was, for all of us.

"Maybe she can tell us who she thinks might send a hitter after her," Quirk said.

Then he added, "When she wakes up."

He had neatly folded his black wool topcoat on the chair next to him. He was wearing a tweed jacket underneath it and a red silk tie and blue button-down shirt with the Brooks Brothers roll to the collar. His big hands, what I knew were old ballplayer's hands that looked more like bricklayer's hands, thick fingers, made the paper coffee cup he was holding look as tiny as a shot glass.

Hawk spoke little. I idly wondered at one point when he had spent a longer time than this in the presence of cops without being interrogated. Neither Hawk nor I had spoken of Donald Harrigan while we waited, or what we had done to him on Rita's behalf. There would be time for that later.

When she woke up.

"Somebody could have held a grudge from back when she was a prosecutor," Belson said.

"Tony Marcus always say the best way to settle a grudge is to wait," Hawk said.

"That asshole could teach a master class in it," Quirk said.

"Waiting?" I said.

"Grudges," Quirk said.

We talked about possible motives while we waited. It was another way of taking our minds off what was happening upstairs.

Or what *might* be happening upstairs. Maybe the guy really had been waiting to finish her with a head shot and didn't get the chance. Maybe the snow coming hard and sideways the way it still was had simply made him miss enough that Rita was upstairs, and still alive.

"Could be an old boyfriend with a grudge," Belson said. "Or a new boyfriend. We all love Rita. But the list of her exes could stretch from here to Providence and back."

I did not look over at Hawk. He did not look at me, mostly because Frank Belson, who missed nothing, was sitting right here with us.

Quirk said, "From what I've heard, just about all of them who were ever with Rita were happy to have served."

"We all know what a hot-shit defense attorney Rita is," Hawk said. "But she hasn't won them all. Maybe somebody who got sent up is playing the long game on a grudge."

"We can get a list of clients from Cone, Oakes," Quirk said. "Past and present."

"Be a lot of names for me to go through," I said.

"And well fucking worth it if you come up with the right one," Quirk said.

Hawk stood up and said he was going to brave the elements and take a walk over to the Dunkin' on Cambridge and get better coffee than we'd been drinking, and donuts. I didn't need more coffee at this point. I had enough in me by now to go outside and start shoveling sidewalks myself.

HAWK CAME BACK about twenty minutes later with large coffees for everybody and a box of donuts with a mixed dozen inside.

When I opened the box I said, "Wait, you didn't bring some for everybody else?"

I saw a smile nearly cross Frank Belson's face. Or maybe it was just the overhead hospital lights.

"Admit it, Frank," I said. "I'm funny."

"I *know* you're funny," he said. "I just don't *think* you're funny."

We drank more coffee and ate donuts and waited some more. We all told stories about what a hot shit Rita really was, and not just inside a courtroom. Quirk asked me, and not for the first time, how I had managed through the years not to give in to temptation where Rita was concerned, the way she kept putting it out there for me, and basically telling me to come and get it.

"Easy," I said. "Susan."

I had called Susan at her office and told her I would update her between patients if anything changed with Rita. Somehow her patients were also braving the elements to see their shrink. Neither rain, nor sleet . . .

"Yeah," Quirk said. "I can see Susan being the one to shoot her."

"And then me," I said.

At about one o'clock the surgeon came down to where we sat, knowing that Martin Quirk, commander of the Boston Police Department, remained in our midst. "Dr. Harman" was on her name tag. Tall, slim, Black, young.

"You all should know that I'm not sure your friend would have made it if she hadn't been brought here as quickly as she was," Dr. Harman said. "But I want you all to know that she came through the surgery very well."

"Define 'very well,'" I said.

19

"She's very strong," Dr. Harman said.

She smiled then and added, "I know Ms. Fiore's reputation as a lawyer. But even on my table, she has turned out to be a very formidable woman."

"Doc," Martin Quirk said, "pardon my French, but you have no fucking idea."

FIVE

The doctor asked about next of kin. I told her that Rita's parents were both dead, and she had no siblings. There was, I added, an ex-husband or even two, but I was fairly certain Rita wouldn't count them.

"Other than the people with whom she works," I said, "we're her family."

I had never thought about it that way until this moment. But knew I was right.

Dr. Harman said that Rita would likely be in the ICU for a couple days. Most of the substantial blood loss, she said, had been caused by the bullet piercing one of her arteries.

"A major artery?" I asked.

"In my experience, Mr. Spenser," she said, "there are no minor ones."

She asked who would act as the primary contact for our group. Quirk said he would, and handed her his card. Dr. Harman stuck it in her pocket, lingered just long enough to smile briefly at Hawk, and left.

It was Quirk who finally spoke, for all of us.

"It's not just somebody going after her," Quirk said. "It's like somebody went after all of us."

"Vengeance is ours," I said.

"No shit," Quirk said.

He was on his way back to headquarters. Belson said he was heading over to Joy Street. Quirk said he'd call me if there was something new to report on Rita's condition, and maybe even if there wasn't.

When Hawk and I were on the street I turned to him and said, "Where's Harrigan?"

"You making the assumption I might know that already?"

"Uh-huh," I said. "You wouldn't have made a donut run in this weather even if Quirk and Belson had threatened to arrest you."

"Boy be at his office," Hawk said. "One hundred State Street. And you're fucking welcome."

His Jaguar was parked on Fruit Street, in a tow-away zone.

"Has Harrigan been at his office all morning?" I said when we were inside the car.

"Thought it would be salt of us to ask him ourselves," Hawk said.

I leaned back in the passenger seat and said, "In that case, drive on, Hoke."

"Don't be starting that Miss Daisy shit," Hawk said.

"I was just trying to lighten the mood with our usual racial irony," I said.

"You can lighten the mood when she wakes up," Hawk said.

He put the Jag in gear.

"And how many times I got to remind you there ain't no such thing as racial irony when you look like me," Hawk said.

"In that case," I said, "I could drive."

SIX

The offices for Harrigan and Sons took up the eighteenth to twenty-first floors. There was a security desk in the lobby of the building. Hawk told the guard we were there to see the junior Mr. Harrigan.

The guard reached for the phone in front of him.

"Names, please?" he said.

I took out my private detective's license and showed it to him, leaning down close, but smiling as I did.

"He's expecting us," I said. "A mutual friend of ours has been shot."

Maybe it was something in my smile, which had about as much warmth as the day. Or maybe it was just me being as big as I was and up into his personal space.

"First bank of elevators on your right," the man said.

As we walked toward the elevators, Hawk said, "I believe you scared that poor man nearly half to death."

"One more thing I learned from you," I said.

"'Least you admit it," Hawk said.

On the twenty-first floor, it appeared that Harrigan and Sons was operating with a skeleton office crew because of the weather. A receptionist was at her post when we came out of the elevator. She had long silver-blond hair and oversized blue glasses that I could see matched the color of her eyes.

"We're here to see the younger Mr. Harrigan," Hawk said.

"Do you have an appointment?" she asked.

"'Course we do," Hawk said.

He smiled at her. This one was different from the one he'd used on the guard downstairs. Her nameplate said "Ms. Brickey." I could see Ms. Brickey blush, or perhaps simply overheat—it happened quite frequently when a woman was this close to what I thought of as the essential Hawk, the full force and presence of him.

"Corner office," she said, her voice sounding huskier than it had originally. "Down the hall to your right."

"Thank you, beautiful," Hawk said.

As we walked away from her I said, "Pretty sure you're not allowed to say that in the workplace."

"Not my workplace," Hawk said.

We entered Harrigan's office without knocking. Harrigan was behind his desk. He was wearing a sweater today, no jacket. Maybe it was dress-down day at the firm.

Hawk closed the door behind us, leaning back against it, arms crossed in front of him.

There was an old-school intercom on his desk, easily within

his reach. Harrigan reached for it. But this time I was the one who moved quickly across the room, grabbing his wrist and shoving him back in his chair.

"What the hell?" he said.

"Somebody shot Rita Fiore a few hours ago," I said.

"Wait . . . *what?*" Harrigan said.

He seemed to shrink farther into his chair. I sat on the edge of the desk, facing him. Outside his windows I could see that the day had darkened further just while we'd been inside. Pretty soon we were going to have as much daylight as they did in Iceland.

"Is she alive?"

"She is," I said.

"Which hospital?"

"You want to send her flowers?" Hawk said from across the room.

Harrigan did his best to ignore him, then turned back to me.

"Who shot her?" Harrigan asked.

"We don't know that yet," I said. "It appears to have been a drive-by."

"Where?"

"Near her home," I said. "She was on her way to the gym."

Harrigan gave a quick, vigorous shake of his head, like a horse shooing away flies.

"Wait," he said. "Are you here because you think I might've had something to do with it? I mean, what the flying fuck?"

"We sure ain't here on account of we been missing you, Donald," Hawk said.

"I've been here since seven o'clock this morning," Harrigan

said. "You can check downstairs. They scan your ID even if your name is on the door when you get up here."

"Who said it didn't happen before seven?" I asked. "Just for the sake of conversation."

He looked around the room as if mulling some way to take back control of it. But Hawk was still at the door while I was looking down at Harrigan, who must have felt trapped behind his desk. I was probably preventing him from calling his daddy.

"I had nothing to do with this, I swear," he said.

"And being an officer of the court, he'd never lie," Hawk said, more to me than to Donald Harrigan Jr.

I turned to look at Hawk, in his black leather knee-length coat, completely still, looking at Harrigan as indifferently as he would have looked at a traffic light changing.

"And lying would be wrong, wrong, wrong," I said, turning back to Harrigan.

The intercom buzzed and Harrigan looked at me. I nodded. He reached for one of the buttons at the bottom.

"Hold all my calls, Christine," he said.

I resumed. "It was effectively an assassination attempt."

"On *Rita Fiore?*"

"The same Rita recently stalked and threatened by you," I said. "Until you were dissuaded by us."

"Listen to me!" Harrigan said, voice rising, sounding shrill. "You have this all wrong. I was in *love* with her!"

I noticed a faint sheen of sweat above his upper lip. He hadn't moved from his chair but suddenly seemed out of breath.

"Funny way of showing it," I said.

"I didn't have anything to do with this!" Harrigan said once

more. He sounded even more shrill now. I hoped for his sake this wasn't his courtroom voice. "Whatever you think of me, I'm not a violent person. And as crazy as I got over Rita, I'm not crazy enough to risk a murder rap because she rejected me. Especially not after the two of you showed up and, ah, 'dissuaded' me, as you put it."

He was rocking slightly in his chair now, hands clasped in front of him. He looked up at me and said, "I called her to apologize, did she tell you that? I told her not to laugh, but that I hoped we could be friends again someday."

"What did she say to that?" I asked.

"She was the one who laughed," Harrigan said.

I stood up and walked back around his desk to where Hawk was standing. Hawk reached behind him and found the knob, opening the door.

As we walked out, Harrigan called after us.

"Are you going to tell the cops about me and Rita?" he said.

"No," I said over my shoulder. "But I might tell your daddy."

SEVEN

Quirk called when I was making dinner for Susan and me at my apartment, saying that he'd just gotten off the phone with Dr. Harman.

"Rita's blood pressure dropped all of a sudden," Quirk said. "When it did, her heart rate went through the roof. Doc said it was a common occurrence for a patient who nearly bled out the way she did. When she did start bleeding again, it was in the area where they'd repaired the artery."

He paused.

"They had to take her back into the OR to stop it and stitch her up all over again."

"Is she all right now?" I asked.

I saw Susan watching me.

"Her heart stopped briefly," Quirk said. "When it did, they had to defibrillate her."

"So is she all right *now*?" I asked again.

"Doc says she is," he said. "They put her back under, and say they're keeping her in the ICU for the time being."

"You back at the hospital?"

"Just left," Quirk said.

"Did they let you at least see her?"

"I could have gotten up there if I wanted to," Quirk said. "But I didn't see any point in bracing them. And all I would have gotten to do is look through a window and see a version of Rita none of us wants to see right now."

I held out the phone then, so she could hear Quirk's end of the conversation.

"What time do visiting hours start tomorrow?" I said.

"When we get there," he said, then told me he almost forgot, one of her ex-husbands had shown up while he was there. I don't know who called him. Somebody did. Another ex-prosecutor from Norfolk County, the way Rita was.

"All I'll say is she sure can pick 'em," Quirk said.

"You talk to the guy?"

"When he wasn't checking his phone."

"Frank learn anything in the neighborhood, by the way?" I asked.

"Yeah," Quirk said. "It finally stopped snowing."

Then he said he was on his way home to have a scotch. Or three.

"We are gonna get the bastard who did this, *maith agus ceart*," he said.

"Good and proper," I said.

"I didn't know you spoke Gaelic."

"I learned that one from you."

"Among all the other things you learned from me," Quirk said, before ending the call.

I WENT BACK to cooking. Susan continued to watch me. If she had a specialty of her own in our kitchen, it was watching me.

Pearl the Wonder Dog was at Susan's feet while she was sipping Sancerre. As I cooked, we resumed talking about Rita, whom Susan had never liked, not even a little bit, because of what Susan called flirtatiousness on steroids. Occasionally Susan would refer to her as "Flora the Red Menace," and I'd be forced to point out how old that show was.

"Almost as old as Rita," Susan had said.

But now everything had changed, maybe forever.

"You're convinced that the lawyer with the dirty pictures was telling you and Hawk the truth?" she asked.

"I am," I said, "as quickly as we could have put a bow on this if he wasn't."

"Would you rather I shut up now and let you further distract yourself with your cooking?"

"No," I said. "It would take more than cooking. Though I might be up for some distracting from you later."

I was preparing what I had described to her as a healthy Italian feast. Susan made the observation that *healthy* and *Italian* were generally an oxymoron. Not tonight, I told her. Turkey meatballs, Rao's Homemade low-fat red sauce, a gluten-free pasta made with corn, brown rice, and quinoa. Roasted broccolini on the side. I'd already held up the box and told Susan that the pasta was free of the top eight allergens.

"Yeah?" she'd said. "Name them."

We both knew it was just more small talk to get us through the night. Another form of distraction. She had offered to drive over with Pearl despite the road conditions when I got back from the hospital. I'd told her she didn't have to do that.

"Yes," she'd said, "I do." And so had come.

She sipped. I was taking bigger sips out of my Johnnie Walker Blue and soda. It was still my first of the night. Maybe I would end up matching Quirk scotch for scotch, the three he said he might have, before I was through dinner. It seemed like a good night for that, after the worst day imaginable.

Susan and I ate at the oval-shaped French dining room table that she had found on an online antiques store and insisted I buy. It could seat up to six, but never had. I mentioned to her, and not for the first time, that I could have done just as well, and for half the money, at Pottery Barn.

"We were going for elegant here, champ," she said.

"Not to mention swellegant," I said.

"That's from an old movie, right?" she said.

I said, "Song is 'Well, Did You Evah!' Cole Porter. Movie is *High Society*. A rare duet for Sinatra and Crosby. I could sing some of it, if you like."

"Pass the broccolini," Susan said.

I did. Then I came around the table and put my arms around her, kissing her gently on the cheek.

"What was that for?" she said.

"You being here," I said. "Or anywhere, for that matter."

As we ate, Susan said I must have already formulated some kind of theory about the shooting.

I said, "Rita somehow angered or crossed the wrong person or found out something she wasn't supposed to know. Perhaps without even knowing what it was, or who it was."

"Someone she knows?" Susan said.

"Or knows about," I said. "When she is awake, alert, and able, we will need to talk about clients, current and former, and former paramours, and come up with a list of suspects."

"'Paramours'?" Susan said.

I shrugged. "I have a swellegant way of speaking, what can I tell you."

By now Susan had eaten perhaps a third of her gluten-free pasta. When she saw me eyeballing her plate, she wordlessly lifted it and handed it across the table, and, just like that, her pasta became mine.

"Sometimes we think and act as one," I said.

"Scares the hell out of me, too," she said.

We ate in silence for a few minutes. More accurately, I continued eating while she watched, which seemed to fit our general dining dynamic perfectly. Neither of us had ever been uncomfortable with silence. Hawk had frequently noted that Susan and I could communicate better not speaking than couples who refused to shut up in each other's presence ever could.

"I've known Rita as long as I've known you," I said.

Susan reached across the table and put her hand on top of mine. "Just not nearly as well as she wanted to know you," she said. "Even before you met the girl of your dreams."

"We would have been all wrong for each other," I said. "Rita and me, I mean. We were meant to be friends."

Susan raised her glass. Somehow there was still wine left in it. I raised my glass, which now contained my second scotch.

"To Rita," Susan said.

We drank.

"I will find who did this," I said to her.

"Bet your ass," Susan Silverman said.

EIGHT

hadn't checked the online edition of *The Globe* before going to sleep. But Rita was on the front page of the print edition the next morning, as big and loud as she had always been, for as long as I'd known her. The news story was accompanied by a photograph of her that she would have found quite flattering, only because it was. The lead to the story was about the most prominent and flamboyant criminal defense attorney in Boston being shot, and on the street where she lived, in Beacon Hill. Assailant at large. Motive unknown.

Somehow the reporter had managed to get a quote from Martin Quirk himself, which I thought should have been a news story of its own, knowing from experience that Quirk liked talking to the media about as much as he liked singing karaoke.

"This was the work of a gutless punk," Quirk said, "but one who will be brought to justice by this department, I assure you.

Whether shootings like this occur in Beacon Hill or Blue Hill in Roxbury, they're always the same. These are shots fired into the heart of this city."

Susan and Pearl had already gone back to Cambridge by the time the paper was delivered, later than usual this morning because of the weather, I was sure. I had considered trying to meet up with Hawk at the Harbor Health Club for a workout, having not been there for a few days, but then decided instead to get my exercise by walking over to the hospital.

Before I left the apartment, I called Quirk and told him that I'd liked what he'd said in *The Globe* so much that the next time I saw him I was going to give him a hug.

"Or die trying," he said.

He mentioned he was about to call me, that he'd just gotten off the phone with Dr. Harman, who'd told him that Rita had made it through the night without any further setbacks but was still heavily sedated, and might be a day, or even two, away from having visitors.

"I'm going to walk there, anyway," I told him. "Through white snow, in a soundless space."

"Roses are red, violets are blue, and fuck off," Martin Quirk said.

I was about to tell him there'd been a breakdown of meter there at the end, but he'd already ended the call.

I then called Hawk, waking him up to ask if he wanted to meet me at Critical Care.

"You telling me something else happened?" he asked.

"No," I said. "The doctor told Quirk she's stable for now."

"You really gonna walk over there?"

"I want to put eyes on her even if it's through a window," I said. "And between here and there, I can work on our plan."

"That mean you *got* a plan?"

"Well, just in broad strokes."

"Taking that as a no," he said, and then he was the one ending the call.

I put on my 1975 replica Red Sox hat, red with the black bill, waterproof Merrells, gloves, and peacoat. No scarf.

By some climate miracle, the sun was out this morning, and there was a blue sky again in Boston. It was still cold, but pleasant enough to help clear my head so I could figure out how I was going to catch the bastard who had shot Rita Fiore. Or the bastard who had ordered a hit like this. Or both, depending on how well I executed a plan I did not yet have.

I made my way diagonally across the Public Garden and eventually took a right on Revere before crossing Cambridge and arriving at the hospital.

The nurse at the front desk remembered me from the day before and was kind enough to call upstairs to the nurses' desk on Rita's floor. When she hung up she said, "Still resting comfortably."

"Better than resting uncomfortably," I said. "Am I right?"

She sighed. "I hate guns," she said.

Having a gun on me—almost always having a gun on me—I didn't know how to honestly respond to that. So I just thanked her and decided not to ask if I could go upstairs. I was lining up with Martin Quirk on not seeing this version of Rita, at least not today.

So I began the walk back to my apartment, invigorated if not totally relieved, having already decided that my next stop of the morning would be the offices of Cone, Oakes.

Before I got to Marlborough Street, I stopped at the Tatte Bakery on Charles and bought myself two egg breakfast sandwiches with Vermont Cheddar and applewood bacon on sourdough bread to take home with me.

Man's gotta eat.

NINE

The law firm once known as Cone, Oakes, and Baldwin and now simply known as Cone, Oakes was the biggest and baddest in Boston, highest-profile and rich as shit, though they resisted describing it precisely that way in their year-end reporting and reviews.

A couple years ago they had moved into the top dozen floors of One Congress at Bulfinch Crossing. I had visited Rita's office a few times, one with a panoramic view of the Charles and the North End and Back Bay and everything, as far as I could tell, except the Green Mountains of Vermont.

Her office was on the top floor. By now, I knew she had gone through secretaries the way she went through men. When I rang her current secretary, Wendy, I was told to come right up.

"As you can imagine, we're in lockdown mode today," she said. "But I was given a checklist when I took this job and one of the things at the top of the list was that if a Mr. Spenser ever called he was to be put right through or shown right in, even if Rita was in conference with Jesus."

"What can I say?" I said as I made my way across the spectacular lobby at One Congress. "She likes me, she really likes me."

"How is she?" Wendy said. "I haven't been able to get through to her doctor so far this morning."

I told her, bumper-sticker-style.

"I assume you're already looking into the shooting," Wendy said.

"More than words can describe," I said.

Twenty minutes later I was on Rita's floor and seated in a much smaller office than hers with her current top associate, a young man who was so blond and pretty I couldn't decide whether I should be comparing him to Ken or Barbie, validating once again that I was an equal-opportunity objectifier. And damn proud of it.

His name was Benjamin Walsh. He was as tall as I was, just not as wide in the chest or neck. He was wearing a white dress shirt that looked to be at least one size too small, likely as a way to show off a hard gym body, and a pair of gray dress pants that fit him the way tight jeans would have, along with a skinny tie that seemed to go with the rest of his annoyingly young, buff, skinny self.

He had started out by telling me that under normal circumstances he wouldn't have been talking with anybody outside of the Cone, Oakes family today, not even me. But that these weren't normal circumstances.

"Just to make sure, though, I ran it by Mr. Oakes," Walsh said. He grinned. "He told me that *not* meeting with you, and Rita finding out about it later, might, ah, slow my roll here at the firm."

I grinned back at him. "If there's a loose ball," I said, "Rita generally comes up with it."

"Is she going to get through this?" he said.

"Are you asking for a medical opinion?"

"Any opinion will do," Walsh said, "as long as it involves you telling me she's going to make it through this."

"I believe she's eventually going to be fine if for no other reason than her being Rita," I said. "And I believe that we're about to find out that she wins even when she goes up against a loaded gun."

He nodded.

"Good by me," he said. "Now, how can I help you, Mr. Spenser—without violating any attorney-client privilege in the process, that is?"

I tried to guess his age. Maybe early thirties. Maybe a little older; it was hard to tell with how pretty he was. Hair a color I'd once heard Susan describe as corn silk, shaved close on the sides, more of it piled on top. I would have described him as having movie-star looks, except that my friend and protégé Zebulon Sixkill, now working as a private detective in Los Angeles, had told me they weren't going for the blond Brad Pitt look with male actors these days.

I took in some air and let it out, slowly.

"Ben?" I said pleasantly. "May I call you Ben? Somebody shot and nearly killed my dear friend and your immediate boss on the street yesterday morning. So even though you have made it sound as if I am truly blessed to be here in the inner sanctum, I need to tell you that whatever patience I have left after what happened to Rita will dissipate quickly if you try to feed me a bunch of happy horseshit about attorney-client privilege."

I noticed that his eyes seemed to widen, as if the movie just got scary.

"Wow," he said finally. "No wonder you and Rita get along."

"My strength is as the strength of ten," I said. "Or thereabouts."

I told him then that the main reason I was there was to get a handle on who in Rita's professional life might have wanted her dead, right on her street, as theatrical as she had always been in her professional life.

"We may be here awhile," Benjamin Walsh said.

TEN

Walsh started in the most obvious place, as I expected he would, with the trial that had ended a few months before Donald Harrigan had begun stalking her.

Brian Tully was a legendary local anchorman who had worked for Channels 4 and 5 and 7 at some point in his career and had become such a popular figure in Boston over the last three decades that he had once considered running for mayor. But then came a sexual harassment lawsuit against him filed by a former coanchor of his: Shannon Miles.

Rita made headlines, as she so often did, by defending the man, and not representing the woman. She told me in the end that she didn't necessarily believe Brian Tully was completely innocent. But she was Rita. She had a job to do, one she thought she did better than anybody else, and could find no evidence that Tully was the man Shannon Miles was accusing him of being.

She planted her flag there, and on her fierce belief that men or women were innocent until proven guilty.

The heart of Shannon Miles's claims was that after she had ended her longtime affair with the extremely married Tully, he had used his immense power with the station and its parent company to make sure that her contract was not renewed. There was more to it than that, messy and complicated and full of counteraccusations from Tully. But Shannon Miles maintained that she had essentially been fired for withholding sex from Brian Tully; that it was a classic quid pro quo harassment case. So she went after him, and the parent company, asking for $100 million in compensatory damages.

Once Miles went public with her charges against Tully, the case was in and out of the headlines for more than a year. The trial itself, which had ended last October, had taken over every newscast in every station in town, including Tully's own, night after night, along with *The Globe* and *Herald* day after day. It had everything: #MeToo, the media, adultery, anchors the viewers considered old and trusted friends, not to mention two of the best Boston TV reporters in history. And there was a lot of money at stake, along with Tully's own career, and hers. When you added in the Internet's overheating climate, what had gone on and was going on with Tully and Miles—Bri and Shan, as they'd been known in Boston for years—was much, much more than simply a kiss to build a dream on.

Walsh said, "In the end, I honestly believe the public reaction to the case, at least from women, was as much about Rita as it was about the woman who'd brought the suit. But Rita honestly believed that Shannon Miles's attorneys never proved that Tully

had gotten her fired. And she was willing to take the heat for doing her job defending the guy."

"She always has taken things on a case-by-case basis," I said.
"Literally."

"You may remember that when the trial ended, Shannon
Miles stood there on the steps at the Moakley Courthouse and
started cursing Rita out."

"I do recall that," I said.

"But just for the sake of where I think we're going with this
particular line of thought," Walsh said. "Why would Shannon,
or someone acting on her behalf, send somebody after Rita and
not the man who did her wrong?"

"She obviously felt Tully cost her a job, at a point in her career
when she admitted under oath she was vulnerable in the television news business because of her advancing age," I said. "In addition, she was looking for a hundred million, which was three
times as much as has ever been awarded in a case like this. In her
mind, Rita had hurt her as badly as Tully had."

Walsh reminded me that there had been pickets outside One
Congress for a couple weeks after the verdict, until people finally
lost interest.

"The dogs bark," I said, "and the caravan moves on."

Walsh raised an eyebrow. When I tried to do that, Susan said
it looked as if I'd developed a twitch.

"First Tennyson with you, and now Arab proverbs," he said.
"Are you absolutely certain you're a private detective?"

"I can't tell you how many times I've asked myself that exact
same question lately," I said.

I asked Walsh if there was anything big Rita had been working on since the trial that might have crossed a line she didn't even know she was crossing. Or, being Rita, perhaps knew exactly what she was doing and didn't give a good rat's ass.

Walsh moved his chair closer to his desk and began tapping away at a desktop computer that looked as big as the flat-screen TV in my apartment.

"She actually downshifted her work a bit this winter," he said. "I mean, she could retire just off of what Tully alone paid her, even if we're still fielding calls from other powerful guys who can't keep it in their pants as soon as they get the first call from Human Resources."

"Rita does like to be wanted," I said.

He did the eyebrow thing again. "Just not by you," he said. "Something she might've mentioned on multiple occasions."

"I've never felt that should be held against her," I said.

"But the thing is," Walsh continued, "Rita has turned down every other #MeToo asshat who's called, and one woman whose name I really can't share with you because of attorney-client, even if you threaten to shoot me for invoking it again. In so doing, she's left some very big change on the table."

He shrugged. "Listen, she also thought Tully was a bit of an asshat. But she just never completely bought into Shannon Miles's version of things. It might not have been particularly noble of her. You know how complicated things are with smart, powerful, successful women, and how they do get unfairly treated by powerful men, whether those men end up getting their asses sued or not. Maybe Rita couldn't get past her own prejudices about strong women."

"Meaning a strong woman like her."

"Listen," Walsh said. "I'm not looking to relitigate the case.

But there was just a part of Rita that felt that Shannon Miles never proved that Tully had been the one who got her fired." He shrugged. "That day Miles cursed Rita out, she also said that she hoped someday Tully's lawyer found out what it was like to be violated."

I didn't mention to him how much I had always liked Shannon Miles's work, just asked if she still lived in Boston. Walsh said he actually didn't know for sure but would be happy to make a call to the district attorney's office and find out. I thanked him, but said I was capable of making a call like that on my own, like a big boy.

"Rita says you're the best," Walsh said.

"Well, yeah, prove it, kid," I said.

"I'll go through my files and see if I can flag any other possibilities, suspect-wise," he said. "And check her schedule over the past month or so. I promise you, Mr. Spenser, I'm going to be as engaged with this as you are."

"And when Rita is back to being her most formidable self," I said, "I'm sure she'll be able to come up with names on her own, even ones that predate you coming to work for her."

"She is going to come back from this, right?" Walsh said.

"Goddamn right," I said.

Walsh asked me where I intended to start.

"Shannon Miles," I said. "After all, a journey of a thousand miles begins with a single step. Or a single Miles, in this case."

Walsh smiled, flashing a line of perfect white teeth.

"You're a pretty funny guy," he said.

"Yeah," I said, "but I'm trying to quit."

ELEVEN

Shannon Miles agreed to meet me at the Oak Long Bar at the Copley Plaza, a great old Boston hotel.

The hotel, near both the Old Trinity Church and the Public Library, was now officially known as the Fairmont Copley Plaza. Just not to me. But then I still called The Newbury the old Ritz, just as I had even when it had become the Taj.

"At least I've stopped saying Scollay Square when I'm talking about Government Center," I'd said to Susan the other day.

"Woo-hoo," she said.

"The Kingston Trio never stopped calling it Scollay Square when they sang 'M.T.A.,'" I told her. "Want to hear it?"

"Maybe another time," she said.

I remembered standing in front of the Copley Plaza a few days after a couple punks had blown up the finish line at the Boston Marathon. Rita was with me that day. A friend of hers had lost a leg in the explosion. Rita had looked over to where it had happened, practically right in front of the Public Library, and suddenly started to cry. I'd never seen her cry before.

"Maybe," she said to me that day, "I'm not as tough as everybody thinks I am," and I told her that I'd try not to let that get around. It would be bad for business.

Now, all this time later, Rita was the one who needed to be tough. I'd never told her that Hawk and I had gone looking for the two brothers who had set off the bombs on Boylston Street that day. The cops found them first, in Watertown, but it was personal for us the way it was for everybody in the city that day.

Just not nearly as personal as somebody shooting Rita Fiore and leaving her to die in the snow.

There was a sign over the bar that read SERVE THE NATION. It really was an uncommonly long bar, with gray cushioned seats and a small fireplace behind it. The bartenders wore white shirts and vests. There was some carpeting in the room, but also a lot of gleaming hardwood floor. It had its own official name, the Oak Long Bar + Kitchen, and Susan and I would come here occasionally for a drink, though not as often as we wanted to. I considered it one of the most underrated bars in town.

Shannon Miles arrived before I did, and was seated at a table across from the bar, in front of one of the floor-to-ceiling windows. Snow was falling again—but soft snow, in a soft winter light.

I hadn't told her what I looked like because I knew what to look out for. Everybody who watched the local news on television was familiar with her, and had been long before her name blew up from the trial.

"I'm Spenser," I said, walking up to the table.

She stood and smiled, extending her hand. I shook it.

"Of course you are," she said.

She looked as she always had on television, and as she had the last time I had seen her on my television screen, standing on the courthouse steps. She had what once would have been called lustrous hair, probably back when gin mills were still all the rage. Her hair was nearly black, the way Susan's was, but longer. A Susan type, all in all, just not as beautiful, because no one was as beautiful as Susan Silverman.

I couldn't recall when she had last been behind an anchor desk. But she had aged very well. She was wearing a black turtleneck sweater and a single strand of pearls. There were no rings on her fingers, which were long and elegant and featured nails the color of lilacs.

"Let's order drinks before you commence grilling me," she said.

"I'm just here to talk," I said.

"No," Shannon Miles said, "you're not."

"You calling me a liar?"

"Are you a man?" she asked.

She ordered a dirty martini and I a Lord Hobo IPA.

We made small talk while we waited for the drinks, about the long, relentless winter, and how there really hadn't been one like this since 2015. When the drinks arrived, she drank. I drank. We did not toast each other.

"I was surprised you agreed to see me when I told you it was about Rita," I said.

I noticed the snow had started to fall harder behind her. Of course.

"Listen," she said, "there is no love lost between Rita and me because there was never any love to begin with. It doesn't mean I'm not shocked about what happened to her."

She took another small sip of her martini. I was already eyeballing her olives. "How is she doing, by the way? News reports have been pretty scarce the last day or so."

"My medical opinion is that she is hanging in there," I said. "My hope is that she will eventually outlive both of us."

This close up, I could see how artful her makeup job was. When you're in the ring with the makeup champ, as I was with Susan, you came to not just notice good work like this, but appreciate it.

"I had nothing to do with Rita being shot," Shannon Miles said then. "Despite the many times during the trial I did dream about actually shooting her out of a cannon."

"She cost you a lot of money," I said, "and you made no secret of the fact after the trial, and in a very public way, that you wished her ill."

She took another sip of her martini. The olives remained untouched. So there was hope. I was playing the long game.

"She is a woman," she said, her dark eyes, almost as dark as her hair, fixed firmly on me. "She was retained *because* she is a woman. Then she proceeded to shame me on her way to making a very large amount of money for herself, and costing me much, much more."

She pushed her glass off to the side and leaned forward, clasping her long fingers together. She smiled then, as if about to welcome everybody back to the six-o'clock news after a commercial break.

"And do you not find it ironic, Mr. Spenser, or at least whimsical, that your friend Rita, of all people, would be in the position of slut-shaming anyone?"

"That's not who she is," I said. "It's not who she's ever been."

"Maybe you should have been sitting where I was sitting," Shannon Miles said.

Before I got the chance to respond to that, she said, "While we're on this subject, let me ask you one more question: Did you ever sleep with her?"

In the moment, I could think of no good reason to avoid the question, or to tell her it was none of her business.

"I did not," I said.

"Oh," Shannon Miles said. "So you were the one."

TWELVE

I smiled at her then. It's the smile I use with women when I'm trying to be disarming, not make them feel suddenly as if they're about to lose control.

"I don't see how you making rude remarks about a friend of mine currently fighting for her life is helpful," I said.

"I'm sorry."

"I've got an idea," I said. "How about we do a reset?"

"You first," Shannon Miles said.

"Rita didn't believe your version of your relationship with Brian Tully," I said. "It means she was simply doing her job the way she has always done it, by which I mean defending the shit out of her client."

"At my expense," she said. "And, I should add again, expensively."

Shannon Miles paused and then said, "Her career went on quite nicely after that until the other day, by all accounts. I, on the other hand, have no career to speak of. Do you appreciate irony, Mr. Spenser?"

"Only when it's used in developed countries."

"One of the biggest ironies of all is that I am as unemployable in television as are all those men from television who did to other women what Brian Tully did to me," she said.

"The jury didn't think Tully was all of those other men," I said.

"He was," she said. "Whether Rita believed that then, and whether or not you believe it now."

"With all due respect, you had to know what the consequences of going after Tully in an extremely public way and losing might be."

I held up a hand, as a way of asking for her to let me continue.

"I would never suggest that I know what you've gone through, or what the cost has been, and not just in money," I said. "But you had to know what you'd be exposed to, and have to endure, going after Tully in such a public way. Whether any of it was fair or not."

"There were people in my business who decided that was such a desperate career move from me, trying to use victimhood to become relevant again," she said. "Those people, and especially the women who somehow believe I did this for fun and profit, should go through what I went through. And am still going through."

"Shannon," I said. "I am sitting across a table from you. And you are extremely persuasive. But I'm not in a jury box. I'm not here to judge you, one way or another. I'm not sitting at Rita's table. I'm not here to prosecute you. I'm just trying to find out who shot her."

It had gotten dark while we had been here. All of the seats at the bar were filled as the place moved headlong into the cocktail hour, and their dinner crowd came in.

A good bar like this, at this time of the day, made you not want to leave. Despite the way our conversation had gone sideways, Shannon Miles gave no indication that she was ready to leave, as angry as she clearly still was, at Rita and me and the world.

"Let me explain something to you," she said. "In the end, whether she meant it or not, Rita Fiore dragged a selfish prick like Brian Tully across the finish line, while the crowd roared. At least the male crowd. And please allow me the right to think that she had to know exactly who, and what, he was as she did it."

She plucked an olive out of the glass and ate it. It was a foolish dream to think it wouldn't happen eventually.

"And you know what the real end result of that trial was?" she said. "I got screwed by him all over again. And all of a sudden, no one wanted to talk about the career I'd had and the journalism awards I'd won. They just wanted to talk about me being some kind of six-and-eleven gold digger."

I had finished my beer but did not look around for a waiter to order another. Sometimes I truly do have the strength of ten. And I could also sense that my time here with Shannon Miles was coming to an end.

"When the trial was over, you stood on the courthouse steps and said that you hoped Rita would find out for herself one day what it was like to be violated," I said.

"And got royally roasted for that remark, I might add."

I nodded. "But now she has been violated," I said. "Literally to within an inch of her life."

"And I had nothing whatsoever to do with it," she said. "You need to realize something, Mr. Spenser. Sometimes hate doesn't make you stupid, or make you want to act on it. Sometimes it's just hate."

She shook her head, almost sadly. "It's funny how things work out," she said. "I started out being the woman scorned and that's exactly how I ended up, because Rita did such a good job in open court."

She theatrically threw back the last of her martini, stood up, and got into the expensive-looking camel topcoat that had been draped over the back of her chair.

"Sex gets us all in the end, doesn't it?" she said, almost in resignation.

There was nothing for me to do with that.

She didn't leave right away, just stood next to the table, looking down at me.

"If I were you," she said, "and knowing what we know about Rita, I'd be asking myself if sex got her in the end."

THIRTEEN

Even though it was past seven o'clock, I called Benjamin Walsh, betting that he was still at his desk. Walsh was just the type.

He answered right away. I asked if he was still at the office. He said he was.

"For how long?" I asked.

"Awhile," he said. "What do you need?"

"To get back into Rita's office."

"Looking for anything in particular?"

"It's like what that Supreme Court judge said about pornography," I said. "I'll know it when I see it."

"Justice Potter Stewart," Walsh said. "And he was talking about obscenity."

"I was just testing you," I said.

"Give me a hard one next time," Benjamin Walsh said.

Half an hour later I was seated behind Rita's desk, Walsh

having made me promise I wouldn't remove anything without telling him.

"My heart is pure," I told him. "And the love I give is real."

"Gonna have to take your word on that last part," he said, before closing her door and leaving me there.

For a few minutes I just sat there, feeling Rita's presence, remembering all the times I had sat across from this desk, and her in this chair. As quickly as it had come, the image was gone, and I was picturing Rita again in her hospital bed, pale, weak, and diminished, and not out of the woods yet, no matter how much we all wanted her to be.

Then I remembered all the days and nights when I had sat vigil next to Hawk's hospital bed after one of Boots Podolak's Ukrainian gunnies had shot him in the back, before Hawk finally recovered and went up to Marshport to kill them all, saving Boots himself for last.

It was the same way Hawk had sat vigil for me after the Gray Man had shot me, then left me for dead in the Charles River. At the time, and with the help of Martin Quirk, we let the Gray Man think for months that he had finished the job that day, until I had my health back and tracked him down in New York City. I had let him live.

In the end, though, both Hawk and I had been hard to kill. But then we had always been hard to kill. The Gray Man and Boots's hitman and all the others who had ever come for us were part of our world, part of our unwritten contract with the universe, all part of the lives we had chosen.

But not Rita's life. It was never in Rita's contract, or her terms of engagement with the world.

At least not until now.

I got up and walked over to Rita's maple cabinet set against the far wall. It was where Rita kept her whiskey. I opened the cabinet and found a bottle of Glendalough Seventeen-Year-Old Irish Single Malt that I had bought for her after she had won a big case a couple years ago, long before she had taken on Brian Tully's case. We were toasting and drinking, and she had finally smiled wickedly and said, "I could lock the door and finally let nature take its course."

"*Mother* Nature?"

"You know what a bad, bad girl that mother can be," Rita said in a husky voice.

Then I told her that day that if I finally did succumb to temptation, after all these years' buildup, she'd probably be disappointed.

Rita had given a big toss to all that red hair and laughed a big, throaty laugh and said, "I'll risk it if you will."

I poured myself a shot of Glendalough now and raised the glass in the direction of her empty chair, and drank. Then I sat back down and methodically proceeded to go through her desk, feeling as I did like I was some ancient cliché about private detectives, peepers peering through a peephole.

We had not been allowed to discover how much of her life she kept on her cell phone, because she was still not awake and only she could give her consent for that. So all of us, Hawk and Quirk and Belson and me, would have to wait. Everybody had secrets on their phone, and I was certain Rita was no different. After all, she had been a big-time player in Boston for as long as I had known her.

And for a lawyer as organized as she was, as precise as she was with her legal mind, with her cross-examination skills in particular, it turned out that her desk was a festival of clutter.

Scattered throughout all the drawers were credit card receipts from some of the best restaurants in town, and even more receipts from what I thought of as the Murderers' Row of clothing stores on Newbury Street.

I found a manila folder filled with clippings from the print edition of *The Globe*, all of them about the Brian Tully/Shannon Miles trial. There was even a handwritten note from Tully, on personalized stationery, that read this way:

> R:
>
> *Big thanks to the greatest of all time.*
>
> B

In one of the bottom drawers I found a selfie of Rita and me, the two of us standing on Boylston in front of Abe & Louie's steakhouse. I happened to remember the day. We had finished a celebratory lunch because she had just helped Jesse Stone, the head cop in Paradise and a former lover of hers, recover land up in Paradise that rightfully belonged to a Native American tribe up there.

Stone had called me the night before to ask about her condition.

"Should I come down there?" he said.

"When she's awake," I said.

"You need anything, all you have to do is call."

"I know."

"World continues to be an extremely fucked-up place."

"Know that, too."

There had been a time when Rita, I knew, had fallen hard for Stone, and he had fallen hard for her. It made him part of that long line, the one that moved.

I was going through the last of the bottom drawers, about to walk across the room to what Rita called her trophy wall, when I found a small silver picture frame, the picture facing down, underneath more folders, almost as if she didn't want to look at it but still wanted to know where it was.

I knew the feeling. There was a framed photograph of me with the original Pearl the Wonder Dog in my own desk, bottom drawer on the right, always there for me if I needed it, even knowing how sad that moment, frozen in time, would make me feel once I took it out.

The photograph I held in my hand now was one of Rita with her arm around a dead guy.

FOURTEEN

I called the hospital before I left Cone, Oaks and was told that Rita was now in a medically induced coma, one Dr. Harman said would last only a day or two. They wanted her body and her brain at rest, "the whole damn thing," Dr. Harman had called it.

"But precautionary," I said.

"Yes," she said.

"How long are you planning to keep her under?"

"Maybe even less than a day," she said, and ended the call, not even saying goodbye.

I was getting to like her. She didn't like small talk any more than I did.

RITA WAS STILL not awake the next morning when Hawk and I were in my office, Hawk stretched out on my couch and studying the photograph of Rita and Nicholas Drummond, once the boy wonder of Mass politics as Senate president, but dead the previous September in a drowning accident off Castle Island in South Boston. Drummond was the kid who'd basically grown up on the streets of Boston, like a character out of a Dickens novel. Foster care and group homes and then a trade school before he got into politics. Then his death had been as dramatic as his life had been.

In the photo Drummond and Rita were standing on the beach, the ocean behind them, Rita in a bikini, he in baggy flowered swim trunks.

Hawk said, "Wasn't she a little old for him?"

"I keep telling you," I said. "Age is just a number."

Hawk smiled. "Bigger number for you than me."

"Focus," I said.

"What you think I'm doing?"

"Did you ever hear that Rita and Nick Drummond might have been, ah, canoodling?"

"Canoodling?" he said. "That what they called doin' it when you were growing up back in Yellowstone?"

"Laramie," I said. "And I wasn't doing much 'doin' it' when I was growing up there."

Hawk sat up. "So what about this bloke piques your interest, Holmes?" he said, lapsing into his *Downton Abbey* accent.

"She never mentioned a relationship with Drummond, is all."

"You ever think how much time it would've taken up, trying to keep up with everybody she ever *did* have a relationship with?" Hawk said.

"Maybe it's the age difference that caught my attention," I said. "Other than who it is she has her arm around."

Hawk said, "You know how well Rita keeps it a secret how old she is. You can't even find out on the Internet."

I grinned.

"So you've checked, too, huh?" I said.

"All I can say is God bless her," Hawk said. "And God bless America."

I got up and poured more coffee and sat back down at my desk, setting my mug down on *The Globe*, which I had long since finished reading after bringing it here from the apartment.

"Sometimes," I said, "when you are trying to assemble a puzzle, the pieces that don't fit, at least at first, are more important than the ones that do."

"I forget sometimes what a deep thinker you are," Hawk said.

"I'm more than just eye candy," I said.

"So you thinking that maybe there's a way we can draw a through line from a dead boyfriend nobody knew Rita had to her getting shot all this time later?" Hawk asked.

"Maybe Drummond had secrets and Rita knew them," I said. "Or found out about them after he died. He'd become such a huge deal in Massachusetts politics, which you may have noticed no one has ever confused with church. He was the one out front on that land deal over at Widett Circle, convincing everybody how good it would be for South Boston to have a casino and hotel built there, like the city would be getting a brand-new downtown area."

"That's where they talked about building the Olympic stadium before the Olympics went somewhere else, right?" Hawk said.

"Uh-huh."

He got up and handed me back the photograph and then poured more coffee for himself. Eventually we would have to start thinking about lunch. It was never too early to start doing that.

"You think maybe the boy's accidental death wasn't so accidental?" he said. "Even though he was one of the heroes of that deal finally getting done?"

"No," I said. "There wasn't even a hint of that at the time, as far as I can remember. All I'm saying is that he was a fast-tracker at the time he died and maybe somebody thinks Rita did find out something about him, even this long after the fact, that is a threat to somebody, for reasons unbeknownst to us at the present time."

"And you're thinking all these deep thoughts today on account of a picture at the bottom of a desk that got turned over and you got no idea why," Hawk said.

"By God, Watson," I said, in my own British accent, one not nearly as good as Hawk's. "It's practically elementary, isn't it?"

"I just think you've got yourself stuck on this shit because that picture is all you got at the moment," Hawk said.

"It might be less refined, and a more cynical way, of looking at our present circumstances," I said. "But yes."

We had begun to discuss lunch far more seriously when Quirk called to tell us that the doctors had decided it was time for Rita to wake up.

FIFTEEN

We'd been informed in advance that we would be allowed to stay for only a few minutes, that the patient was still quite weak, and groggy, and not close to being out of the woods.

"Whose woods those are I think I know," I said to the doctor.

"Is that from a poem?" the doctor said. "I don't think I know it."

"No worries," Quirk said. "As long as he knows."

"Promises to keep," I said.

"Oh," Dr. Harman said. "Robert Frost."

Quirk shook his head. "It's like they say in football, Doctor," he said. "You can't stop him, you can only hope to contain him."

Quirk paused, jerked a thumb in my direction, and added, "Him. Not Robert Frost."

Then we were inside the room and standing next to the bed, amid all the tubes and monitors and the claustrophobic hospital smell of the room.

Rita's eyes were closed. She looked pale and even smaller than she had when I had seen her through the window in intensive care, as if somehow she had shrunk inside herself some more. Only the red hair looked normal, splashing over the pillow behind her in waves, framing a face that made her look, as pale as she was, like a little girl.

The only sounds, other than our breathing, were from the monitors.

She opened her eyes then, saw us all standing there, and smiled weakly, with a smile so small I felt as if I could have palmed it.

"Shit," Rita said. Even her voice was small. "This can't possibly be heaven."

She reached out to me and I took her hand, which felt like she was still lying in the snow, and made us tell her what had happened to her. Quirk did that quickly, in cop shorthand. When he finished, I asked what she remembered and she said none of it.

She asked how long she had been here then, and I told her.

In the small, hoarse voice, one nothing at all like the big voice that could fill a courtroom, she asked, "So how come you hotshots haven't solved the case yet?"

"How do you know we haven't?" Martin Quirk said.

"Because if you had," she said, "you all wouldn't be standing here looking sadder than pallbearers at my funeral."

I heard Hawk whistle, turned, and saw him smiling. "Well, girl," he said, "you must be gettin' better, 'cause you still spicy."

Rita was still holding my hand, almost as if she needed it for warmth. When she finally took it away, it just fell next to her on the bed, as if she didn't have the strength to hold it up any longer.

She closed her eyes again and was still, and I was afraid she'd gone back to sleep. Three tough guys in here with her, as tough as she had ever known, but she had always considered herself to be as tough as we were, even making her way in a mostly man's world. But now she had found out what all of us found out eventually, that tough was always the one with the gun.

Quietly, Martin Quirk said, "Rita?"

She opened her eyes.

"You sure you don't remember anything?" he asked.

"I remember I was on my way to the gym," Rita said. "That's it. Now I'm here."

We heard a rap on the windowed part of the door behind us. Dr. Harman was already pointing to her watch. I was secretly hoping that she might actually try to tell Martin Quirk to leave before he was ready.

"Anything happen lately to scare you?" Quirk asked. "Before this happened, I mean."

There was a flicker of light in her eyes then. "I have noticed a few wrinkles lately," she said.

"You know what I mean," Quirk said.

"I do, Martin," she said. "And I know why you want to know. But the last time anybody wished me ill was Shannon Miles at the end of that trial."

"I've spoken with her," I said.

"Of course you have," Rita said.

"She told me she had nothing to do with you being shot," I said. Then I grinned at her and added, "She did call you a bitch, however."

"Of course she did," Rita said.

Hawk said, "Other than her, you got any thoughts on who'd send somebody to shoot you?"

"No."

It was as if she were doing everything possible, with whatever strength she could muster in the moment, to still be Rita, for her own benefit almost as much as ours.

"We will find out who did this to you," Quirk said. "And when we do—not if, but when—we will prosecute *their* ass to the full extent of the law. The good news is that whoever it was won't have you to defend them."

From behind Quirk, Hawk said, "Let me and Spenser find them first, and do that 'vengeance is ours' thing he already mentioned."

Dr. Harman had quietly slipped into the room, and told us now that the patient needed rest. Both Quirk and Hawk leaned over and touched Rita on the shoulder before heading outside.

I leaned down and said, "When I come back tomorrow, we need to talk about Nick Drummond."

She reached for my hand then, as a way of keeping me there.

"You know?" she said.

"I found a picture in your desk," I said.

She said something in a voice too faint for me to hear.

"Mr. Spenser," Dr. Harman said. "This particular visiting hour is now over."

Rita squeezed my hand and tried to pull me closer, as if there was something more she wanted to tell me. But then she closed her eyes again. I stood over the bed and looked down at her one last time. I reached down and touched the side of her face, which felt even colder than her hand had felt. I wanted to ask her more about Nick Drummond, but she was already asleep.

Susan always said that the problem with a good idea was that once it got inside your head, it was almost impossible to get it out.

I thought I might have one now.

One in a row.

SIXTEEN

Susan drove over from Cambridge with Pearl after she finished work. We were now having dinner at Toscano on Charles Street, both of us having decided that Toscano had fallen out of our restaurant rotation for no good reason. It was too close to my apartment, and too great of a neighborhood place.

Richard was still the owner, and the stone and red-brick walls looked as I remembered them. I told Susan once we were inside that the smell of the food made me want to sing like one of the Three Tenors. She told me to go ahead, but that by the time I concluded my aria I would be dining alone.

"Where have you been?" Richard said to me as he seated us, having made a traditional and predictable fuss over Susan.

"Keeping the city safe for decent people," I said.

"Is that the truth?" Richard asked Susan.

"It hurts his feelings to suggest otherwise," she said. "Best just go with it."

71

I ordered a martini. Susan ordered an Aperol spritz.

"Isn't that more a summer drink?" I said.

"I'm trying to think summer thoughts," Susan said. "But it's really, *really* hard."

I waited until our drinks arrived to tell her all about our visit to Rita's hospital room, and our brief conversation about Nick Drummond before Dr. Harman had given me the boot.

"Rita and Nicholas Drummond," Susan said. "Hard for me to wrap my head around that one."

"Because he was younger than she was?" I said.

"Because she was Rita," Susan said, "and he was the hot kid in politics around here, with an image that people were already thinking was too good to be true."

"You know what they say about things that seem too good to be true."

"So Drummond is up on your radar?"

"He died under mysterious circumstances, even if the cops couldn't find evidence that he did anything other than drown," I said. "Now Rita gets shot under mysterious circumstances, at least in terms of who did it. And I find out that she was having some kind of thing with him."

I drank some of my martini, with great pleasure. A good martini, at this time of the night, with Susan Silverman sitting across from me, at least briefly restored some order to my world, if not more clarity.

Susan hadn't yet opened her menu. Nor had I. She probably didn't think I could wait her out. I'd show her.

"When you've got nothing," I said, "anything seems like a lot."

"What about a disgruntled ex-client?" she said. "Even Rita, as good as she is, must have one or two of those."

"That's occurred to all of us," I said. "But Rita hardly ever loses a case, which means that most of her ex-clients are extremely *gruntled*. Is that even a thing?"

"Go with it."

"Shannon Miles suggested it could be an ex-boyfriend."

"But you said that you and Hawk had eliminated the lawyer with the dirty pictures as a suspect."

"It might have had something to do with the fact that Hawk looked ready to hang him out a window if he didn't tell us the truth, but, yes, we believed him."

"So you are now shifting your focus to a dead boyfriend nobody knew Rita had," Susan said, "and one who drowned accidentally. Or not."

"I am," I said.

"But Frank Belson emphatically ruled out homicide at the time," Susan said.

"I'm going to meet him for coffee in the morning," I said, "to ask him about that."

She finally reached for her menu.

"I don't suppose you'd be interested in changing the subject to food, would you?" she asked.

"I mean, if you're hungry, we could think about ordering," I said casually.

Susan did what she usually did, even at a restaurant at which we'd eaten before, studying her options as if still studying for her Ph.D. at Harvard. I decided right away, the portobello-and-zucchini appetizer and the penne with Tuscan meat sauce.

After we had ordered, Susan said, "You know, it occurs to me that one thing never changes with politics in our city."

"What's that?"

"It remains as difficult as ever to tell the good guys from the bad guys, even when the good guys look too good to be true. And to identify who the biggest liars are."

"Ain't that the truth," I said.

BACK AT HOME, Pearl was snoring softly from our living room, and I could feel Susan's eyes on me in the darkness of our bedroom.

"I can't let this stand, Suze," I said.

"I know," she said, and pressed herself more closely to me. "You will do what you do, and do it as well as you always do."

"Why not?" I said. "I have no other skills."

She kissed me again then, with far more follow-through this time, sticking the landing, I thought.

"Well," she said. "Maybe one or two others."

"I thought we had concluded the evening's festivities," I said.

"And you call yourself a detective," Susan said.

SEVENTEEN

Frank Belson and I met on Washington Street at Mike's City Diner, which was within walking distance of police headquarters at Schroeder Plaza. The old Berkeley Street headquarters, built a hundred years ago, was now Hotel AKA Back Bay. Like the old place, it was now going under an assumed name.

We were both just having coffee.

"You're not eating?" Belson said. "You must have brought me here to tell me you're dying."

"I ate too much at Toscano last night," I said.

"Wasn't aware there was any such thing with you," he said.

The sky was the color of gunmetal and looked to be full of more snow, but nothing yet.

"Rita make it through the night okay?" he said. "I haven't talked to Quirk yet."

"No news is good news," I said.

"Not in my line of work," Belson said.

He looked tired. No news there.

"Quirk said you might have a thought on who might have done this," Belson said.

"One thought," I said. "Generally all I can handle at a time."

I told him then about the photo of Rita with Nick Drummond I'd found and that my one thought was that there might be some way that his death and her shooting were connected.

"That's it?" he said.

"Call it a hunch," I said. I sipped some coffee. It was always strong and good at Mike's, and you didn't even have to give the waiters the nod to get a refill, no matter how busy the place was. "Tell me about Drummond's drowning," I said.

Belson took me through it, the way he did, with not a single word he didn't need. How Nick Drummond had lived in the Castle Island neighborhood. How it was an established fact that he liked to go for early-morning swims in the summer, was still taking them even after Labor Day.

Sometimes, Belson said, Drummond was even out in the water before the sun came up. He must have been out there early the day he died, even though a Category 3 storm had blown up the coast a couple days before, leaving behind amazing waves. People who had tried to swim the water there the day before had complained of riptides.

"Wouldn't an experienced swimmer like Drummond have known that?" I asked.

"And he wasn't just any experienced swimmer," Belson said and nodded. "Maybe you don't remember that big-assed photo-op swim he took for charity the summer before he died, Cape to Martha's Vineyard. Seven freaking miles."

"Could somebody have dumped him and made it look like a drowning?" I said.

"Could have, sure." Belson shook his head. "But no unusual bruising. Nothing sketchy in the tox screen, only salt water in the lungs. We canvased that neighborhood pretty good, trust me. Nobody saw him go into the water. He was just there, washed up, when a couple cuties out for their morning run found him, got hysterical even before they realized who he was, called nine-one-one."

"Was the tide right to bring him in where they found him?"

Belson hit his forehead with the palm of his hand. "Shit, why didn't I think of that? And the answer is yes."

I was actually starting to get hungry now. The smell of the bacon had a lot to do with it, along with the stack of pancakes a uniformed cop was tearing into at the counter, which looked so delicious I was suddenly willing to fight him for it.

"Drummond have enemies?" I said.

"He was a politician," Belson said. "A *Bah*-ston politician. Does a dog have fleas?"

"Any notable enemies?"

"Truth is, the bastard had made a lot more friends than enemies on the way up, and he wasn't just on his way up, he was a rocket to the moon," Belson said. "Remember, he'd just saved that land at Widett Circle from getting turned into more rail-yards."

Some of it I remembered. Some I got from reading back on Drummond, and his role in the entire process. The Massachusetts Bay Transportation Authority had bought that land and watched it grow in value and finally had to decide whether to sell it to one of the developers who wanted to build a casino and ho-tel on the property or to sell it to some other developers who wanted to turn the former Meatpacking District into the rail-yards that Belson had just mentioned, ones the city really could have used as a way of providing relief for South Station.

Nick Drummond had been the most vocal advocate for the building of the casino and hotel, talking about jobs, jobs, jobs, eventually gaining the support of the Redevelopment Authority, telling anyone who would listen how this project would be the centerpiece of modern and reimagined South Boston, almost like a city of the future.

It became a hot-button issue, over a very hot property. The casino plan, though, was the one that finally won the day. And by the end of the long and torturous and typically Boston politi-cal process, a crowded field of bidders had, almost inevitably, worked its way down to the two biggest developers in town:

Kevin McManus and Thomas Mauro.

Which one would get the land became the hot new debate. Finally the governor and mayor, for one of the rare times since both had been in office, managed to get together on something, signing joint executive orders mandating that both the State Sen-ate and City Council had to be in agreement on whose plan made the most sense for the city, financially and otherwise.

McManus's proposal won, by two close votes, which most people in town felt had fallen his way because of stories *The Globe* had run in the days before both votes that connected Thomas Mauro to Joe Broz, which meant to the Mob.

Broz, for whom Vinnie Morris had once worked, was long since dead, and there wasn't much left of Broz's old outfit. But one of Joe's nephews, John, had built a pretty successful construction company in Boston over time. John Broz had done business with Mauro over the years, and Mauro didn't run from the fact that John Broz's company was in line to get at least one of the building contracts if Mauro ended up with the land.

It didn't put Mauro directly into contact with what had once been a famous Boston crime family. But it still put him in the same story with Joe Broz, which turned into Mauro's story. He tried to fight back, but it was too late by then. McManus was the last man standing, and a new hero of the city.

Him and Nick Drummond.

"McManus gave all of the credit to Drummond," Belson said, "and Drummond let him. They even managed to shove the governor and mayor out of the picture."

He checked his watch. I pointed to his wrist and grinned.

"An Apple Watch, Frank?" I said. "What's next, one of those rings that measures your heart rate and tells you if you're getting enough sleep?"

"My wife got it for me," he said. "So fuck off."

He threw some cash on the table. "I never told you this, because Rita asked me not to tell you, she said you never got wind of her and Drummond," he said. "There were a couple times when she asked me to take another look at Drummond's death. It's just that there was never any new information, so it was one of those open cases that stayed closed. But I'm telling you now.

"By the way?" he said. "One more thing I forgot to mention, now that I think about it. But you're not the first person lately to ask me about Drummond."

"Who was the other?"

"That television guy Rita just got out of the shit," he said.

I stared at him.

"Brian Tully?" I asked.

"Prince Charming himself," he said. "You know him? He told me something funny might have been going on over there at Widett Circle."

"I don't know him," I said. "But I just had drinks with Shannon Miles."

"You think the universe might be trying to tell you something?" he said.

"About time," I said.

EIGHTEEN

I got Brian Tully's number from Benjamin Walsh.

Tully answered right away when I called. I told him who I was and he said he knew of me from Rita.

"She talks about you like you're some kind of superhero," Tully said.

"As ageless as Captain America," I said. "Just with a neck as thick as the Hulk's."

"How is she doing?" he asked. "I've been meaning to get over to the hospital."

I was about to ask what had been stopping him, but thought better of it. He might have information on Nicholas Drummond, or at least be willing to expand on the theory he'd mentioned to Frank Belson. Maybe when we knew each other better.

"The doctors are hoping the worst is over," I said. "And I'm hoping to check in on her again later."

"Give her my best," he said. "I owe her a lot." He paused and said, "Everything, actually."

"I heard," I said.

There was a pause, and then he said, "Why do I get the feeling this call isn't so you can give me an update on Rita's condition?"

"It is and it isn't. When can we meet?"

"Now's as good a time as any," he said. "Where are you?"

I told him where my office was and he said he could stop by on his way to the station. Now that he was no longer radioactive in the television business, he had been hired to do both the five-o'clock and ten-o'clock news at Fox 25.

If he'd lost in court, he would have been the latest guy in a job like his to get banished to Weinstein Island, and likely unemployable, the way Shannon Miles now was.

Fox 25's studio, I knew from having passed it plenty of times, was at the corner of Beacon and Park, within walking distance of the State House, just on the other side of the Public Garden and the Common from me.

Tully told me he was currently living on Gloucester Street, in a small town house between Beacon and Commonwealth, his wife having kicked him out of their Wellesley house even before the verdict had been reached, clearly declaring how she would have voted if she'd been in the jury room.

"Those jurors didn't believe Shannon," he said on the phone. "But Bonnie, my ex, she sure as hell did. But I guess things could be worse."

"Yeah," I said. "Nobody shot you."

"Not yet, anyway," he said.

———

IT'S ALWAYS ODD, and even disconcerting, when you see people in person you've only ever seen on television. I'd experienced the feeling with Shannon, and was now experiencing it in real time with Brian Tully.

He was about my height, just not as wide, with dark brown hair that had to have been colored, even though it was artfully flecked with gray. His eyes were very blue. But it was Tully's voice that was most striking, a rich and familiar baritone that didn't just fill the room, but had me half expecting him to start talking about an overturned tractor-trailer on the Pike.

He wore a down parka and a thick Irish-wool sweater underneath, with corduroy jeans and high duck boots.

When he had settled into one of my visitor chairs he asked, "How close did Rita come to dying?"

"Close enough."

"You ever been shot, you don't mind me asking?"

"Yes."

"*You* ever come close to dying because of it?" Tully asked.

"Yes."

I'd asked him if he wanted coffee, or tea if I could find a tea bag. He had declined both.

"So," he said, with a sigh.

"So," I repeated. "Tell me about your interest in the late Nicholas Drummond."

"Who said I had an interest in Nick Drummond?"

"Frank Belson is a friend of mine," I said. "You should hear us. Sometimes we swap gossip like high school girls."

"I should have told him our conversation was off the record," Tully said.

"Trust me," I said, "it wouldn't have made much difference."

"That means he told you why I reached out to him."

"He did."

"And now you've reached out to me," he said. "But I'm not entirely clear why."

"I'm inquiring about Drummond because it's come to my attention that he and Rita were involved in a relationship before his death," I said. "And so we are entirely clear about something, Brian: If you mention that to anybody outside this office, I will come over to your studio and drag you out from behind your desk by your hair."

"Why do I think you're not kidding?"

"Mostly because I'm not," I said. "But I believe we might be able to help each other out here, as long as I am also of the belief that I can trust you."

"Understood," he said.

"Belson said you got some kind of source telling you that something funny might have been going on with the casino deal, which might mean Nick Drummond was involved in the fun," I said.

He nodded. "I don't know you nearly well enough to trust you with one of my sources," he said. "And whether you believe it or not, I actually *do* have sources. And still consider myself a reporter, Mr. Spenser, no matter how many years I've been behind that desk."

It was increasingly apparent how much he liked the sound of his voice. I had to admit: If his voice was my voice, I would have been pretty sweet on it, too.

Tully grinned again. "Remember a few years ago when the wrong people were trying to build that casino at the Seaport?"

"The Encore."

He nodded. "Do you also recall that I was the one who broke that story?"

"I do," I said.

It was a harmless enough lie. But I didn't want to disappoint him, since the TV people I had met in my life were often delicate flowers off camera, whether they considered themselves rough, tough news busters or not.

"Well, a few days ago I got a call from one of my sources on that story that something similar might have been going on with the casino they're going to build at Widett, and money changing hands to get the thing done, before and after they decided not to build the railyards."

"And this source mentioned the hands might have belonged to Drummond? Really? Because we both know that would fly in the face of everything anybody knew about this guy."

Tully nodded. "Shocked the shit out of me, too, frankly."

"Your source tells you this now?" I said.

"I asked about that, and was told that the information had just come to him."

"Better late than never."

"I'm not saying that I believe Nick was guilty of anything, I'm just telling you what I heard," Tully said. "And that I'm going to keep digging."

"Make sure to watch your ass while you do," I said. "I know from experience that sometimes the witches be real."

He smiled now. "Hey," he said. "I'm not just another pretty face."

85

When he got to my door, he turned and said, "If there is a way for us to help each other, I'd be on board with that. So feel free to give me a call if you find out anything."

His hand was still on the doorknob.

"Just so you know," he said. "I'm not the guy Shannon Miles says I am."

"I'll have to take your word on that," I said.

"One of these days I'm even going to prove it to her," he said.

"But until you do," I said, "I've got a question for you: Where does she go to get her career back?"

Tully started to stay something but stopped himself short of doing that. Maybe he needed a prompter, and a tagline. He just quietly shut the door behind him and left my office, on his way to do the five-o'clock, and then the ten, just because he did have a career still. Susan had said on multiple occasions that it really was a man's world, and if I still didn't believe her, I should google it.

NINETEEN

They had moved Rita into a private room, one now filled with several floral arrangements.

"They must have been waiting to deliver the flowers until I had my own room," she said. "It looks like I'm lying here at my own wake."

"Have any of these lovely flowers been sent by admirers past or present?" I said.

"Only if you count my bosses," she said. "But they only love me for my billable hours."

I pulled a chair up next to her bed. "For lack of a better question, how are you feeling?"

"I feel like shit," she said.

"Well," I said, "having recently eaten some lead myself, I do know the feeling."

"With all the stitching they did, no more bikinis for me," Rita said.

"And the world will be poorer for it."

"Talk, talk, talk," she said.

Someone must have brought her makeup supplies, or she had ordered them in. Maybe Uber delivered cosmetics now the way it delivered everything else except good government. But there was some color back to her face, even if artificial, and she had clearly shampooed the red hair today, which was now back to looking like the Eighth Wonder of the World.

"There's something we need to do," I said.

"I'm not sure I have the strength to play doctor with you," she said. "But I'm game if you are."

"I'm being serious."

"So am I," she said.

"We need to talk about Nick Drummond," I said.

"No," she said.

But then we did.

It was either my bedside manner or the drugs.

RITA DID MOST of the talking, which meant that even in a hospital bed that much remained unchanged for us.

She told me that she had loved Nick Drummond, and truly, despite their age difference, and how it had never bothered her that they had never gone public with their relationship.

"Amazingly for the modern world," she said, "we kept the story of us between us for the most part."

"I would've thought he would have strutted like a rooster to show you off," I said. "Everybody would have seen you as Boston's new power couple."

"Pretty to think so, as you insist on saying," Rita said. "But I *was* older than he was and, on top of that, I was the lady in red, in just about all the relevant ways. And Nick and I were both honest enough, especially with each other, to know that where he wanted to go, I'd never have been able to go with him."

"But you loved him still," I said. "Even if the love was unseen."

"You quoting poetry to me even after I've had a near-death experience?"

"Yeah."

"Well, I gotta admit, that line pretty much nails it."

"I need to ask this," I said. "At the time of his death, did you have any suspicion at all that it might somehow have been murder?"

"Short answer? Yes," she said. "Just because he was such a good goddamn swimmer. I'd been with him in the ocean plenty of times, usually when we'd sneak down to my house in Nantucket. He loved it down there so much. Sometimes he'd go down without me, he had his own key, just used it as a way of getting away from the world, and even me, if you can believe it. He started calling it Neverland."

She sighed. "Anyway, even though I couldn't imagine why anybody would have wanted him dead, I got pretty fixed on the notion that somebody might have, even though that land deal was going to be part of his legacy. Everybody was on fire with how many new jobs it was going to mean and the affordable housing in the area, and all the rest of it. He really had become the most popular politician in town."

"But a good goddamned swimmer."

"I kept bothering the DA, who's a friend, to ask him to reopen the case," Rita said. "And I'd bother Frank Belson from time to time. They both said there was simply no evidence that foul play was involved. So eventually I dropped it. But about a month ago, I went back to my friend the DA and said I didn't want to sound crazy, but Nick dying that way still made no sense. But pretty much got the same answer."

I told her then about what Brian Tully had told me about the Widett Circle deal, and those twenty-four extremely desirable acres of prime real estate, and the chatter he was hearing about Drummond.

"Nick Drummond on the take?" Rita said. "Tell Brian Tully he can go fuck himself."

"I'm just telling you what he said."

"But even if Nick was—which he wasn't—what would that have to do with me?" she said.

"Humor me for a second, which means without getting pissed off," I said. "Let's play it out. Say it was a dirty deal, and even if Nick wasn't involved, he found out about it. Maybe McManus or Mauro or both of them were willing to do whatever it took in the run-up to those two votes. Maybe the finding out did get him killed. And somebody who knew about the two of you being in a relationship made the assumption that before he died, he might have shared whatever he knew with you. Maybe the DA mentioned to somebody that you were bothering him about the drowning all over again."

She grinned. "'Bothering'?" she said. *"Moi?"*

"Almost impossible to fathom," I said. "But stay with me on this. Has there been anything at all out of the ordinary lately that might somehow have rung a bell with the wrong person?"

"Listen, pal," she said, "I'm having a lot of trouble remembering the time before I got shot. It's still kind of a jumble. Sometimes I don't know what really happened and what's one of the fever dreams I've been having. Last night, I swear, I thought Nick was in the room with me."

"I know the feeling," I said.

She closed her eyes again. I saw her frowning with what few frown lines she had left. She had told me more than once that filler had become one of her very best friends in the whole world.

"Wait, there was something," she said.

She looked up as if she could see clouds parting.

"I found this key," she said.

TWENTY

Rita told me then about how Drummond kept clothes at her house, for times when he needed to go straight to the State House after a sleepover. Told me that for the longest time after he died, she hadn't been able to remove them from her closet, or go over to his apartment in Southie and clean that out; she'd left that to his chief of staff.

So she'd just left the clothes where they were, undisturbed, telling me that the idea of packing them up was still too raw and painful, and that even the lingering scent of him might be too much for her to bear.

But, she said, she'd finally decided to put on her big-girl pants, that the closet wasn't some kind of shrine, they were just clothes and he wasn't coming back for them. So she went in, even having a sense of what she was going to find. A couple Brooks Brothers

92

suits. Sweaters. Jeans. Dress shoes. Sneakers. Shirts and under-
wear. His stuff.

Nick's stuff.

"I knew it was time to stop acting like the pathetic widow
woman," she said. "Past time, really."

She still wasn't sure why she'd even gone through the pockets
of the suits. But she had. Not because she was suspicious that she
might find something that would lead her to another woman.
Just some small piece of him that she could keep without creep-
ing herself out. Some scrap he'd left behind.

She'd found the key in the second suit.

"He was always losing things," she said. "He acted almost
pathologically absent-minded. One of those people who'd start
looking around for his phone when it was still in his hand.
Maybe he planned to go to the bank the day he died. Who knows?
Or maybe he'd just forgotten the key was there. Or it was one
more thing he couldn't find."

Some banks, she said, didn't have the name of the bank on
keys like that. This one did. The Longfellow Bank on State Street.

So she called them. Explained who she was. Told them she
wanted to access the safe-deposit box. Whomever she spoke to
took it all the way to the bank president. He did some checking
and told her that when Drummond had first rented the box a
couple years ago, there were three names approved to access it:
Drummond himself. His chief of staff, a woman named Delores
Thompson. And Rita.

"So I went over there and he took me down to where the
boxes are kept," she said. "Then they brought the box into a
small conference room and left me alone to open it."

"What was inside?" I said.

"Nothing," she said. "It was empty."

"And nobody saw you open it," I said.

She shook her head.

"When was this?" I asked her.

"The day before somebody shot me," she said.

TWENTY-ONE

After I left Rita I called Hawk to see if he wanted to have lunch. He said no, he had things to do this afternoon, and had a date later.

"May I ask with whom?"

"Cecile," he said.

"Whoa," I said. "Cecile the hotshot surgeon who dumped you because you wouldn't share your feelings with her after you got shot? *That* Cecile?"

"One and the same."

"I thought she moved away."

"Girl's back," he said, "and now doing her surgeoning at Mass General, it turns out."

"And she's willing to give you another look?"

They had in fact been going out together when Hawk had been shot in the back by Boots Podolak's goons. Cecile had told Hawk she could no longer abide his trust issues, being that the only people he really seemed to trust were Susan and me.

"She say she's hoping I've evolved since she left," Hawk said.

"This is great," I said. "We can start double-dating again."

"Yeah, Grandpa," Hawk said. "Maybe at the sock hop."

I started the walk back to my office, already looking past lunch and ahead to dinner and where I might order takeout, as Susan had a board meeting for the Jimmy Fund. The Upper Crust on Charles was an early favorite, just because pizza from The Upper Crust was never far from my thoughts.

Even with the cold, I had found myself starting to embrace the Back Bay winter wonderland. I cut across the Common and the Public Garden, struck all over again by the beauty of the place when it was covered by snow. It reminded me, and not for the first time, of my boyhood in Wyoming, the winters there, the snow-covered ranch land that seemed to stretch forever in all directions, and the boy that I had been, imagining that covered wagons would be coming through any day, even in winter, as part of the Great Western Migration.

Once I got home, I spent the rest of the afternoon reading even more about Nick Drummond, failing to discover anything that I needed to treat like breaking news. At one point I went to *The Globe*'s website and reread the coverage of his death and the overwrought reaction to it at the time.

By then I had drunk enough coffee to chase down the Green Line shuttle. Darkness had once again come early today. I finally turned off my overhead lights in favor of the antique desk lamp, which somehow seemed to enhance the quiet solitude of the hour.

I then fixed myself a Bushmills Black, neat, sat back down at the desk, and considered how little progress I'd made on Rita's shooting.

I was in this because of her.

I had no proof that she had been shot because she had paid that visit to the bank, and just that act set off alarms. But if she had been shot because of that, if this was about cause and effect, then she was still at risk, which meant I had to protect her.

I thought about the men who had engaged in the very public fight over the Southie land, Kevin McManus and Thomas Mauro, slugging it out in the middle of the ring for months. Then there was Brian Tully, who Shannon Miles thought was a rat, but who had sat in this office and told me he might have smelled the presence of a different kind of rat involved in the proposed site of a new casino and hotel for South Boston.

In the old days, just because I thought more about the old days than anyone really should, the tennis guy Bud Collins used to write a general sports column in *The Globe*, and had created a fictional character named King Rat, who lived at the old Boston Garden when that place was a dump.

If I could pull all these pieces together in the imaginary puzzle on my desk, maybe I could identify a different kind of King Rat, someone who might have had the Senate president killed, and who maybe also tried to kill the most high-profile defense attorney in town, one who happened to be my dear friend.

It was night now. If I poured myself another glass I was going to end up sleeping on my couch, like one of those football coaches.

Had Belichick ever slept on his couch?

I got up, rinsed my glass, and shut off the desk lamp, the only lights in my office coming from the headlights of the slow-moving traffic up Boylston.

It was in that moment that my phone chimed.

Belson

There were no preliminaries with him, but then there rarely were.

"I told you there was one other guy who came around asking me about that Drummond?" he said as I answered the phone.

"Brian Tully," I said.

"Put it this way," Frank Belson said. "He won't be doing the ten-o'clock news tonight."

TWENTY-TWO

It was Tully's housekeeper who had found him, shot dead in his bed, two times in the chest.

"He actually wouldn't've been doing the ten o'clock," Belson said, "it being a Saturday."

"I assumed you were just being colorful."

"You're not the only one with the words."

Belson informed me then that Tully's town house was on Gloucester Street.

"Between Comm Ave. and Beacon," I said.

"You know this how?"

"He told me when he came to my office," I said.

"When and why did he come to your office?"

I told him that I had talked to Tully about Nick Drummond.

"You think this might have had something to do with all that?" Belson asked.

"No clue."

"Not the first time," Belson said. "Place was tossed, by the way."

"Robbery?"

"Or not," he said.

By the time I made the turn onto Gloucester off Comm Ave., I could already see that the crime scene festival was in full force, some TV trucks here, some on Gloucester, some in the distance at the corner of Beacon. The coroner's van passed me as a couple more flashing cruisers arrived, parking next to a crime scene Sprinter van. I had seen this movie before, most recently in Brookline, when the body of a client of mine named Laura Crain had been found.

There were onlookers on their side of yellow police tape, despite the cold. By now these people surely knew what had happened, and to whom, maybe even how it had been done. A light snow had begun to fall, of course. What looked like just a dusting tonight.

Belson was waiting for me on the street.

"Dead celebrity," he said. "Such a joy."

"Which floor?"

"Bedroom is on the first."

"Anybody hear anything?"

"Shooter must have used a suppressor."

"Security camera?"

"Frozen, like every other freaking thing in town," Belson said. He jerked his head in the direction of the front door.

"ME figures he'd been dead about twelve hours when the woman found him," he said. "Maybe after he got home from doing the Friday-night news. So late. Quiet street. Night was cold as shit. Nobody remembers seeing anybody go in or out."

"You said the place was tossed?"

"Like somebody was looking for something," Belson said. "Maybe he kept a lot of cash on hand. Maybe the shooter put a gun on him and told him what he'd come for. Or just put a couple in him and decided to look around himself."

He paused.

"He say anything to you of interest he didn't say to me?" Belson said.

Tonight he was actually taking occasional puffs on his cigar, something I hadn't seen him do, at least not in my presence, for a long time. This close to him, the thing smelled like a landfill.

"All he told me about the land deal was that he had a source who thought something funny might have been going on."

"Not ha-ha funny, I assume."

"No, sir."

"I don't suppose he might have mentioned who his source might've been?"

"You know better than that," I said.

"Unfortunately, I do," Belson said. "Even talking hairdos play by the rules."

"Same as us."

"Same as me, you mean," he said. "We couldn't find a phone, or a laptop. Guy did have a gun of his own. Smith & Wesson 686. It was in the top drawer of the nightstand next to the bed, not that it did him any good." He blew out more foul-smelling smoke, at least having the courtesy to do it out of the side of his mouth. "They all buy into that 'good guy with a gun stopping a bad guy with a gun' until the bad guy blows them to kingdom come."

We stood there on the sidewalk, outside the place that Brian

Tully had been renting after his wife had kicked him out of the big house in Wellesley.

"Is there any chance that this robbery, if it even was a robbery, didn't have anything to do with Drummond or what Tully's source dropped on him about the casino deal, and all the rest of that jazz?" I asked.

"No," Belson said. He held up a hand. "Sorry, I meant to say 'Fuck no.' I think it was you who told me you didn't believe in coincidences, because there's no way God would leave that much shit to chance."

"I think somebody else said it before I did," I said. "Just can't remember who was referencing a Higher Power at the time."

He turned back toward the town house. "Going to go back in and give the place another look," he said.

It would be more than just a look, because Belson wouldn't come back outside until he saw everything he needed to see and had convinced himself that he hadn't missed anything that he shouldn't have missed. And later tonight, or tomorrow morning, he would be able to describe where everything was, despite the mess inside, as if he'd taken a series of pictures with his phone.

"Guy was trying to be a reporter again," I said. "Show he still had the chops."

"And it might've got him killed," Belson said.

"Yeah," I said.

"You gonna stay on this?" he asked.

I was sure he could see me grinning in the flashing lights. "Rhetorical question?" I asked him.

"Let's try to do it differently for a change, because it would mean so much to me," he said. "You find out anything useful, you tell me before you start poking bears."

"You forget something, Frank," I said. "I *am* the bear."

I WAS BACK at my apartment and getting ready to call The Upper Crust, the night still young, when the hospital called about Rita having gone into cardiac arrest.

TWENTY-THREE

called an Uber so I didn't have to waste time looking for a place to park. By the time I was out in front of the Critical Care Center on Fruit Street, Dr. Harman was downstairs in the lobby to tell me herself that they had managed to stabilize her, and that the latest crisis was over, at least for now.

"Does *stabilized* mean safe?" I asked her.

"It means stabilized," she said.

"I thought she was getting better."

"She was."

"But the bullet missed her heart."

"Well aware," she said. "It doesn't change the fact that what happened to your friend and my patient, Mr. Spenser, was a severe shock to her entire system. And what happened an hour or so ago was a form of system failure; that's the best way I can describe it to you."

"Can I see her?"

"Not even if you were the one with a badge," she said.

I had called Quirk after I'd gotten the call from the nurse. He was at a birthday party for one of his granddaughters. I don't know how many grandchildren he had in all, but I sometimes got the sense that there were almost enough to field a soccer team. He told me to call if anything changed.

"When she wakes up," Quirk said. "Tell her that I told you that she needs to cut the shit now."

I knew where Belson was, probably still on Gloucester Street. I could call him later, and do the same with Hawk. What mattered now was that one of us was here. I was glad it was me. It made me feel like I was doing something, even though I wasn't doing much for Rita at the moment.

"Please tell me she's going to make it," I said to Dr. Harman.

"If there are no further setbacks," she said.

"But you're not in control of setbacks," I said.

"I wish," she said.

She smiled then, reached up, put a hand on my shoulder.

"Go home, Mr. Spenser," she said. "If anything changes, you will be my first call. For now, go get yourself some rest."

I told her I had an even better idea.

"And what might that be, if you don't mind me asking?" she said.

"I'm going to see a good shrink," I said.

TWENTY-FOUR

We were on Susan's couch. We rarely used her fireplace, but tonight was an exception. It was the only light in the room. My arm was around her, and she was curled into me, with Pearl curled up at the other end of the couch. My scotch and soda, in a tall glass, was on the coffee table.

Susan had made a Kir Royale for herself because she said that as good a bartender as I usually was, I was consistently deficient in getting the combination of champagne and cassis in the flute glass exactly right.

"But it doesn't mean I don't still love you," she said.

"Whew," I said. "That was a close one."

We had talked about Brian Tully's death. Mostly we had talked about Rita nearly dying, again. We each leaned forward at the same moment, as if synchronized, reached for our drinks, took our sips, and settled back into her couch.

"Why is this affecting me as much as it is," I asked.

"Rita?"

I nodded. "I know Rita is my friend. I know how often we have worked together. And how often I have worked around her flirtations."

Susan looked up. She was smiling. "'Flirtations' is putting it mildly."

"You know what I mean."

"I almost always do," she said. "But are you asking me for my professional opinion here, or the opinion of someone watching the hot chick in the tight dress who keeps putting moves on her boyfriend?"

"You're hotter," I said. "The fact that you're also a therapist just makes you even hotter, in my own professional opinion."

"I was making a larger point."

"As you so frequently are." I leaned over and kissed her hair. As always, just the smell of it was intoxicating. But then almost everything about her was, in a timeless way that still made me feel like an overheated high school boy.

Under the ancient trees we lay ourselves down again and again.

It was too late in the evening and too much had happened today for me to remember who had written that line, or why it was another that had stayed with me, standing the test of time and memory.

"But since I am getting advice for free," I said, "let's do go with your professional thoughts."

"Not the only thing you get from me for free," she said.

"Oh, ho," I said.

We sat in silence and watched the fire a little more until Susan said, "The most obvious answer is this one: You love Rita, even if you might not have ever thought about your feelings for her that way. And you know that despite all the teasing and joking the two of you have done, she loves you, too."

"I'm aware that it's more than just a deep friendship between us," I said. "And I've always known she wanted more out of the friendship."

"Even unrequited love is idealized, and self-focused," Susan said. "Whereas a love like ours is more focused on the other person's happiness, and their needs, often more than your own."

"I've never felt unrequited love for Rita," I said.

"I was talking about the red-haired hellcat's point of view," Susan said.

She angled her body now and leaned up to kiss me, softly, on the lips. Before she settled back into me, she took another quick sip of her drink.

"And I think there is something else in play here," Susan said, "and that is mortality. You've faced death plenty of times, and that means more times than I care to remember. Rita has not. Now this has affected you the way Hawk nearly dying that time affected you, which means profoundly."

"I'm not afraid to die, Suze," I said.

"But you are, ah, deathly afraid of people you love dying," she said. "It's why you protect them so fiercely, starting with me."

"I need to help her get through this," I said. "And protect her, if I have to."

"It's what you do," she said. "First, though, you need to wait for the doctors to do what they do."

"Thank you, Doctor." I reached over and took a last sip of my drink. I told myself I might need another one before we went to bed. But for the moment, I needed this talk more.

"There's one more piece of this," I said. "I feel bad for Rita, and not just because she got shot."

"Because she is alone," Susan said. "I sense that she is alone even when she is with somebody." I looked at her face and saw her smiling again. "As often as she's with somebody."

"She says she loved Nick Drummond when she was with him. Now she has no one to love her back," I said.

"Wrong," Susan said. "She has you."

I pulled her even closer to me.

"Not the way you have me," I said.

"No shit, Sherlock."

TWENTY-FIVE

awk met me at the Critical Care Center at eight the next morning, which I knew from his body clock was like him showing up in the middle of the night.

We were having second cups of cafeteria coffee. It wasn't great. But in my worldview, to actually have a bad cup of coffee you had to make it with dishwater. And maybe not even then.

We were once again waiting for Dr. Harman to come down and talk to us.

"How'd your date with Cecile go?" I asked.

"Put it this way," he said. "Doc might be willing to give me a second opinion, though maybe not as soon as I'd like."

I grinned. "Not like you haven't been on probation before in your life. Look at it that way."

"Says she still got warm feelings for me."

"Who doesn't?"

"But says she still might have some trust issues, and whatnot."

"The only woman in your life who doesn't have those issues with you is Susan."

"We really need to keep talking about this?" he asked.

"Until Rita's doctor gets here with her own opinions," I said. "And whatnot."

Dr. Harman had called me a little after seven. I was still at Susan's. She told me that Rita's heart was back to functioning normally, that she'd had a peaceful night, and explained that what had happened to Rita was known as a myocardial contusion. She said that events like hers could sometimes occur even months after a gunshot wound like Rita's, and that Rita was lucky that this particular event had occurred while she was still in the hospital.

"All in all, a good night for her," she said. "Which means a good night for all of us."

"Beats the alternative," I said.

"Wow," she said dryly. "You could do my job."

Dr. Harman came out of the elevator a few minutes later.

"Still all good," she said.

"When can we see her?" I asked.

"Maybe later today," Dr. Harman said. "What she needs more than anything right now is rest."

She started to walk away, turned, and came back.

"I'm aware of what you do for a living, Mr. Spenser," she said. Turned to Hawk.

"Less clear about you," she said to him.

"Aw, shucks," he said.

"But for the time being," she said, "and as much as possible in the short run, I want you to leave her out of whatever the two of you're doing in regard to her shooting, because the last thing in the world she needs right now is stress."

"Understood," I said.

She studied me a little more. "Somehow I doubt that," she said.

"Aw, shucks," I said.

TWENTY-SIX

Two hours later I was sitting and drinking more coffee with the woman who had been Nicholas Drummond's chief of staff.

Delores Thompson had suggested we meet at Blank Street Coffee on Charles, which was around the corner from the State House, where Nick Drummond's office had been, and hers still was.

It was becoming more and more troublesome for me to guess people's ages, male or female, but Delores Thompson was neither young nor old, her features both strong and beautiful at the same time, her looks reminding me of the actress Viola Davis. There was a presence of both authority and competence about her, and I had gathered quite quickly that she wasn't in the habit of taking shit from anybody, or suffering fools gladly, no matter how well intentioned they were.

I had ordered regulation coffee. She had ordered a matcha

latte with almond milk. When she did, she must have detected something on my face, perhaps a look of amusement.

She smiled, in very much a no-bullshit way.

"Don't judge," she said. "I could have gone with sencha green."

"I am not a tea guy," I said, "of any color or political persuasion."

When we had our mugs in front of us, she got right to it.

"In case you were wondering," she said, "I knew about Nick and Rita. It made me one of the chosen few."

"I read somewhere that you were Nicholas Drummond's brain," I said.

"Hardly," she said. "He hadn't been at this very long, but he had as sharp a political mind as I've ever encountered, and even sharper instincts. But me knowing about his relationship with Rita was simply a cost of doing business, not me prying into his personal business. I needed a number other than his in case of an emergency. He'd reluctantly given me hers, and I had reluctantly taken it."

There was a hint of something now, if not disdain, then perhaps displeasure.

"You didn't approve of them?" I said.

"*I* don't judge," she said.

"Listen, I'm not here to discuss his sex life," I said. "Or hers."

"Then why are you here?"

She wore her hair short. I noticed that even when she smiled, her dark eyes did not. They were fixed on me now, and with purpose.

I told her then about my meeting with Brian Tully before he died, and how he was clearly asking questions about the land deal, and how it had come to pass.

"He seems to have intuited that he thought money had changed hands to get the deal done," I said.

"'Intuited,'" she said.

"I know lots of big words," I said, "and can often use them in an efficacious manner."

This time she smiled with her eyes, too.

"Brian Tully is all anybody in town is talking about," Delores Thompson said. "He had a lot of friends at what I call Da House."

"I only met with him the one time," I said. "He'd been asking questions about Widett Circle, and about Nick's death. So now I am doing the same thing with you."

"Efficaciously," she said.

"You betcha!"

"Mr. Spenser, I am going to say this as plainly as possible," she said. "I am not going to sit here and let you insult my former boss. He may be gone. But I still consider myself the keeper of the flame."

"Not my intent," I said. "But until someone disavows me of the notion, I think that somebody might have thought Nick Drummond at least knew something he shouldn't have known. And that if he did, Rita did. And that it might have gotten him killed and gotten her shot."

"That is a lot of blue smoke and mirrors, as we say in my world," she said.

"I've gone down rabbit holes before," I said, "but somehow managed to find my way out."

She drank some of her tea, and then spooned more sugar into it, which I thought defeated the purpose of drinking green tea in the first place.

"Nick Drummond died far too soon, in a tragic accident," she said. "And, in my own opinion, died a hero of our city. I haven't heard anything resembling proof, from you or from Brian Tully or the Boston Police Department, that it was anything other than that."

She closed her eyes and shook her head.

"It was like that young man was living in the wrong time," she said. "He didn't like to email or text. Didn't believe anything was really private in the modern world once it got up in those Clouds. Sometimes was secretive to a fault, and not just about Rita. Most people who wanted to email him had to go through me. He was a bit of a charming Luddite that way. He even liked sending actual letters, if you can believe it. Ones he wrote himself on an old manual typewriter. An Underwood."

"A classic, that typewriter," I said. "I used to have one, too. Still have it in a box. When the Internet falls apart, I've got no worries."

"You know what I miss?" she said. "Well, I miss a lot of things. But I miss the *clack-clack-clack* of those keys when he was in his office."

Now I told her about the key to the safe-deposit box, and Rita calling the bank to inquire about it, and discovering that the box was empty.

"Nick might've mentioned having that box, but it was a while ago," she said. "I always wondered why he needed it, or what he kept inside it. Now you're telling me he'd emptied it out before he died?"

"Someone did," I said.

She sighed. "A man of the people who liked to be a man of mystery," she said. "I'd always wanted him to share more with the public about the life he'd led as a foster kid. He'd just smile and say, 'The good old days are now' and leave it at that. Said he didn't want anybody's pity then, and didn't want it now." Now she smiled, almost wistfully. "Put me down as one more person who didn't know as much of his story as I would have liked."

I smiled at her then. "Are you telling me as much of it as you do know?" I said.

"I believe I'll ignore that question," she said.

She glanced at her watch. I knew I had taken up more of her time than I'd told her I would.

I said, "Do you think that your boss might have been murdered?"

"And there it is," she said. "The elephant in the coffee shop."

"Do you?"

"I'll tell you what I told the police at the time, and what I'm sure Rita Fiore has told you. The only thing that troubled me, and troubles me still, is that he was such a world-class swimmer. But the police told me, because believe me, I asked, that they had never found anything suspicious about his death except that he was a good swimmer who picked the wrong day to go swimming and drowned."

"There was a lot of money associated with that land deal," I said. "Whether it was over the table or under the table. Now your boss, who did the most to help broker that deal, is dead. A media guy looking into it is dead. And your boss's girlfriend, and my friend, is in the hospital because somebody tried to kill her."

The dark eyes were on me again, more fiercely than before. Delores Thompson stood.

"You find out somebody did something to Nick," she said, "you call me again, Mr. Spenser. Until then, enjoy the rest of your day."

She walked briskly out of the coffee shop. I paid the bill and walked back to my office.

When I got there, Shannon Miles was standing outside my door, looking frantic.

"You have to help me," she said.

"Help you with what?"

"I think they might be coming after me next."

"Who might be coming after you next?"

"Whoever it is that shot Brian Tully," she said.

She took in a lot of air, let it out, and said, "I may have shot someone myself last night."

TWENTY-SEVEN

quickly got Shannon inside my office. She took off her low-hanging knit cap, shook her hair loose, and took off the sheepskin jacket she was wearing.

But even sitting in one of my client chairs, she seemed as agitated as she had been in the hallway, unable to keep herself still.

I asked if she wanted coffee. She said what she really wanted was a drink. I told her that as a skilled barista I had the ability to provide both, and proceeded to make her a cup of Dunkin' in my Keurig before lacing it with a generous slug of Bushmills.

"I don't know where to start," she said, taking the mug from me with both hands and taking a sip.

I told her that shooting somebody seemed to me to be as good of a jumping-off point as any.

"You said you *might* have shot somebody," I said. "You mean you don't know?"

Shannon Miles shook her head. "I fired one shot and then I ran."

"Hit who?"

"I don't know," she said. "The man who'd broken into my house. He was wearing one of those wrestling masks."

"Where do you live?"

"Newton Street," she said.

"Brookline," I said. "Not all that far from Boston College."

Now she nodded, before drinking more of the Spenser version of Irish coffee.

"I'd been on the Vineyard, the night before, the small place I have there," she said. "It's where I was when Brian called me."

She sighed, as if to hit a reset button.

"Let me back up," she said.

I knew from experience that she had to tell it her way, even if she might be the only one to whom her story made sense, at least until I'd heard all of it.

"Before you start," I said. "Why did Brian call you?"

"He said he wanted to make things right between us," she said.

She absently reached up and brushed some hair away from her eyes. There was a tremor to her hand as she did. I could see why she was keeping both hands firmly on the mug when she would bring it back to her lips.

She shifted again in the chair, and recrossed her legs.

"I asked if he were joking." A harsh sound that tried to be a laugh came out of her then. "He said no, he was being serious, that the way things ended up between us had been eating him up inside. I said, 'Poor thing.' But then he was talking so fast I could barely keep up, telling me to please hear him out, he was working on a story that would blow the lid off the land deal in

Southie. Said he had a source and a good one, and that he wanted us to work it together, like it was the good old days for us all over again. At which point I informed him that the only days I remembered now were truly, amazingly lousy ones."

"But you heard him out," I said.

"I'm still a reporter, Mr. Spenser, if one without a portfolio these days," she said. "So, yes, he had my attention, though I wasn't entirely sure for how long. But I was stuck at the Vineyard for the night, one of those winter nights when it felt like one of the most isolated places on earth. And even talking to someone who'd helped ruin my life made me feel less alone in the moment."

She drank more of the whiskey-laced coffee. Or maybe it was whiskey with a splash of coffee.

"But then he told me he didn't want to talk too much about it on the phone, you never knew who might be listening," she said. "I told him he sounded paranoid. He said bet your ass he was, this story involved powerful people, and when could we meet?"

I watched her twist again in the chair. It was like watching a cat move around in a sack.

For now she put the mug down on my desk. I was betting it wouldn't be for long. This wasn't the angry person I'd met at the Oak Long Bar. This was someone clearly scared out of her wits.

She was still telling it her way.

"I told him I would try to come back to Boston in the morning," she continued. "He said that just in case I was delayed, he was going to leave something for me at my house, what he said was an outline of the information he had. He'd typed it out so there wouldn't be any record on his laptop, or the Cloud, or whatever. I told him he couldn't just leave it in the mailbox, or on my doorstep. But then he sounded like the same old cock-of-the-walk Brian, and reminded me he still had a key. Then he said he'd explain the rest of it to me in much greater detail when he saw me. Before I ended the call, I asked him again to explain why he'd reached out to me and he said that he didn't want me to think he was *that* guy. And when I told him he absolutely had been that guy, he said, 'Not anymore.'"

She got up then and walked over to where the bottle of Bushmills was sitting next to the Keurig and poured more of the dark liquid into her mug.

I sensed she was finally getting to it now, what had happened at her house. There was no reason for me to rush her. I had nowhere else to be.

"I was on my way up 93 when I heard that he had been murdered," she said. "But I remembered that he said he was going to leave something for me at the house. I'd tried to call him a couple times from the road, but he didn't pick up. Now I obviously know why."

"But you wanted to know what he knew, or even thought he knew, that might have gotten him killed."

"*Needed* to know, is more like it." She shrugged, and smiled as if she were mocking herself. "The business we have chosen," she said. "A lot of people thought I was a whore during that trial. Well, maybe just a news whore."

Her driveway, she said, was more like a long access road leading up to her house, one that hadn't been plowed by the people she'd hired to plow it while she'd been away. So she parked at the end and made what she said was nearly a quarter-mile walk up the hill. There were some footprints in the snow, but she just assumed they belonged to Tully and thought nothing more of it.

As soon as she opened the door, she saw that the place had been trashed. That was when she instinctively reached for the gun in her purse.

"It was actually Brian who'd bought me the gun and taught me how to use it," she said. "He said that it was insane for a public figure, especially a single woman, not to arm themselves."

She said that once she was inside, everything seemed to happen at fast-forward speed. The intruder was on the second level, and came charging down the stairs at her, either not thinking she was armed or not noticing the gun in her hand right away.

"I had time to fire one shot," she said. "I know you think it sounds crazy, but I really am unsure as to whether I hit him or not, if he just stumbled down the steps on his own when I startled him by firing at him."

"Then what?"

"I ran."

"Did he have a gun?"

"I swear," she said, "I don't know. And didn't stay around to find out."

"But you didn't call the police."

"I didn't know what to do," she said. "I might've just shot an unarmed man, whether or not he'd broken into my house." She ran another trembling hand through her long hair. "They say getting shot is a shock to your system. Well, so was shooting someone, at least it was for me. I ran back to my car, going down in the snow a couple times, afraid to look back. Then I drove to the Marriott in Cleveland Circle, which is just a few minutes away. I might have slept for an hour, if that. When I woke up, I kept checking the Internet every few minutes to see if a shooting anywhere near my street had been reported, or if there was anything new on Brian's death."

She said she was afraid to go back to her house this morning, not knowing what she might find there. Or who.

And then she thought of me, she said. Not a cop. But close enough. I had given her my card when we met at the Copley Plaza. She told me it was still in her purse.

"Now here I am," she said, leaning forward. "What am I going to do? Whoever killed Brian is clearly after me now."

I pointed to her mug. She shook her head.

"You did the right thing by coming here," I said. "I'll protect you."

"You barely know me," she said. "You're probably as surprised to see me as I was to hear from Brian."

"Force of habit," I said. "And while this may sound politically incorrect, I've always been a sucker for damsels in distress."

I stood.

"Get your coat back on."

"Are we going to the police?"

"No," I said.

"Why not?" Shannon Miles asked.

"Force of habit," I said again.

TWENTY-EIGHT

Since Shannon Miles had left her car at the hotel and taken an Uber to my office, we walked back to my apartment and I drove us to Brookline in what had once been a new Grand Cherokee in the fall but now looked as if I'd parked it in a snowbank for the past couple months.

It was slow going, even the plowed roads feeling like the ice at the Garden. We left the Cherokee at the bottom of her hill the same as she had the night before, which was perhaps why she was able to surprise the person who'd broken into her house.

There were a few hundred yards between her and the nearest house on her block, so it was unlikely that any of her neighbors had heard a shot being fired.

She had shown me the gun before we'd left my office. It was the same model Smith & Wesson Belson said Brian Tully had owned, the one Tully never got a chance to use on his own intruder.

My .38 was in the side pocket of my peacoat. I took it out and pressed it to my leg as we approached Shannon Miles's front door. The exterior was red brick, with blue trim around the windows and a fireplace to our left. An expensive house in an expensive neighborhood in an expensive Boston suburb. Shannon Miles hadn't gotten the monetary settlement she'd sought from Brian Tully, but if she was still living here she had not yet reached the point where someone would have to run a benefit for her.

She looked nervously at the gun in my hand.

"You don't think someone is still inside, do you?" she asked.

"The odds of that are unlikely," I said. "But think about how long they were for the Sox when they came back against the Yankees that time in '04."

Despite our circumstances, and what had happened to her and her former coanchor the previous evening, she smiled. "You're an interesting man," she said.

"Remind me to show you sometime how I can read upside down."

I gently tried the knob. The door was unlocked. I motioned for her to stay behind me and stepped inside, the .38 now extended fully in front of me.

From behind me Shannon Miles said, "He was right there at the bottom of the stairs."

There was beige carpeting on the stairs. But there was no blood that I could see anywhere, nor on the hardwood floor between the bottom of the staircase and the living room to our left.

No blood, no body.

Maybe the bullet she'd fired hadn't hit the guy in the mask after all.

I heard a sharp intake of breath from Shannon Miles. "This can't be," she said.

"What can't be?"

"The place was a complete shambles last night—I could see the mess in the living room, the pillows on the floor and the coffee table turned over, right before I saw the guy coming down the stairs," she said. She walked toward the living room ahead of me. "And now it looks as if my housekeeper has been in."

I kept my gun out as the two of us walked through the house, room by room, downstairs and then upstairs. The rest of the place was as neat as the living room, as if Shannon Miles were getting it ready for a house showing.

"Why would he . . . whoever it was . . . clean up after?" she said.

I said, "Maybe the guy wanted it to look as if you were looking for attention if you did call the cops. Attention or sympathy."

"You mean like I cried wolf?" Shannon Miles asked.

"Something like that."

We were back to the first floor by then. She was pointing to the area at the foot of the stairs.

"It happened the way I said it did," she said. "You have to believe me."

"I do believe you," I said.

"Somebody must have been able to listen in on Brian's phone," she said. "Can people make that happen?"

"More often than you think."

She said, "And then somebody came looking for whatever it was Brian said he was going to leave for me, and was still searching my house when I walked in on him."

127

"Except you don't know if he left it, if he got the chance to leave it," I said.

"I'd have to do a more thorough search than we just did to see if he might've left something my intruder didn't find," she said.

She told me I could search the first level of the house. I did. She was upstairs for more than a half-hour, then finally came back to the living room, said she'd found nothing in all the possible hiding places in the house she could think of, sat down on her L-shaped couch, as if suddenly exhausted, as if the last several hours were now fully catching up with her.

"I can't stay here alone," she said, almost as if talking to herself. "And if they came for me here, it will be easy enough for them to find out about my place at the Vineyard if they haven't already, so I wouldn't feel safe hiding out there."

"I'm going to call somebody," I said.

"Who?" she asked.

"Somebody who will keep you as safe as I would," I said. "And is an even better shooter than I am, if it ever comes to that."

I walked out of the room, and back outside, and made the call. He answered on the first ring, as he almost always did; he was as obsessive and compulsive about that as he was about everything else.

I explained, in conversational shorthand, what I needed.

"You must be shitting me," he said.

"Would that I were."

"Here the fuck we go again," Vinnie Morris said.

TWENTY-NINE

The only concession that Vinnie had made regarding the current weather conditions were a pair of what I assumed were waterproof lace-up boots, black, that looked as if they had just come out of the box.

"Nice boots," I said when I met him at the top of Shannon Miles's driveway.

"Thursday," he said. "And before you say something stupid, it's the name of the brand."

"Thanks for clearing that up," I said.

When I introduced him to Shannon Miles, Vinnie said, "I used to watch you do the news, when you worked with the other guy."

"Thank you," she said. "I think."

"I'm talking about the guy got shot," Vinnie said.

"He still tries to keep up with the news," I said to her.

"What do you do for a living, Mr. Morris?" Shannon Miles asked.

"Entrepreneur-type work, you could say," Vinnie said.

"But Mr. Spenser said you're quite good with a gun," she said.

"It still comes up from time to time in my entrepreneuring," he said.

She excused herself then to go back upstairs, ready to search more thoroughly for what Brian Tully might have hidden, if he'd gotten the chance. She'd already gone back over her emails, and checked her phone, discovering no messages from him after she'd spoken to him from Martha's Vineyard.

"Thank you for coming on such short notice," she said to Vinnie before heading up the stairs.

"Why not," Vinnie said.

He had casually draped his cashmere topcoat over a chair. Underneath was a royal-blue suit, starched white shirt, no tie. He had sharp features, dark eyes, was as lean as a knife. And really could, if necessary, slice the address off an envelope.

"I assume this would be a paying babysitting job," he said when she was out of earshot.

I told him it was and that I was being compensated, quite generously, by Rita's bosses at Cone, Oakes.

"How's she doing?" Vinnie asked.

"It's like they say in sports," I said. "She's day to day."

"Aren't we all?" he said.

Then he said, "I'm guessing that me being here has something to do with her being where she is. Or we wouldn't be where we are."

"Beautifully put," I said.

"On the phone you said it looks like the same people who capped her old partner sent somebody here last night," he said.

"A somebody she might've shot."

"And you think the guy was up and around enough to tidy up?" Vinnie said.

"If he didn't, somebody did," I said.

"If this is making any sense to you, could you maybe help it make better sense to me?"

"The only working theory that I have, one I've shared with her, is that maybe they wanted to set it up, just in case she was trying to play the victim card all over again, over a break-in that wasn't."

"So as to maybe make it easier for them to take another swing at her down the road," Vinnie said.

"Somebody thought that Rita knew something, and she didn't, but she got shot anyway," I said. "I'd like to do everything in my power, and yours, to ensure that the same thing doesn't happen to Ms. Miles."

"You think she might be dead already if she didn't shoot first?" Vinnie asked.

"It's why I've once again enlisted you to join my band of merry men."

"To save another Maid Marilyn," he said.

"Marian," I said.

"Whatever," Vinnie said.

Then he said, "Just out of curiosity, how long you think it might take for you to roll this thing up? I'm just looking for a ballpark estimate, I won't hold you to it."

"I've only been in it since Rita got shot."

"I'm only asking on account of a thing coming up in Chicago that might require my attention, and is probably gonna pay more than you're paying me."

"I didn't tell you what I'm paying."

"Chicago is more," Vinnie said. "Trust me."

"Stay with it as long as you can," I said, "and then I'll figure out who I need to bring out of the bullpen."

Then I told him what Brian Tully had told me about the land deal, and asked if he'd ever heard anything about Thomas Mauro being hooked up in some way with what was left of Joe Broz's operation, since Vinnie had once been Joe's number one.

Just because Mauro hadn't gotten the land didn't mean the Mob hadn't been involved in the whole thing at least somewhere.

"My opinion?" Vinnie said. "That story was mostly Grade A crap. We both know Gerry Broz basically turned the family business into an ink spot by being such a screwup. And the nephew's business is legit, leastways as legit as anybody else in construction in this town. But people read 'Broz' and it was like they were reading 'Corleone.'"

"So if Thomas Mauro is connected, it's not to them," I said.

"Yeah," he said, "no."

"Anybody I could ask about any other possible connections to organized crime in our city?" I said.

Vinny rolled his eyes, for my benefit.

"A lot of people you could ask who *might* know," he said. "But Tony Marcus *would* know."

"Here we go again," I said.

THIRTY

It had been over a year since I'd visited Buddy's Fox, the bar and restaurant in the South End where Tony Marcus kept his office.

The last time I'd been there I'd been trying to help the son of a friend get out of a gambling hole he'd dug for himself, and since he owed money to Tony, I had gone there to negotiate a peace.

Now Hawk and I were back, seated across from Tony's desk, which he liked to say was his version of the *Resolute* desk in the Oval Office.

"Just on account of there being nobody more fucking resolute than me," he said.

As always, Tony looked more dapper than all of Savile Row. His two body men, Junior and Ty-Bop, were positioned on either side of his office door.

Junior remained as big as an Amazon truck. Ty-Bop was

outfitted today in a Rafael Devers No. 11 jersey and a Yankees cap, which I thought wasn't just an odd fashion statement, but somewhat counterintuitive. As always, he seemed to be buzzing like a power tool even standing still. He was also the best shooter I knew outside of Vinnie.

"You only come here when you want something from me," Tony said to me. "So I'm telling you straight up that whatever it is you do want, I ain't just giving it away."

"Can't old friends just connect in an increasingly isolated world?" I asked.

Tony shifted his attention to Hawk. "You still not tired of listening to his jive-ass bullshit?"

It came out sounding like *bool-shit*.

Hawk smiled. "Look who's talking," he said.

"How's Rita?" Tony asked.

"Improving," I said.

"How close the girl come to passing over the other side?" Tony asked.

"If it was football," I said, "they would have had to bring out the markers. She was that close to the yard to gain."

"Now tell me what you come here for, I'm a busy man."

I told him as much as he needed to know, about Rita and Nick Drummond and the bank and Brian Tully and what Tully had told me about the land deal before he got shot. And about somebody coming for Shannon Miles after Tully did get shot.

"Sounds like a shitshow," Tony Marcus said. He smiled. "Your specialty. But you still ain't told me what you need from me."

"I was wondering what you might know about the sell-off in Southie having been, ah, illicit in some way," I said. "Or at least a lot less *licit* than people might have thought it was."

"Oh, hell, yeah," Tony said.

He said he'd tried to get in on the deal himself, through a couple City Council members who, as he informed us, had partaken of his various escort services from time to time over the years.

"I am shocked," Hawk said, "to discover that some of our various elected officials couldn't keep it in their pants."

"What's the damn world coming to?" Tony said.

I studied his face, fascinated by it, and by him, as always. I remembered reading once about a breed of cat, Chartreux, known for being smiling cats. That was Tony Marcus's smile, in total.

"But I take it you weren't able to cut a piece of the pie for yourself," I said.

"By the time I tried to come through the back door with a bag full of cash," he said, "I was told that my old friend Tommy Mauro, another partaker of my girls, just so you know, might've been way ahead of me. And the other guy, McManus, might've been spreading some sugar around, too."

"Both of them?" I said.

"What I heard," Tony said.

"Is Mauro mobbed up," I said. "The media tried awfully hard to tie him to Joe Broz's old shop."

"Are you shitting?" Tony said. "Talking about Joe Broz would be like going to New York and acting like the Gambino family was still a thing. Those damn wings got clipped a long time ago. Same with Joe Broz's people, after it turned out that Joe's son took over and acted like someone got his front lobe removed at the same time."

Tony then went through the motions of taking a cigar out of the humidor on his desk, clipping the end, slowly lighting it as he rolled it around in his mouth, being as careful with the whole process as if performing gallbladder surgery.

"Mauro don't have clean hands, none of them boys in real estate do, you ask me," Tony Marcus said. "But I never heard he was all the way crooked, leastways not like you meant."

He blew a rather perfect smoke ring toward the ceiling and watched it until it disappeared.

"Go ahead and smoke if you want," I said. "Don't worry about us."

The smiling-cat smile was back then. "You don't like it, Ty can open the door and Junior can throw your ass out it."

"Well," Hawk said, smiling mostly to himself, "they could try their very hardest."

"I know Mauro a little bit, on account of the girls," Tony said. "And we done a little this and that and the other in real estate together, off the books, I guess you could say. But the boy's too smart to be dumb, if you're feeling me on that. There's no way, with him wanting that land as badly as he did, that he'd jam himself up with, well, someone truly was organized."

"Organized" came out a little bit at a time, like he was cutting it up into pieces and tossing it at us.

"But somebody wanted it out there that he was connected," I said.

Tony nodded.

"You think maybe Kevin McManus is the one who got that story out there?" I said. "He's the one who ended up with the land."

"Whoever put it out there, it worked," Tony said. "Maybe McManus was gonna get the land no matter what. But in the end, he won, Mauro lost, and it didn't matter who might've been on the take and who wasn't, who was connected and who wasn't, game over."

"It sounds so simple when you put it that way," I said. "Like logical decomposition."

"More jive-ass bullshit," Tony said. "It just don't never end, do it?"

THIRTY-ONE

Hawk and I drove to the hospital from the South End, as
Quirk had called to tell us that Rita, who'd been moved to
a private room, could have visitors again. Quirk was waiting for
us outside. Dr. Harman accompanied us all inside, somewhat
like a hall monitor, I thought.

"Just to make sure you don't bother the decent people," she
said in explanation.

I said, "You must know by now that Martin Quirk is one of
the most decorated and respected policemen in the history of his
department."

"It doesn't change the fact that he's now sitting with the bad
kids in the back of the class," she said.

Rita tried to raise her energy level in our company, but that
didn't last for very long. It was as if she started running out of
battery power after just a few minutes. As much as we were
told that she was getting better, at least incrementally, she still

looked a size smaller, in all ways, than she had been before being shot.

When Dr. Harman asked us if we had any leads yet, her admonishing look wasn't directed at one of the most decorated and respected cops in the history of the BPD, it was directed at me.

"Let's just say our investigation is ongoing," I said.

Quirk reached over with one of his big hands to take hold of Rita's. "Hey," he said to her. "He stole my line."

"Okay, you're all done now," Dr. Harman said.

I told Rita then that if we weren't back later, we'd be back tomorrow.

"Well," she said, grinning up at us, "it won't be as if you didn't warn me."

When we were in the hall, Dr. Harman looked up at Hawk. "You never say much," she said.

Hawk smiled brilliantly at her. "Makes it easier not to miss much," he said.

She smiled back at him, and walked toward the nurses' station.

"Don't even think about it," I said when we were in the elevator.

"Think about what?"

"You know what."

"I didn't do nothing," Hawk said.

"Yeah," I said. "You did."

"You think I'd even consider hitting on Rita's doctor?" he said.

"Yes," I said.

Quirk asked where we were going. I told him my office. He

said he'd meet us there, and I could give him an update on whatever I had. Martin Quirk then looked at Hawk and said, "Shame you can't ride with me, it would be like old times for you, being in a cop car."

"I have always felt a bond with law enforcement, can't lie," Hawk said.

"You call it a bond," Quirk said. "We call them handcuffs."

QUIRK SAID HE couldn't stay long, he said there was a meeting at City Hall for which his presence was required. So I quickly took him through everything I had learned, all the way to having just been with Tony Marcus.

"So Vinnie is gonna stay with Shannon Miles for the time being?" Quirk asked.

"He said he might have to go out of town at some point, on what sounds like an exciting career opportunity."

"What," Quirk said, "shooting out the lights at Wrigley Field?"

Quirk put eyes on me now as if I were in an interrogating room.

"Is that really everything?" he said.

I nodded.

"I can't prove that somebody staged Drummond's death," I said. "And we both know that if anybody could prove it, Frank would have done it long ago. But you know the rest of this, Drummond being dead and Tully being dead and Rita being nearly dead. Now somebody goes after Shannon Miles after Tully tells her he might have new information on how the casino deal got done."

Quirk took it all in, waiting until I finished.

"I know how much you want to put this in the same picture frame," he said. "And as much as it sounds like it could end up there, it's sure as shit not there yet."

Hawk grinned from the couch. "See how he made commander?" he said.

Quirk looked at him and shook his head. To me, he said, "You obviously believe Shannon Miles is still in danger or you wouldn't have called in one of your All-Stars."

I nodded. "And Rita could be in danger once she's out of the hospital."

"I can help with that, when the time comes," Quirk said.

Then he said, "Where you going with this next?"

"I need to talk to Thomas Mauro," I said.

"*If* he'll talk to you."

"People often open up to me, Martin," I said. "It's like a gift."

"Mauro around?" he asked.

I told him that Thomas Mauro was doing the only sane thing for someone with his money: spending the winter in Palm Beach, which meant if JetBlue had seats I was going to be on a plane later this afternoon.

"He don't just want to crack the case," Hawk said. "Boy really just looking for any reason to see the sun again."

"What," I said, "I can't do both?"

THIRTY-TWO

I got Thomas Mauro's phone number from Delores Thompson. When I'd asked if she might have one for him, she said, "I have everybody's number. Want to talk to Tom Brady?"

"Not a chance," I said. "They shoot deserters in the Army."

But before I called Mauro I called Edward Oakes. He had told me that if there was any way he could help me, I only had to reach out. I asked if he knew Mauro. He said that Mauro was a Cone, Oakes client.

"I should have assumed," I said.

"Should I assume that you're going to annoy my client in some way?" Oakes said.

"Don't take this the wrong way," I said. "But guilty."

Oakes called me back about ten minutes later and told me that Mauro would see me first thing in the morning, then gave me an address on South Ocean Blvd. in Manalapan, which even a plebian like me knew was south of Palm Beach.

"Basically, go to Mar-a-Lago and take a right," Oakes said.

"Easy for you to say," I said.

MY FLIGHT LANDED at Palm Beach International a little after eight o'clock. It could have landed in the middle of the night for all I cared. All I knew once I walked out the terminal doors to where the Hertz bus would pick me up was this:

I was warm again.

Susan and I had once stayed at the Ritz in Manalapan, which was just over the Lantana Bridge. I had discovered when I tried to book a room that it was no longer a Ritz, but was now known as the Eau Palm Beach Resort and Spa. Something else they'd changed on me. But the place was only a few minutes from Thomas Mauro. Better yet, it wasn't my money, it was Edward Oakes's.

The hotel was pretty much as I remembered it. I checked in and went upstairs and when I opened the terrace doors and stepped out onto my balcony and felt the ocean air on my face and saw the star-lit ocean seeming to stretch all the way to the Bahamas, or whatever land mass came next, I managed to not burst into tears.

I ate downstairs at the Angle restaurant, ordering their sweet potato soup as an appetizer to my rib-eye steak. By the time my entrée arrived, I was on my second glass of cabernet.

I had already decided I would call Susan when I got back to the room. But before I went back upstairs, I walked outside and past the pool closest to the restaurant and took off my shoes and socks and walked down the beach. If I wasn't thinking deep thoughts as I headed south along the water, I was definitely thinking much happier thoughts than the ones with which I'd left Boston.

I didn't know what I would get out of Mauro, what he might volunteer or let slip. But if Tony Marcus, without any skin in the game, was right about Mauro, then there might at least have been some kind of arrangement between him and Nick Drummond, at least until there wasn't.

And if all that happened to be true, then Mauro was connected to Rita, whether he was mobbed up or not.

I thought about a nightcap in the lobby bar when I got back, but decided that a whiskey from the minibar would do me just fine. When I was back in the room I got out a small bottle of Glenlivet, poured it into a glass, got on the bed, and called Susan Silverman and asked if she might possibly be interested in talking dirty.

"As exciting an opportunity as that sounds like," she said, "I think I'll resume watching *Slow Horses* after we've chatted, and then call it a night."

"I feel as if you may have answered in haste," I said.

"Well, you're certainly entitled to your opinion," she said.

There was a lengthy pause at her end of the line and then she said, "I went to see Rita."

THIRTY-THREE

told her to hold the thought as I walked back over to the mini-bar for more scotch, phone in hand. Then I continued to the terrace and sat down on one of the chairs.

"Before I tell you all about it," she said, "are those crashing waves I hear in the background?"

"If you were here," I said, "we could go down to the beach and make out like Burt Lancaster and Deborah Kerr in *From Here to Eternity.*"

"Yet another movie only you think isn't too old to reference," Susan said.

I drank more Glenlivet. It went down pleasantly and smoothly. Not like a crashing wave. More like warm water.

"So did I just hear correctly that you, Dr. Susan Silverman, went to see your nemesis Rita Fiore?" I asked.

"You did," she said. "And I did."

"Without giving me so much as a heads-up."

"What I'm going to say will hurt, but only for a second," she said. "It wasn't about you."

"You're right," I said. "That does hurt."

The view of the water and the sound of it combined with the sound of her voice only made me miss her more.

"I've been thinking about doing it the last couple days," she said. "I just wanted her to know that if she wanted to talk when she was out of the hospital, or even before that—and even to me, God forbid—I was here."

"I'm just glad that the sight of you showing up in her room didn't make her heart stop all over again."

"I didn't stay long," Susan said. "But I'm glad that I went. And she seemed genuinely glad that I'd made the effort."

I raised a glass to that, and to the ocean at the same time. *Hello darkness, my old friend.*

"This gives me just one more reason, not that I needed another one, to love you beyond all human understanding," I said.

Susan laughed. It had always been a wonderful, full-throated laugh, absent of inhibition, the way she was absent of inhibition.

"Oh, please," she said. "Even baristas love me that way."

"So how was she?"

"Scared," Susan said. "Scared about what happened to her. Scared about leaving the hospital. And, as we've already discussed, scared of being alone once she has left the hospital."

"She knows I will protect her," I said.

"I know that, and she knows that."

There was another long pause from her. I could picture her in her bed, Pearl at the end of it. Susan in her T-shirt. Sweatpants. Reading glasses at the end of her nose.

"This whole thing is a hot mess, isn't it?" she said. "And Rita being shot is just one part of it and you're trying to figure out how big a part."

"Yes."

"And you think that this man Mauro will give you a bit more clarity?"

"Ever hopeful."

I finished what I promised myself would be my last scotch of the evening, took one last look at the Atlantic, and walked back into my room.

"Do you believe that Nick Drummond was murdered?"

"I have no proof of that being the case and neither does Frank Belson," I said. "But yes."

I pictured her again. Perhaps she had her hair pulled back, as she sometimes did before bedtime. I had no way of knowing that. What I did know was that she was as beautiful to me over the phone as she was in person, and that I never required Face-Time to verify that. I had frankly never liked FaceTime when we were apart. I just preferred imagining her. Seeing her only made me miss her more. Girl of my dreams.

"You wouldn't be talking to Mr. Mauro if you didn't think he's involved in this in some way," Susan said. "If only on the perimeter."

"Correct."

"But if it isn't just the perimeter, you need to be careful."

"Suze," I said, "if he is involved, he's the one who will need to be careful."

I told her then that I loved her. She said she loved me. I told her that unless tomorrow brought any surprises, I would be back in time for dinner.

As often happened, neither one of us wanted to be the one to end the call.

Then I heard her laugh again, bigger than before.

"What's so funny?" I asked.

"I just realized you wore me down."

"In what way?"

"Let's do talk dirty," she said.

And we did.

THIRTY-FOUR

In the morning I took a run on the beach, one that did not tax my increasingly creaky knees, despite the soft sand.

"You only supposed to end up with knees like yours you played a contact sport," Hawk liked to say, at which point I would remind him that I did play a contact sport, just without a helmet and pads.

Mauro had told me to pull up to his gate just past Hypoluxo Beach, and that it would open automatically upon my arrival.

I slowly made my way up the gravel driveway, a huge expanse of lush green grass on either side of me. Beyond the house seemed to be even more water and blue sky than I could see from my balcony. I knew it was the same ocean we had in New England. But right now, I liked theirs much better.

Mauro was waiting for me when I got out of the car. He was as tall as I was, with way too much white hair, too much of a tan, and, as I was about to discover, a big handshake that tried way too hard.

"Spenser," he said.

"It is me," I said. "Some say 'It is I,' but *me* is the more acceptable object pronoun."

Mauro gave me a brief, knowing nod and said, "Eddie Oakes warned me about you," and then showed me in.

A Hollywood agent with whom I had done some work in the past had once told me a story that had become a legend out there. The first time Bob Newhart had been invited to Johnny Carson's Malibu home, as Carson was giving him the tour, Newhart finally asked, "Where's the gift shop?"

I imagined that place was like this mansion except, perhaps, smaller. As we made our way through the foyer it was impossible for me, as a closet art lover, not to notice a horse sculpture that I knew to be a Damien Hirst, only because both Susan and I were fans of Hirst's work.

Eventually I followed Mauro up a winding staircase to the second floor, where there was an even better view of the water than there had been downstairs. Mauro seemed as pleased with himself for his view of the ocean as he was for owning a Hirst.

"Little quieter down here than it is further up South Ocean," he said. "I didn't need to be on Billionaires' Row."

"More of a criminal element up there?" I said.

We took seats in the study, in front of a floor-to-ceiling window. And before I could even begin to explain more fully why I had made the trip down here from Boston, Mauro said, "Just so you know? Nick Drummond wasn't the living saint everybody thought he was."

He let that settle.

"Do tell," I said.

"I'm sure you know Saint Nick's bio."

"I know he put himself on the map by getting elected to the Senate in First Suffolk," I said. "Crowded field. He didn't get a lot of votes, just the most."

"Good old Southie," Mauro said. "Want me to sing some of 'Southie Is My Home Town'?"

"You're from there?"

"Only for a year when I was little," he said. "But when I went after that land, I made it sound as if I practically grew up at Fort Independence." He gave a little shrug to the broad shoulders. "You do what you have to do before somebody does you."

"Somebody should put that on a pillow," I said. "But you were saying that Drummond wasn't who people thought he was."

Mauro turned to me. "You like old movies?" he asked.

"More than anyone should."

"There's this expression from *The Grifters*," he said. "Annette Bening, I can't remember if she was married to Warren Beatty yet or not. But she was a hot ticket in those days. Anyway, she talks about a 'short-con operation' to Roy. The Jon Cusack character. Well, that was Nick Drummond, Spenser. For a young guy with longer ambitions, the land was a short con for him. And a means to an end."

"But it sounds as if there was a time when your own ambitions about that land were aligned with his," I said.

"They were," he said.

"Does that mean he was in your pocket?"

"Fuck off," he said.

"Maybe later," I said. "I guess what I'm trying to figure out is how much of a sore loser you were, now that Drummond is dead at the present time, as Casey Stengel used to say."

He angled his chair so he was facing me squarely. "Is that why you're really here? Because you think I might have had something to do with Drummond dying?"

"Did you?" I said.

"Fuck off," he said again.

I grinned before the heat got turned up. "You didn't even answer your own question."

He stared at me for a moment, trying to give me the hard eye. But then he grinned. "Hey," he said. "I think I might like you."

"Don't worry," I said. "The feeling will pass."

"You want something to drink?" he said.

I told him I was good. But he got up and walked over to the bar set up against the wall near his desk, took out some tomato juice, splashed in some Tabasco, then added so much vodka it turned the Bloody Mary he'd just made for himself pink. He gulped down half of it on his way back to his chair.

"First of the day," he said. "Always makes me want to salute the nearest flag, and I don't even care what country."

Then he said, "Where were we?"

"You had mentioned small cons and long games, as I recall."

"It was like this with Drummond," he said. "Everybody thought he was some kind of Boy Scout. But a realist is what he was. And a very practical politician. He worked enough of the right people in the district to get himself elected in the first place. Along the way he ginned up his own coverage like he was a goddamn Kennedy. Then all of a sudden he was Senate president, consolidating his power there in a hurry, and making enough City Council members, the women members especially, act like groupies." Mauro snorted. "You want to know how confident that kid was of his own charm? He was a white guy who actually thought he could still get elected mayor of Boston."

"We used to lead the league in those," I said.

"Not anymore," he said. "You read *The Globe*?"

"Every day," I said. "Cover to cover."

"You're obviously not reading it closely enough," he said. "They're the minority majority paper now."

"This is all fascinating," I said. "Truly, it is. But I'd still like to know if Drummond was in the bag for you, and if he was, how it is that somebody else ended up with that land."

"So are you asking me if I had something to do with him dying," Mauro said, "or him taking bribes from me while he was still alive?"

"I'll take what I can get," I said.

"I did offer him cash inducements as a way of getting him on my side," he said. "Sort of like my own personal super PAC, just without the filing."

I grinned at him again. "Well, now that we're sharing," I said, "I'd also sort of like to know if you're as connected as some of the coverage of that deal indicated."

The pale Bloody Mary was gone. I was of the opinion that it wasn't going to be his last of the morning.

"Total BS, is what that was," he said. "Had I done business with John Broz in the past? Yeah, I had. Would he have gotten the inside track on the bidding for at least some of the project? You bet your ass. But all of a sudden people treated him like he was the gangster and not his dead uncle, and the story was in *The Globe*, and social media went insane, like I was the one who had been a freaking Mob boss. All because of John's last name." He shrugged. "And then I was the one who was dead."

"You lost, McManus won."

"I had a salary cap, as it turned out," Mauro said. "He didn't."

"You're saying he outbid you for Drummond's support?" I said.

"Wait," Thomas Mauro said, "and I'll draw you a goddamn picture."

We both stared back out at the water then. I could see boats in the distance, but they were as sparse as clouds in the sky on this day. I was already starting to think about flying back to the snow.

"By the way?" Mauro said. "Drummond's death was an accident, unless you know something I don't."

"I don't," I said. "But I'm a naturally suspicious person, and am of the growing belief that Drummond somehow got in over his head on this thing, or knew something that he shouldn't have known, or overplayed his hand and it got him killed. And that whatever he knew, somebody thought Rita Fiore knew, and it nearly got her killed."

"You got some imagination, Spenser, I gotta hand it to you."

"I'd be a writer, but everybody says it's too hard."

Mauro stood suddenly. I thought he might be on his way to a second Bloody Mary. He was not. This was him being a big guy and letting me know that we were done here.

"I didn't kill anybody," he said. "Like I told you, I'm the one *got* killed, in the newspapers, and then on that deal."

I stood then.

"We clear on this shit?" Mauro asked.

"For now," I said.

"Good," he said. "Now get your ass out of my house."

I was about to tell him I had been thrown out of nicer places than this, but then realized that I probably hadn't.

THIRTY-FIVE

Back in Boston the next morning and feeling like a snowbird who'd made a wrong turn, I was working out with Hawk at the Harbor Health Club.

Henry Cimoli, the owner of the place, was "supervising"— his word—a Pure Barre method class in another room, now that Harbor Health had mostly been turned over to Pure Barre, Pilates, yoga, Peloton bikes.

Hawk and I knew full well that Henry, an ex-boxer, really didn't know the difference between the barre method and a corner bar. He just liked to watch women of all ages doing all manner of stretches in Lululemon tights.

"Keeps me young," he told us.

"Pretty sure there's pills you can take for that," Hawk said.

Out of consideration for Hawk and me, Henry had left a heavy bag and a speed bag in a weight room that had once again shrunk recently, after Henry decided he needed even more space for Peloton bikes, which I felt were multiplying like rabbits.

Hawk and I first spotted each other on the weights before I went to one corner to work the heavy bag while Hawk worked the speed bag hanging in another, once again making me envious of how fast his hands still were—as much of a blur as the bag.

We were sitting side by side on a bench drinking water when Henry, clad in silver boxing pants with a navy stripe down the side and a matching silver top that I thought made him look like a drum majorette, sat down on the bench across from us. He looked even smaller now than he'd been as a featherweight, but still as trim as a bullet.

"What do you know about Kevin McManus?" I asked him.

Henry grinned. "A pirate," he said. "But a gentleman pirate. I didn't tell you two at the time, because I was afraid you'd probably go try to beat him up, but McManus even tried to buy this whole block once, when he was in the process of trying to buy up the whole freaking world."

"Hold on," I said. "You mean there was something he wanted to buy and didn't end up getting?"

"That is correct," Henry said. "Maybe ten years ago, maybe a little more. I meet with McManus, and I keep waiting for the point in the conversation where he's going to screw me. But what he ends up asking is where I'd relocate if he did a teardown. I tell him I'd be headed for the home. Then, just like that, we get to talking about boxing, and he's asking me who I fought, since he knew I'd boxed professional. I tell him, and then it turns out his old man had boxed in some shows that Suitcase Sam Silverman used to put on at the Arena, may God bless the soul of that shithole joint, and that me and his old man had even fought some of the same guys. That's that. I'm still waiting for him to screw me, but the next day he shows back up and says he's changed his mind and I can keep the place, that he's doing it as much out of respect for me as his old man."

"Ah," I said, "the enduring romance of the sweet science."

"Whatever," Henry said. "You know what happens after that. Now you get the idea McManus owns every block in town *except* this one."

Henry had some kind of pink energy drink in the bottle in his hand, and drank some now.

"I keep reading from time to time that he still thinks he's going to own the Red Sox someday," I said.

"He can have 'em if you ask me," Henry said.

"You think you could call up your old friend Kevin and set up a meeting for me?"

"Do I get to ask what for?"

With Henry, the last word still sounded like *fir*.

"He might be able to help me out on Rita's shooting," I said.

"Do I get to ask why you think he might be able to do that?"

"Long story, Henry," Hawk said. "But we all here know what a short attention span you got." Hawk smiled at him. "Even shorter than you."

Henry nodded. "Neither one of you is as funny as you've always thought you are," he said.

"I am," I said. "He's not."

It took some doing, but Henry finally got his phone out of a side pocket in his tight pants.

"If I do set this up," Henry said, "you're going to say something that will piss him off, right?"

"I'm insulted that you even feel the need to ask me a question like that," I said.

"I'll take that as a freaking yes," Henry Cimoli said.

THIRTY-SIX

Kevin McManus told Henry Cimoli he would meet me at around six o'clock for a drink at the 21st Amendment, a low-key, Bowdoin Square bar I very much liked.

The timing with McManus worked out for me, as I planned to go visit Rita in the late afternoon, wanting to have one more conversation with her about the land deal and the part Nick Drummond had played in it, in what had been the last triumph of his rising political career.

On the level or not.

It was a conversation I had been putting off with Rita until she was well enough for it. But I was hopeful she knew more about Drummond's business than she had so far revealed, or perhaps even remembered. Or might somehow know something she didn't even realize she knew, something that would help move me off my spot, because at this point I needed all the help I could get.

I had spoken to Thomas Mauro about Drummond. I was about to do the same with McManus, who became king of the hill and top of the heap when Mauro did not. I had now spoken to Delores Thompson, as guarded as she'd been with me. And had even chatted with the charming Tony Marcus.

Now I was back to Rita, who had loved Nick Drummond and believed that he loved her back, and had been in a relationship with him when he was on his way to becoming the toast of the town.

Dr. Harman was not present on Rita's floor when I arrived. The nurse in charge was a young woman I had previously met named Bertini. She couldn't have been much more than five feet tall, but in the brief interactions I'd already had with her, I felt certain she could probably take me in a fair fight.

"I have been told by Dr. Harman to tell you that you have ten minutes," Bertini said.

"Does the clock start now, or not until I'm actually in the room?" I asked.

"Don't start with *me*," Nurse Bertini said.

As I walked in, I saw that Rita had propped herself up in her bed, a heavy wool shawl draped over her shoulders. The shawl seemed to diminish her even more than her condition did. It also seemed to age her, though I would have jumped out the window before making an observation like that to Rita Fiore.

She looked as pale today as she had the first time I'd been allowed in to see her, even with the makeup I could see she had applied.

"I must look like my grandmother," she said, as if she'd just read my mind.

"You never told me you had a smoking-hot grandma," I said.

She smiled. It wasn't much of a smile. Like one on training wheels. But it made her look less tired, and less weak. Just slightly more like the real Rita, and the force of nature she had always been.

"So how can I help you?" she said. "Do you have some sort of legal problem?"

"I wish," I said, then told her about my meeting with Tony Marcus, the meeting in Florida with Mauro, the appointment I had scheduled for tonight with Kevin McManus.

When I finished she said, "Both Tony and Mauro are lying about Nick. I'm sorry, but that's it, and that's all. I'm not saying Nick was an altar boy. I'm sure he did cut some corners and maybe even cross some lines to get elected in the first place, and then to get that deal done in Southie. That's who he was. A get-things-done guy, learning how to do that on the fly. I hardly have to tell you that politics in this city, or any city, isn't the Lawn Tennis Association. But I knew this man. And I'm telling you he wasn't for sale."

"I'm not being pejorative," I said. "I'm just telling you what they said."

"Look at you with the big words," she said.

"The ladies love it when I flex my big brain muscles."

She smiled again. "You're telling me what they said," she said. "But I'm telling you about the man I knew."

"I'm not trying to upset you," I said.

"You're not," she said.

"Sounds like I am."

"Don't try to out-argument somebody who argues for a living," she said. "Or the one who'll get wheeled out of here is you."

I idly wondered if Nurse Bertini really did have the clock on me, and if I was already starting to run out of time.

"Nick is dead," I said. "Why would Tony and Mauro be lying about him?"

"To stay in practice?" Rita said.

I leaned closer to her from my chair. "Can you remember him ever talking much about his dealings with Mauro, or Kevin Mc-Manus," I said, "especially when the rubber was about to meet the road?"

She shook her head. "I only talked about the whole *mishegoss* when he'd bring it up. It was as if he was talked out about it by the time we'd be together, at night or on a weekend. And when it was finally—and mercifully—over, he just told me that he thought the better man, and better businessman, had won. And that the city, too, had won big."

I saw her eyes start to fill up then.

"It was his last good thing, Spenser," she said. "Don't let any of these people turn it into a bad thing."

She stopped herself then, but only briefly, before adding, "And don't you turn it into a bad thing, either."

I took in some air, and let it out more slowly than I needed to. "Something bad happened to you," I said. "And I can't let that stand, even if something Nick Drummond did, even with the best of intentions, might have played a part in that. That's not good or bad, just the way things are."

"You never stop, do you?"

"You know better."

"Just promise me one thing," Rita said. "Keep me in the loop on anything and everything you find out. Don't just tell me what you think I can handle because I'm in here. I'm still me, goddamn it."

"Understood."

We sat there in silence until I said, "We haven't talked about Susan coming to see you. There was a time when I would have tried to sell tickets for something like that. Or made it a pay-per-view event."

"Can't lie, pal," Rita said. "Did not see *that* coming. Meaning her coming."

"Nor did I," I said. "But she said it was a good talk."

"We didn't end up swapping recipes," she said. "But as much as it pains me even more than my current aches and pain, I liked her."

"Wow," I said. "Now that Boston has frozen over, hell can't be far behind."

She reached out, rather feebly, with her left hand. I took it. Even her hand felt smaller than normal.

"I really do love you," she said.

"Not so fast, Red," I said, and then told her there was one more thing I needed to tell her, about Shannon Miles basically being in protective custody.

She took her hand away.

"Please tell me you mean police custody," she said.

"Not exactly," I said.

THIRTY-SEVEN

Nurse Bertini chose that precise moment to rap on the window, jerking her thumb like an umpire to throw me out of the game.

I held up one finger. She actually grinned and held up a different one. I knew we'd connect on a human level eventually, but I would wait to tell her that when I was back outside.

"Shannon Fucking Miles?" Rita said. "Are you *kidding* me?"

"I can explain," I said.

"Explain what? That you're somehow helping the one person in the whole world basically on record as wanting me dead?"

I told her all of it, as quickly as I could. Tully's call to her the night before he died. The intruder Miles had shot, or not. Her showing up at my office the next morning. Me recruiting Vinnie to be with her, if only temporarily, and until I came up with a better plan.

"Spenser's Home for Wayward Girls," she said. "It's still a nonprofit, right? You don't want the IRS coming after you."

"She's a part of this," I said. "And she's in trouble."

Rita rose up in bed, making me feel as if the chair in which I was sitting was now the witness stand.

"*She said she hoped I would find out what it was like to be violated!*" she snapped. "Well, girl, mission accomplished."

Nurse Bertini gave another rap on the window, her look now saying *Don't make me come in there.*

"Did she hire you?" Rita asked.

"I am working for Cone, Oakes," I said. "I have only one client. You. And as generously as Mr. Oakes is compensating me, and not treating me like a nonprofit, you know I would have done what I am currently doing for nothing."

"Shannon Miles hates me," Rita said, not letting this go, because she didn't let things go: she was Rita. "But now you're working for her at the same time you're working on my behalf, whether she's paying you or not."

"Before Mini Nurse Ratched rousts me, let me say one more thing," I said. "You and me and Shannon Miles are on the same side here, like it or not."

I saw her soften then, just like that, if against her will.

She sighed.

"Okay, then," she said.

"Wait," I said. "*Did* I just out-argument the great Rita Fiore?"

"I'm obviously in a weakened state," she said.

"Hey," I said. "A win is a win."

When I was at the door, I heard her say, "Spenser?"

I turned back to her.

"Am I allowed to still think of Shannon Miles as a bitch?" she asked.

"I'd expect nothing less," I said. "Weakened state or not."

THIRTY-EIGHT

I arrived at the 21st Amendment a few minutes early. As it turned out, Kevin McManus had arrived a few minutes earlier than that, which meant he'd chosen not to make an entrance, as people of his rank so often did.

He had scored a table right around the corner from the stucco wall featuring a row of hooks for coats and hats. Or perhaps had the table on a time share. Right above him was a sign that read MY GOODNESS MY GUINNESS.

We were close, but not too close, to the crowded bar area. As I passed the bar I couldn't help but notice two guys, dressed in black leather jackets, both of them with eyes on McManus, neither one holding a drink. One was on the smallish side, sleek, with slicked-back black hair. The other, bald and broad, looked big enough to comprise the entire right side of the Patriots' offensive line.

McManus stood. He was around six feet tall, with closely cropped white curly hair and eyes that would have been called Paul Newman blue in another time. I was vaguely aware, having done some reading up on him, that he was in his sixties. But he wore it well, and seemed to have maintained at least the remnants of a summer tan. Maybe he spent as much time in Florida in the winter as his buddy Thomas Mauro did.

Unlike Mauro, though, he didn't overdo it with his handshake.

"From the description I got from our friend Mr. Cimoli," he said, "you're Spenser, unless they're looking for a new bouncer here."

"Accept no substitute," I said.

I noticed he already had a glass of Guinness on the table, maybe to be a team player, and a shot of whiskey next to it. He immediately asked what I was drinking, and I told him I'd have what he was having.

McManus nodded at a waiter standing next to the offensive lineman.

"I wouldn't have figured you for a shot-and-beer guy," I said. "Or a patron of this particular saloon."

"I've done my share of horse trading at the golden dome," McManus said. "And there was a time in my life when this place would have been way too fancy for me. I'm a Dorchester kid, for one thing. And Henry probably told you I was the son of a boxer who lost more than he won and spent the rest of his time working on Long Wharf when it used to stretch from the end of State Street nearly a mile into the water. In my neighborhood, shot-and-beer places were homes away from home."

He drank some of his whiskey then, before washing it down with Guinness. Then smiled at me with a lot of teeth almost as white as his hair.

"Not that you asked for my family history," he said.

When the waiter brought my drinks, I reached for my whiskey. We clinked shot glasses.

"*Sláinte,*" he said.

"To Nick Drummond," I said.

I saw something change in his eyes at the mention of Drummond's name. I wasn't quite sure what. But something.

"Henry said you don't fuck around," he said.

I grinned. "Want to drink to that, too?" I said.

We did.

"So Nick Drummond is the reason you wanted to meet with me?" he said.

"Thomas Mauro suggested that Drummond was bought and paid for," I said. "By you."

For some reason, I looked down at his right hand then, the one resting next to his drinks. The raised knuckles made me think he might have done some boxing himself at some point in his life. They were permanently swollen, the way mine were, and Hawk's were, and Henry Cimoli's. With ex-fighters, the battle scars weren't just around the eyes, or noses not nearly as straight as they had once been before people started punching us in the face.

"You're in the right church," McManus said. "Just the wrong pew. Mauro's the one who thought he could buy that kid. But then the poor bastard learned the hard way that Nick Drummond might have been the only politician in town who wasn't for sale."

"Not to belabor the point," I said, "but that's not the way he tells it."

"Being full of shit is a full-time job with Mr. Mauro," McManus said.

He drank more beer then, before wiping his lips with the back of his hand.

"And when the guy wasn't able to put a fix in on that land," he said, "it wouldn't shock me if he had him killed."

THIRTY-NINE

By now there was even more of a bar crowd than there'd been when I came through the door, loud in the way after-work crowds were. I didn't think anybody could overhear the conversation that Kevin McManus and I were now having at the 21st Amendment. Or maybe McManus didn't care whether someone was eavesdropping or not. Maybe he just said whatever he wanted to say, about anybody, whenever he wanted to say it.

And wherever he wanted to say it.

Either way, the preliminaries with the son of a boxer were clearly over.

"Do you have any proof that Mauro is the one who got it done?" I said.

"Nope," he said. "There's just things you know in your gut. And mine has rarely steered me wrong."

"You're lucky," I said. "Mine sure has."

"You think Drummond drowned?" McManus asked.

"Not so much," I said.

"Me neither," he said.

"But Mauro is firmly convinced that before he did, he took a dive for you," I said.

McManus nodded sarcastically. "I know he tells people that. It's like some kind of fever dream with him. But I'm telling you that it never happened. I came to love Nick Drummond like a son, and not just because I knew he could help me get something I badly wanted. I knew from the start that as big as the Widett Circle deal was, the kid was going to be bigger. And probably bigger than this city when he was through, if you ask me. He was going to end up in the U.S. Senate, or end up governor."

"Pays to have friends in high places," I said. "Especially if you're the one getting paid."

"I frankly don't give a rat's arse whether you believe me on this or not," McManus said. "But the only thing I ever gave him was a promise that I would do whatever I could do to help him get wherever he wanted to go."

I turned slightly to take a closer look at the bar area. I assumed this was primarily a State House crowd this close to the place. But I had no way of knowing for sure without taking a poll. I just saw mostly young, well-dressed people, men and women, pumping up the volume as if it were the bleachers at Fenway.

"Do you honestly think," I said, turning back to him, "that Thomas Mauro was a bad enough loser, and crazy enough, that he had the most popular young politician in town killed?"

"Mauro's a badass," McManus said. "Always has been. It's why

171

it made me laugh like hell when people were wringing their hands when they thought he might be 'associated' with organized crime." McManus put air quotes around *associated*. "He didn't have to associate with people like that, because of all the gangster in *him*."

"Let's say you're right about that," I said. "Why kill off Drummond after the deal was already done? It was your land by then. Your development. You were the one who was going to build the casino and hotel and remake South Boston."

"Don't forget the affordable housing," he said.

I grinned. "What they all say."

Something else changed with his eyes then, and I momentarily thought I could see the Dorchester kid he had been. Son of a fighter and a fighter himself, and maybe not just in the ring.

"When I say it, I mean it," he said.

He leaned closer to me, finally lowering his voice. "I never thought Mauro just wanted a casino for himself. I had no way of proving it, but I heard he might be fronting for people a lot more badass than he is, out of Vegas. You ever run into guys like that in your line of work?"

"Unfortunately," I said, "I have."

"They still bury people because they can," McManus said.

"Over a piece of land in Boston?"

He waved our waiter over. When the kid got to the table, McManus waved off the bill and just stuck a wad of cash in his hand. A lot more than two beers and two shots would have cost him. Maybe everything was a big deal with Kevin McManus, even paying a bar bill.

"You ask me," he said, "maybe Mauro somehow went from

thinking Nick Drummond could be an asset to him being some kind of threat. Maybe you should be looking into that, and not fucking around with me."

He was starting to get up. I put a hand on his arm to keep him where he was. He looked down at my hand, then back at me. But didn't do anything about it. Maybe because he was out of his weight class.

"Somebody shot a good friend of mine," I said. "And somebody shot and killed Brian Tully after he came to see me. On top of all that, someone went after Tully's former TV partner." I pulled him a little closer. "So you really need to know that the last thing I'm doing here, Kevin, is fucking around."

I could see his two bodyguards starting to inch closer to the table. McManus put up a hand to stop them. Then he grinned at me.

"Hey," he said, "just a figure of speech."

"What they all say," I repeated.

"I've got an idea," McManus said. "How about I hire you right here and now to find out if somebody killed Nick? How would that be?"

"I have a client," I said. "But thanks for asking."

"Never bullshit a bullshitter, Spenser," he said. "You just don't want to work for me?"

"You know what they say," I said. "When you're right, you're right."

Now he stood, and so did I.

"Last question," I said. "Say Nick Drummond did know something he shouldn't have known. What do you think it might have been?"

McManus smiled then, and actually seemed to mean it. Then clapped me on the back as if we really were shot-and-beer boys.

"Hey," he said, "you're the detective."

He left. I watched him go. I would have told myself that I'd just made another rich friend, except that I didn't much like bullshitting a bullshitter, either.

FORTY

awk and I were taking a long morning walk along the Charles. The sun was out for a change, but there was a high wind dead against us after we'd made the turn at Mass Ave. I had promised to cook breakfast for both of us when we got back to my apartment.

"Maybe next time you go visit somebody in the Sunshine State you should take your trusty sidekick with you."

"You're always telling me you're not a sidekick, not to make too small a point of things."

"Comes and goes," Hawk said. "Like the damn snow."

"But it is good to know you'll travel anywhere in the pursuit of truth," I said.

"The truth?" Hawk snorted. "The only truth we got so far is a bunch of people got themselves shot."

He wore a thick Canada Goose parka that I knew was a Canada Goose only because he'd told me, at the same time he told me how much it had cost. He had the hood up over a knit cap stamped with the Harvard logo, which an old girlfriend had given him during a brief period when we were both in relationships with Harvard-educated women. I just couldn't recall her name. So many of them with Hawk, so little time.

"Which one of them two rich men you believe more?" Hawk asked.

"Neither," I said.

"Dated an actress for a while in L.A. once," Hawk said. "I asked her what was the thing struck her most about the movie business. Girl didn't hesitate. 'The lying,' she said."

There was another huge blast of wind from our left off the water this time, enough to make us put our heads down and stop for a moment.

"Goddamn, I hate this weather," he said. "You know what North Face really is? Mine."

"Bitch, bitch, bitch," I said.

We were finally on David G. Mugar Way, and close to Marlborough. But I felt as if we were coming to the end of a cross-country skiing event at the Winter Olympics.

"Okay," Hawk said, "put it another way. If you had to pick one of those boys more *likely* to be telling you the truth, which one would it be?"

"McManus, I suppose. He did seem to have genuinely cared about Drummond."

Hawk smiled. It wasn't as big as his normal smile, but that was probably because he couldn't move his face. "I'm the same way, acting genuine and caring and whatnot when I'm after a woman."

"Must it always come back to sex with you?" I said.

"Uh-huh," he said.

"So how are we going to find out which one of them might be telling the truth?" I said.

"Here we go with that *we* shit," he said.

I TOOK A hot shower when we were back in the apartment and then started cooking while Hawk took a shower of his own. When he came out, I'd already prepared a shameful amount of crispy turkey bacon and had pancakes going in two skillets.

When everything was ready, we ate and discussed the case further, touching a lot of bases. What information did Tully have? What did the shooter think Rita might have known? What kind of evidence, and in what form, could Tully have left for Shannon Miles, if he'd even gotten the chance to leave it?

What kind of evidence might have been in that safe-deposit box at the bank before somebody cleaned it out?

What I thought was another excellent question.

"Whatever Tully had, or thought he had," Hawk said, pouring more maple syrup over his second stack, "might have been what got all these people shot. And maybe what got Nick Drummond drowned."

"That land turned out to be more expensive than anybody thought," I said. "Remember, there were more bidders in that auction than just Mauro and McManus once they abandoned the plan about the railyards, but then they began to take themselves out of the running one by one."

Hawk reached over and took a piece of bacon off my plate. I did not offer any protest, as I constantly did the same thing to Susan Silverman.

"You think McManus could've been telling the truth about Mauro maybe fronting for somebody else?" he said. "And they the ones turned out to be the bad sports because they think Drummond might've screwed them over along with Mauro?"

"Fronting for whom? The Vegas guys McManus hinted at?"

"Like McManus say," Hawk said. "You the detective."

"I don't see how that's helpful," I said.

Hawk said, "How come I always got to be the one helps you find your way out the forest?"

"I see it more as a maze," I said.

He got up from the table, rinsed his plate and his cup, put them in the dishwasher. Then he put his parka back on and said he had to go meet Cecile for breakfast.

"You just had breakfast," I said.

He smiled. "Just me acting genuine and caring," he said.

"One more thing you might think on," Hawk said at the door. "If more thinking won't make your head hurt somethin' awful: Who other than Rita was closest to Drummond?"

"Probably his chief of staff," I said. "But I already talked to her."

"Yeah, but maybe that girl know more than she letting on," he said. "She a politician, too, remember."

When he was gone, I called Delores Thompson's cell phone, the one she said had everybody's number in it, and went straight to voicemail. I left a message and asked her to call me.

When she still hadn't called half an hour later, I tried again.

Straight to voicemail again.

So I went online and found the main number for the State House, now that the Internet was the new Yellow Pages. Someone finally picked up on my third attempt, and I asked to be connected to the office of the Senate president, a job that wasn't

178

going to be permanently filled again until a special election in March.

A man answered. He said his name was Barnett, and that he was the incoming communications director, and that somehow my call had been transferred to his desk.

"I'd like to speak to Delores Thompson, please," I said.

Barnett asked who was calling. I told him, adding that I'd just met with Ms. Thompson a couple days ago.

"She was helping me out with a case," I said. "I just had a few follow-up questions."

"Good luck trying to ask them."

"What's that mean?"

"Ms. Thompson's gone," Barnett said

"Did she quit suddenly?" I said. "She didn't mention anything about that to me."

"If she did quit, nobody here knows anything about that, either," Barnett said. "She just said she was going out the other day and still hasn't come back."

"Has she ever done anything like that before?"

"I've only been here a couple months. But no."

"Did she at least say where she was going?"

"As far as I know, she didn't say anything to anybody here," Barnett said. "Security sent somebody to her apartment, to make sure she was all right. But there was no one home."

Barnett paused.

"Like I said. She's just gone."

FORTY-ONE

Before Barnett, who said he had to run to a meeting, ended the call, I asked if he'd ever heard Delores Thompson mention any family. He said all he knew was that she was a widow, and another chief of staff in the building had mentioned to him one time that she and her late husband never had any children.

"I liked her," he said. "Everybody here liked Delores. One of the other senators once told me she could only wish that somebody might ever care for her the way Delores cared for Senator Drummond. It was like he was her only child."

I asked for an address. He gave me one on Kenrick Street in Brighton. Then he asked if he could put me on a brief hold, he wanted to check one more thing. When he came back on, he gave me the number for the superintendent for her apartment building, which he said he'd gotten from State House security.

I thanked him.

On my way to Brighton, I called Rita.

"What can you tell me about Delores Thompson?"

"Why do you ask?" she said.

"She's gone missing."

"As in a missing person, that kind of missing?"

"Nobody has filed an official report on her," I said. "I checked with Belson. But, yeah, she seems to have disappeared."

"And you think this could be connected to Nick and me and the whole damn thing?" Rita asked.

"You know what I think about coincidence," I said.

"You believe in it as much as you believe in Bigfoot."

"So how much *do* you know about her."

"Nick and I had dinner with her a few times," Rita said. "I got the impression that Nick was pretty much her whole life. Not in a romantic way. More a mother-hen way. Nick said he practically had to threaten her to make her take a day off. I think she'd even go down to my house in Nantucket and work with him on weekends when he needed her to do that."

Rita paused.

"I want this to be over," she said.

"Join the club," I said.

Instead of taking the city streets, I'd taken the Mass Pike to save time, and gotten off at the Watertown exit. When I finished talking with Rita, I called Martin Quirk.

I explained about the situation with Delores Thompson, said I had a number for her super, but that I needed to get inside and search her apartment, and was wondering if he could call ahead.

"I'm curious about something," Quirk said. "When exactly did the highest levels of the Boston Police Department become your personal concierge service?"

"Got a bad feeling about this one," I said, then read off the super's number.

Quirk called back a few minutes later as I was circling around the Crowne Plaza hotel built over the Pike.

"Guy's name is Mauricio," Quirk said. "You won't have any problems."

He paused then.

"Anybody gonna file a missing on this Thompson woman?"

"I can do it later or have somebody at the State House maybe do it," I said. "Except that I think it might be too late for that. From what I'm told, this woman never missed a day of work. Now she's missed two without notifying anybody."

"You think they went after her, too?" Quirk said.

"Hoping no," I said, "but thinking yes."

There was another pause, longer than before. Someone less experienced at interaction with Martin Quirk might have thought he'd ended the call without telling me.

I knew better.

"Maybe you need to start worrying when they might come after you," he said.

"What for?" I said. "I really don't know anything."

"Not like you haven't been down that road before," Quirk said.

Then he ended the call.

FORTY-TWO

Delores Thompson's apartment was tasteful, elegant, neat. And still.

The refrigerator seemed completely stocked with the essentials: milk, juice, plastic bottles of Hint water. Cheese. What appeared to be an unopened bag of grapes. A bottle of KRIS pinot grigio. A pint of half-and-half not even close to its sell-by date. Unopened deli turkey and ham. A new loaf of whole-wheat bread. Eggs. Wherever she'd gone, she certainly hadn't thrown out any food.

This was the way your refrigerator would look when you got back from work.

There were some framed pictures in all the rooms of the two-bedroom apartment, most of them of her younger self standing next to a tall man I assumed to be her late husband. In the one on her nightstand, he was wearing an Air Force uniform.

There was no laptop in the apartment, no modern tablet of any kind, no landline.

Her closet, though, was bursting with clothes. Work and casual. A lot of shoes. The drawers of her antique dresser were similarly full. There was nothing out of the ordinary, nothing resembling a clue or that there had been some kind of struggle. Or abduction. Or murder.

No hidey-holes or clues in her desk.

The only object of interest in the second bedroom, which she clearly used as a home office, was an antique Underwood typewriter. It had to be the one Nick Drummond had owned, the one she'd spoken about with me. She must have kept it after Drummond had died.

The counter in the bathroom, the medicine cabinet, and the drawers underneath the counter were full of makeup items, so many of them, in sheer volume, she could have given Susan Silverman a run for her money.

I went back into the bedroom and got on my hands and knees and looked under the old-fashioned four-poster bed. There were three TUMI suitcases of varying sizes. The middle size one had wheels. Susan had bought me a similar roller bag for Christmas, telling me that it was time to retire my ancient duffel bag once and for all. The first time I'd used it was on our trip to Santa Barbara, when I realized how much easier it was making my way through airports with it. I told her that I thought the whole wheel thing with luggage had a chance to really catch on.

But Delores Thompson hadn't taken a trip, because she hadn't taken anything at all.

Somebody had taken her.

Or done far worse than that.

I took one last look around, then went into the second bedroom, walked over to the desk, and hit a few keys on the Underwood.

Clack-clack-clack.

Just as she'd described it. And a pretty wonderful sound in and of itself.

I locked up behind me, dropped the key off with my new friend Mauricio, and got into my car.

I was about to check in with Shannon Miles and Vinnie Morris when I saw that I had a new voicemail message. I hadn't heard my phone ring since I'd arrived on Kenrick Street.

The message had been left by Delores Thompson, in starts and stops:

"This is Delores . . . Thompson . . . I found what they've been looking for . . . Maybe they did kill him . . ."

She ended the message this way:

". . . Please call me as soon as you get this . . ."

I played it again from the beginning, then took a closer look at my phone.

The call had been placed yesterday.

FORTY-THREE

knew uncovering why Delores Thompson's message had spent twenty-four hours lost in cyberspace wasn't going to help me find her, or figure out what had happened to her, or how her going missing fit into the whole cockeyed grand scheme of things.

Didn't tell me what she'd found.

I still wanted some sense of how it had happened. Every time I would complain about my phone to Susan, usually part of a lengthier presentation about the ills of technology in general, she would either ask some question about my settings that I could almost never answer or want to know if the phone had undergone its most recent update. Then she would invariably solve the problem herself. And I would just write it off as one more mystery of a modern world that no longer worked the way I wanted it to—and worked contrary to what I thought should be the natural order of things.

Luckily, my friend Lee Farrell, now commanding the Sexual Assaults Unit of the BPD, was a tech guy, which made one of us.

"How does something like this happen?" I asked Farrell.

"What else you got today, where the wind comes from?" he said.

He was a good cop and a better friend, so good at being both that the small-minded idiots that remained in the department at this point no longer cared that he was gay. My own position on that particular subject had never varied:

As long as we're talking about consenting adults, I don't care who you fuck.

And if you do, you should probably just go fuck yourself.

"There are all sorts of reasons why this can happen from time to time, to everybody," Farrell said. "Sometimes the fix is as simple as disabling and then reenabling the voicemail feature on your phone. Or it could be a flaw in your phone. Or have something to do with data connections, Wi-Fi connections, or third-party applications that can conflict with your device's OS."

"Sure," I said. "Everybody knows that."

"But none of that is going to do a damn bit of good for you right now, is it?" Farrell said.

"It is not," I said, "and would only waste more of your time before I get to the real reason for my call."

"At long last," he said.

"Is there any way for you to ping her phone and figure out where she made the call if I give you her number?"

"Let me ask you something first," Farrell said. "How long has she been missing?"

"Maybe a little under two days, or a little over," I said. "But no one she works with has filed a missing person's, and neither have I."

"It's different with adults than kids," Farrell said. "Kids aren't allowed to just disappear, as we all know too damn well at SAU. Adults are, as long as there's no sign of foul play." He took a fast beat and then said, "*Is* there any sign of foul play?"

"No," I said. "I just came from her apartment in Brighton."

"Okay, then," Farrell said. "Give me as much information on her as you can."

"I don't have all that much."

"You say she worked at the State House, right?"

I told Farrell she had stayed on there after Nick Drummond's death.

"I've got some free time right now," Farrell said. "I'll call over there and speak to whomever I need to speak to, and tell them a missing person's has just been filed by a neighbor, and we'll go from there."

"Hold on," I said. "You're telling me that cops lie?"

"Like champions when we have to," he said. "As soon as I have what I need, I actually will file a report, and then we can run her phone number through the NCIC. You know what that is, right?"

"National Criminal Intelligence Center," I said. "I'm not an idiot."

"Sure, why not," Lee Farrell said. "Anyway, once they've got her information, they can ping the phone. If you want to know how, I could give you a quick tutorial on IP addresses."

"No, thank you," I said. "But I owe you for this."

"I'm glad you brought that up. Don't you still owe me an expensive meal at The Newbury because of a previous favor? Pretty sure you promised."

"I lied," I said. "Just like a cop."

———

A FEW HOURS later, I was back in my apartment, waiting for Farrell to call me back, not knowing if the call would come before tomorrow, because Farrell probably didn't know that, either.

Still thinking about the message Delores Thompson had left me.

I found what they've been looking for?

But who?

Darkness had fallen even earlier than usual in the Back Bay, after a light late-afternoon snowfall that had come and gone as if it were a force of habit in Boston at this point.

Susan and I had a dinner reservation at Henrietta's Table in Cambridge. The reason I'd picked the place was because I was going to have their Yankee Pot Roast tonight and nobody was going to stop me.

"I like a man who knows what he wants," she said.

"And not just with Yankee Pot Roast," I said.

"Oh, great," Susan said. "Here we go talking about *that*."

I had called Rita again when I returned from Brighton and asked if Drummond had become more secretive near the end of his life, as if he were hiding something.

"I've told you before," Rita said. "Even though he was a public figure, he was a very private guy. And really did do his best to keep business separate from us, almost as if he were trying to protect me from the muck of his world."

I was allowing myself one can of Boomsauce IPA before I drove over to Cambridge. I drank some now.

"I need to ask you again," I said. "What if I find out things about Nick Drummond you don't want to hear?"

"You won't," she said.

I had ended the call with Rita and was about to head down to the car when Farrell called.

"Got something," he said.

I waited.

"Your friend Ms. Thompson was either standing inside or right outside 99 High when she placed that call to you," he said.

"The old Keystone Building."

"So you know where it is," Farrell said.

I told him I knew exactly where it was, between the Leather District and the waterfront.

"Does this help?" Farrell asked.

"The short answer is maybe," I said. "But I really have no goddamn idea."

"Not to sound cynical," Farrell said, "but it's not as if you haven't been there before. And I don't just mean with that building."

"Quirk said something similar to me earlier today," I said.

"We kid because we love."

I went over to where I'd left my laptop on the kitchen table and typed Tenants, 99 High, Boston into Safari.

The first ten names on the list of tenants appeared almost immediately, top of the page.

They weren't in alphabetical order.

And didn't need to be, as it turned out.

The seventh company, right there after AGF Investments, was this one:

Thomas Mauro Inc.

FORTY-FOUR

Thomas Mauro didn't return the message I'd left until Susan had ordered our first round of drinks at Henrietta's Table.

"You may be starting to get on my nerves," Mauro said. "Not sure we're all the way there yet, but could be we're getting close."

"I thought we got there when you told me to get out of that house of yours that isn't on Billionaires' Row," I said.

"And yet here we are," he said.

"Gets on a guy's nerves, doesn't it?" I said.

I had stepped outside to talk to him, always thinking that people talking on their phones in restaurants, often loudly enough to be heard the next block over, should be treated as public nuisances and arrested on the spot, the charge being obstruction of fine dining.

"I really had assumed we'd concluded our business," he said.

"Not quite," I said. "Are you in Florida or here?"

"'Here' being Boston?"

"Yes."

"Here," he said. "I flew back into Hanscom yesterday morning."

Hanscom meant he'd flown privately and wanted me to know. Or perhaps needed me to know. Boys with toys, a private jet being the ultimate toy for guys like Mauro, unless you were taking a trip into outer space.

"I only need a few minutes of your time," I said, "and then I will stop bothering you."

Mauro said, "And if I believe that, you've got some prime real estate near the expressway you want to sell me."

"Pretty sure it's already been sold to somebody else," I said.

To my surprise, he laughed. "You do have some brass ones, Spenser, no shit."

"May I come by your office in the morning?" I said.

"Why the hell not?" he said, gave me a time, and asked if I knew where his building was.

"As it turns out," I said, "I do."

I STOOD AND looked at Susan before she was aware I was staring at her from across the room. She was wearing a charcoal-gray turtleneck sweater, and black jeans and knee-high boots. She'd had her hair cut today, slightly shorter than was her normal practice. It somehow framed her face even more, made her even lovelier, if mortal man—in this case, her stylist, Tyler—was capable of such a thing.

She turned and saw me then and smiled and, as often happened when she looked this beautiful and this happy, the world stood still.

Her Sancerre, I could see, had been delivered, and so had my martini. I walked back to our table and said, "I don't usually do this with strangers in restaurants, but would you mind if I joined you for dinner?"

"Why not?" she said. "Then afterward we could go back to my place and experience unbridled passion together."

"Okay," I said. "But in that case, we'll need to split the check."

She gave me a quizzical look, as if sizing me up. "I'm wondering if you're worth it."

"I give references," I said.

"Name one."

"There's this hot shrink who only lives a few blocks from here."

I sat. We drank.

"Mauro's back in Boston," I said.

"So Ms. Thompson could have been on her way to see him when she called you," Susan said. "Did you tell him about her message?"

"I thought I'd surprise him."

"You know, of course, that the call being made from the vicinity of his building doesn't mean he was there at the time, or that she was able to see him even if he was," Susan said.

"But of all the buildings in all the city, she called me from his," I said.

"You're not going to do Bogie, are you?"

"That hot shrink I mentioned? She keeps urging me not to."

I ordered the Maine Rock Crab and Corn Chowder, and my pot roast. Susan ordered what the menu actually described as a Wilted Green Salad, and salmon as her main course.

When the waiter had taken our menus and walked away,

Susan said, "Sometimes supposed connections that make perfect sense to you turn out to be random in the end."

"I can't make that determination until I'm in possession of all available facts."

"And just how many facts do you believe Mr. Mauro will make available to you?"

"Probably not as many as I'd like," I said. "But perhaps more than he intends."

Susan smiled.

"You remain as inner-directed as ever," she said.

"Wait until we change the subject back to unbridled passion," I said, and then Susan raised her glass again.

"Okay, then," she said. "We can definitely split the check."

FORTY-FIVE

Hawk stopped by my office in the morning, an hour or so before I was heading off to meet with Thomas Mauro, on his way to Chestnut Hill to spell Vinnie Morris for a few hours at Shannon Miles's house. Vinnie had informed me earlier that there was a "thing" that had come up, local and not Chicago, that required his immediate attention.

He said he could tell me where he was going and what he was doing if I really needed to know.

"Better that I don't," I said, "just in case I need plausible deniability later."

"That supposed to be funny?" he said.

"I thought so," I said.

Hawk had picked up a box of Dunkin' Donuts. Fortunately, he had told them to include extra Boston Kreme. Sometimes they didn't include any at all if you didn't ask. Sometimes experience was all.

I had come to the office a little after eight today. With the numbers I'd gotten from my new best friend, Barnett, I had then spent the time before Hawk arrived speaking on the phone with folks at the State House who had worked closely with Delores Thompson, making more new friends but learning nothing of consequence about where they thought she might be. Lee Farrell had called me, just to let me know that an actual missing-person report had been filed, but that he had no new information about Delores Thompson, either.

Delores's Instagram page remained unchanged, mostly showing old photographs from when Nick Drummond was still alive, almost all of them of him, a handful featuring the two of them. I still had the nagging feeling that she had told me far less than she knew, about everything, back when she was still around to tell me anything.

When I finished telling Hawk about all that Farrell had said, Hawk said, "You're aware that the number-one job for us is still finding out who shot Rita, right?"

"As always, I remain fixated on the end goal," I said.

"Me, too," Hawk said. "But you always more worried about the why and the how. Only thing I give a shit about is who."

"I'm convinced it's all connected, all the way back to Drummond dying, to Delores Thompson disappearing," I said. "I am further convinced that all of these people, including Rita, are collateral damage because two arrogant rich guys both wanted the same thing and didn't care how they got it."

"Keep forgetting to ask," Hawk said. "We talked about my fee yet?"

"You can have the rest of the donuts," I said.

"I *bought* the damn donuts," he said.

"Bitch, bitch, bitch," I said.

THOMAS MAURO INC. didn't occupy the top floors of his building. But he was high enough up, at 99 High, thank you, with what turned out to be a pretty great view of the Seaport and the Financial District and a lot of other tall buildings in between. The rich really were different from the rest of us. It often started with the views.

Somehow Mauro looked just as tanned as he had when we'd first met. He was wearing a red V-neck sweater with a gray T-shirt underneath, jeans, and a pair of hiking boots. Hi, I'm L.L.Bean.

"So what's so important that you needed to see me?" he asked, as I took a seat across from him. "Or should I just say that we need to stop meeting like this."

I had considered various ways to get into it with him, as I didn't know what he knew about Delores Thompson's disappearance, if anything. Or if he'd had any contact with her, at least in person, after Nick Drummond had died.

"When's the last time you spoke with Delores Thompson?" is the way I began.

"Drummond's chief of staff?"

"She thinks of herself that way even now."

"Why do you ask?"

He wasn't wary, exactly. But definitely more alert.

"It was a pretty simple question, actually," I said. "It's not as if I asked you to explain escrow holdings to me."

He put his boots up on the desk, leaned back in his chair, and clasped his hands behind his head. Trying to appear casual and in control of the conversation even though he really was not, at least not right now. Mauro wasn't making a deal with me, or even trying to screw me out of some money. But that seemed to be his attitude. The effect of the pose.

"She called me the other day, as a matter of fact," he said.

"Why did she?"

"Why do you care?"

"Because she's disappeared," I said. "And because the last place she used her phone, to place a call to me, actually, was near this building, if not inside it."

"You were able to track her phone?"

"I didn't," I said. "But the police were."

"The police are in on this?"

"They are."

"How about you tell me why she called you," Mauro said.

I grinned. "We can keep doing it like this if you want, and keep wasting each other's time. But it would streamline everything if I asked the questions."

"Good point," he said. "And my time is a hell of a lot more valuable than yours."

"She left me a message saying she'd found what they were looking for, without saying what," I said. "I was wondering if you might know who 'they' are, and what she might have."

Mauro processed all that. The hands came out from behind his head. The boots came off the desk.

He leaned forward.

"After Drummond died," he said, "I got curious about what he might have had on McManus. Or what she might have known

198

about what he had on McManus. And if it might be something that could still have that deal fall apart on him. So I reached out to her, one time, and said that if she ever came across anything that could hurt McManus and maybe help me at the same time, she should give me a call, and that I would make it worth her while."

"What did she say to that?"

"She said she had no idea what I was talking about," Mauro said.

"But now she leaves a message for me, telling me that she did have something," I said. "But what I don't know is whether that meant she had something on you or him."

"You don't give up, do you?"

"Hardly ever."

Mauro's cell phone then buzzed on the desk in front of him. He reached for the phone, looked at it, said, "Asshole," and put it back down. His iPhone was bigger than mine. Of course it was.

Now he clasped his hands in front of him.

"First you act as if I had something to do with Drummond's death," he said. "Now you're about half accusing me of having something to do with his chief of staff's disappearance. So maybe this meeting needs to be over."

"Not just yet."

"It's my office."

"Think of it as being ours until I leave," I said.

He laughed then, and seemed to mean it. In some odd, big-guy way, though, Mauro suddenly seemed to be enjoying the back-and-forth. He reached into the top middle drawer of his desk then, took out a vape pen, puffed on it a couple times, and put it back. He had spoken of me annoying him. But for Thomas

Mauro to annoy me further, he would have had to start talking about his net worth.

"I just want to know what you talked about with Delores Thompson," I said.

"As usual, you've got this all wrong," he said. "The only time I talked to her was when she did call me and said she had something urgent to talk about, and asked if she could come by, she'd rather have the conversation in person." He took the vape pen out of his drawer and took another hit. "Since she had my attention, I told her I'd be waiting for her when she showed up."

"So what did you talk about once she got here?" I said.

"That's the thing," Thomas Mauro said. "She never *did* show up."

FORTY-SIX

By the time I got to Shannon Miles's house, Vinnie had returned and Hawk was gone. Vinnie informed both Shannon and me that a certain situation in Chicago still hadn't been resolved, and he now needed to be there tomorrow.

"You shouldn't take it personal," Vinnie told Shannon Miles.

"I won't," she said. "I'm sure you have more important things to do than babysit me, Mr. Morris."

"You got somebody to replace me?" Vinnie asked me.

He was wearing another dark suit. It was dark suits or blazers for Vinnie, no matter the temperature or season. But regardless of the choice he'd made on that day, he looked as if he'd just stepped out of a catalog, if there were catalogs for people in his line of work.

I said, "As irreplaceable, or irrepressible, as you are, you know me well enough to know that I always have a backup plan."

"Sure," Vinnie said. It came out as *shoo-ah*. Then he said he was going back to the kitchen to make himself another cup of coffee. While he was in there, I quickly filled in Shannon Miles on Delores Thompson's message and my visit to Thomas Mauro, and how eventually I knew I'd have to circle back to Kevin Mc-Manus, just because he was the one who'd ended up with the pot of gold, and was probably one more person withholding information I wanted, or just flat-out lying to me, just because I assumed practically everyone was these days.

"Brian told both of us that he had a story to tell," she said. "Delores told you she had a story to tell. Now Brian's dead. Delores is gone. Rita is in the hospital. Someone came after me."

She was drinking tea. It was still hot. She put two hands on her mug, blew on it, and took a sip.

"And the Senate president might have been murdered," she said and sighed. "Good Lord."

I looked at Shannon Miles. She wore a flannel shirt, the sleeves rolled up, and some faded jeans. Somehow, she still looked as attractive and put-together as she had on television, perhaps just a little older and a little more tired after everything she had been through, with Tully and the trial and now all of this.

It was still difficult for me to process that our lives were now intertwined, especially since she and Rita had once regarded each other as enemies.

"It all seems so . . . what?" she asked. "Byzantine?"

"Until you figure it all out," I said. "And then it often makes perfect sense."

"And you're confident you will figure it out?"

"Always confident," I said. "Occasionally right."

"I'll bet it's more than occasionally."

"Let's not get overconfident," I said.

I asked her to go back over the phone conversation she'd had with Brian Tully when she'd spoken to him that night from the Vineyard. She put her head back on the couch and closed her eyes, going through it again, as if trying to see the words she was speaking. But her retelling was the same. I asked her if she was sure she hadn't left anything out. She smiled and told me that when she was a kid out of college and working as a reporter at *The Providence Journal*, she quickly realized that when it was time to sit down and write her story, she rarely had to open her notebook, because she'd had the ability to remember the quotes word for word.

"I wish I could be more helpful," she said. "Because I'm aware of the stakes if you do figure this out."

"In what way?"

"Because then it becomes my story, too," she said.

She got up from the couch and walked across the room and stood in front of her fireplace.

"Listen, I actually *can* be helpful, Spenser," she said. "I can be that reporter. I can make calls for you. I can do research." She breathed deeply. "I *need* to be that reporter. It will make me feel like myself, even if all I'm doing is working search engines and the phone."

She smiled. It was still a winner. "Anyway, that's my offer to you."

"I accept," I said, without hesitation.

She tilted her head. "Wait," she said. "What about Rita?"

"What about her?"

"Are you going to tell her that you're not only looking out for me, but that we'll be working together?"

"Sure," I said. "Rita doesn't scare me." Then I smiled. "Well, maybe a little bit."

"Tell me what you need," Shannon Miles said. "I'll get to work this morning."

"I need to know who Brian Tully's source might have been on the casino deal, the one he said was a source on that other casino deal at Boston Harbor."

"The Encore," she said.

"Whomever his contact was is another string to pull on," I said.

"On it," she said. "And, Spenser? I can carry on with my life without a bodyguard."

I shook my head.

"Sorry," I said. "If you're going to start asking the kinds of questions we want answered, you're still very much in the barrel."

"So do you really have a replacement for Vinnie?" she asked.

Vinnie came walking back into the living room then.

"I have someone in mind, actually," I said.

"Who?" Vinnie said. "Hawk?"

"Hawk will be otherwise occupied."

"Watching your back?"

"If it comes to that."

"So who's the guy, then?" Vinnie asked.

"Not a guy," I said.

"Is she someone from Boston?" Shannon Miles asked.

"Paradise," I said.

Vinnie grinned.

"That girl cop works for Jesse Stone?" he said.

"I think Molly prefers to be called Deputy Chief Crane," I said.

FORTY-SEVEN

hief Jesse Stone of the Paradise PD, with whom I had worked previously, and his deputy, Molly Crane, had been planning to drive down one of these days to visit Rita.

One of these days turned out to be today, and so, as it turned out, we didn't have to go to Paradise because Paradise came to us.

Jesse's relationship with Rita had burned bright for a while, as a lot of relationships did with Rita, but it hadn't lasted. They had, however, managed to remain friends. Rita had intimated, on more than one occasion, that sometimes the friendship that had endured between them had occasionally come with benefits, when the flesh was weak for one or both of them.

"And I'm not speaking to my overall fitness," Rita said.

Now Jesse and Molly were the ones seated with Shannon Miles and me in her living room, absent Vinnie Morris, who, before leaving, had made sure I knew he would come back from Chicago if needed.

"Kind of funny," he said, "me being replaced on this job by a cop."

"I keep telling Hawk that irony isn't dead," I said. "It just occasionally takes some time off."

By now I had explained everything that needed explaining to Stone and Molly. I left out the parts I knew they would have skipped over if they were the ones telling it. Even working in a twelve-person police force in a small town on the North Shore, Jesse and Molly were as good as Quirk or Belson or Lee Farrell.

Stone, I knew, had been a minor-league ballplayer when he was young. He still looked fit and trim enough to play. Once a jock, always a jock. But he was the kind of cop who didn't have to tell you how tough or smart he was. Today he wore a blue PPD vest with jeans and black high-top sneakers that must have been his version of snow shoes. Molly Crane, just as tough and far prettier than he was, wore the same vest. It looked much better on her. When they'd walked in with their matching jackets, I'd asked how they'd done in their paddle tennis match.

"Watch it, smart guy," Molly said, smiling at me, her dark eyes flashing. "You need me, remember?"

I nodded at Stone. "Not as much as the chief does."

Molly smiled across the coffee table at Shannon Miles then. "House arrest will be a lot more fun with me," she said, "I can assure you."

"You're sure you're okay with getting a stranger forced on you as a roommate?" Miles asked.

"I've done it before," she said. "Even with one of Chief Stone's former girlfriends."

"Sunny," Stone said to me.

I knew he was referring to Sunny Randall, another Boston private detective of my acquaintance, and a damn good one.

"Forgot about you and Sunny," I said.

"Jesse hasn't," Molly Crane said.

Shannon Miles had made tea for herself. Stone and Molly and I were drinking coffee.

"How was Rita today?" I asked them.

Molly said, "Well enough to make an indecent proposal to Chief Stone."

"With you present?" I asked.

"Yes, she did, the brazen hussy," Molly said.

Then I told them I hoped we wouldn't need Molly's house as a safe house for too terribly long. But with Delores Thompson missing and, to my thinking, presumed dead, I couldn't take any chances.

"My offer still stands," Jesse Stone said. "Whatever you need from me, you got, and not just with Molly."

I nodded. "You got a lot of rich guys up in your town, right?" I said.

"It makes us feel awfully good about ourselves, I don't mind telling you," he said.

"Maybe you could ask around and find out if some of your rich guys know the rich guys all tied up in this thing," I said. "Or anyone who has done business with them. And just so you know, both Mauro and McManus think the other one is dirty."

"Hope it doesn't hurt the snowflakes' feelings," Stone said.

He drank some coffee. "When Drummond died, I assume the cops here went through his Cloud and all of the other magical mysteries of our world."

"They did," I said. "But it turns out he might have been the one guy his age who didn't need much of a storage plan, at least not that anybody could find. And he wasn't fond of the notion of Big Brother having access to his accounts. He even wrote on an old typewriter, according to Ms. Thompson."

"My hero," Stone said.

"Every time I send an email I sometimes imagine people from here to Thailand being able to check it for grammar," Molly Crane said.

"The message you got from Ms. Thompson said she had evidence of some kind that made her think Nick Drummond got himself murdered," Stone said. "Be nice to know what it was. And where it is."

"Wouldn't it, though," I said.

I felt myself grinning. Stone didn't miss things the same way Frank Belson didn't miss things. And he listened every bit as intently as Belson did, whether he showed it or not.

"Somehow in this work it always comes down to finding the thing," Stone said, "whatever the thing is."

"The Holy Grail," I said.

"Except probably not so holy in this case," Jesse Stone said.

He stood and asked Shannon Miles, "You ready to go?"

Her suitcase, computer bag, and purse were near the front door. She had already informed Stone and Molly Crane that there was a registered gun inside the purse.

"Soon as I'm settled in," Shannon Miles told me, "I'll get back to work. And as soon as I find out something interesting, I'll call."

"Goes for me, too," Stone said.

When Molly and Shannon Miles were outside, packing her bags into the back of Stone's Explorer, the doors of the house already locked and the alarm set, it was just Stone and me standing on the front porch.

"You think the Holy Grail you're looking for really did get Drummond murdered?" he said.

"All day, every day."

"If it did go down that way, you think it had to be one of your rich guys who might've got 'er done?"

I said, "See previous answer."

We shook hands.

"You find out who shot Rita, I'd like to be your first call," he said.

"Second."

"Who's first?"

"Hawk," I said.

FORTY-EIGHT

I had offered to meet Wayne Cosgrove, outgoing editor of *The Globe*, at his office. He said I didn't have to bother. And besides, he said, he was always looking for reasons to get away from the office these days.

"Depressed because you're leaving?" I said.

"I've been about the current state of the business for so long," he said, "it'd be like saying the ocean just got deeper."

We met at City Table at the Lenox Hotel, a place on Boylston that had stood the test of time the way I supposed Wayne Cosgrove and I both had.

Cosgrove was a reformed hippie, both dogged and smart as hell, someone who'd been a star reporter at the paper, then the best columnist in town, and finally editor-in-chief. *The Globe* had been struggling when he took over. Cosgrove had explained it to me once over a drink:

"I kept waiting for somebody else to raise their hand. When they didn't, I did."

Now he had elected to walk away from the paper, and the newspaper business. His hair was a lot shorter than it was when I'd first met him, with a lot more gray in it. Once he'd worn corduroy sport jackets, jeans, and cowboy boots. Now he wore suits.

We settled in at a high-top table in the middle of the room. City Table was mostly empty when we got there, brunch having ended and their lunch crowd not yet arriving.

"Do I look more woke than the last time you saw me?" Cosgrove said with a crooked smile.

"Not only do I not know what woke looks like," I said, "I'm still not entirely sure what it even means."

We'd both ordered cheeseburgers. Cosgrove was having a Bloody Mary to go with it. I stayed with coffee.

He plucked an olive from the Bloody Mary. Something else of which I wasn't entirely sure was why olives looked more appetizing when they were in somebody else's drink. Maybe Dr. Silverman could explain it to me.

"Sorry to tell you this, pal," Cosgrove said, "but if you don't know what woke is, you've got no shot at being my replacement."

He drank some of his drink.

"So why are we here, really?" he said. "It's never because you missed me."

"I want to talk about the paper's coverage about that prime real estate at Widett Circle," I said.

"You mean you want to know how we screwed the pooch the way we did?" he asked.

We talked our way through while we ate.

"It's on me as much as anybody else," he said. "In the end, you gotta trust your people. I know how it works because I was one of those people back in the day. And I know how many guard-rails are on sourcing, because I put even more of them in place when I got this job. But my reporter had the best source in the world on that story, and fell in love with him."

"Who was the source?"

"I can tell you now," he said, "because the guy's dead."

"You're saying it was Nick Drummond," I said.

"Himself," Cosgrove said.

He drank more Bloody Mary.

"Turns out he'd taped a conversation with Tommy Mauro where Mauro bragged that it had been Joe Broz who'd helped him out when he was first starting out in the real estate business. And how, even though the old man was gone, he felt like he'd just be repaying him by getting John Broz's company into play if he got the land."

"Good old Grade A quid pro quo," I said.

"Yes, sir."

"Who heard the tape?"

"My reporter," Cosgrove said. "And me. And the lawyers."

"Was it all on the record?"

He shook his head. "Drummond made it clear to Matt Vallone—our reporter—what was and what wasn't," Cosgrove said. "But he wanted us to know that we weren't wrong with Mauro's con-nection to Broz. That we were doing the right thing with our coverage, that the bare bones of the story were solid, and that we were good."

Cosgrove took a sip. "'We' meaning him, and us," he continued. "He told Vallone there was more evidence if we ever needed it. But the tape was just his sign of good faith."

"He say what other evidence he had?"

Cosgrove shook his head again. "Just that he had it," he said. "But we never saw it. And after the deal closed, Vallone stopped asking for it."

"But Mauro was the one who was screwed by then."

"You know what they say," Cosgrove said. "You torture facts long enough you can make them tell you whatever you want them to. We had that recording, which meant the story on Mauro and Broz wasn't wrong. But looking back, it doesn't feel right, either. McManus got the land, Mauro got shut out, and while McManus has lived happily ever after, Nick Drummond sure did not."

"I don't even know," I said. "But is Vallone still with the paper?"

"He quit not long after Drummond died," he said. "And I wasn't sad to see him go. He'd gotten too close to Drummond and I let him. Everybody ended up using everybody, which is the way it works with sources sometimes. Or a lot of the time."

"Where's Vallone now?"

"Still in town, pretty sure," Cosgrove said. "But it's not as if we've stayed in touch." Cosgrove sighed. "Like I said: You trust your people."

He jabbed a french fry at the pool of ketchup on his plate as if stabbing it with a knife.

"Drummond picked the lane that he thought would do him the most good, and it was the one with Kevin McManus in it," Cosgrove said. "And my reporter pretty much got in the same lane."

"Mauro is still convinced McManus paid off Drummond," I

said. "But I asked McManus straight up and he said no, the only thing Drummond got from him was a promise that when it was all over, he'd do anything he could to help Drummond get to where he wanted to go in politics."

"Probably so," Cosgrove said. "But if you're asking me if I think money could have changed hands along the way, the answer is yes."

"What was in it for Vallone?"

Cosgrove sighed again. "What's always in it, for all of us," he said. "A big story."

I asked if he still had Vallone's contact information. He pulled out his phone and tapped away at it and said he was sending it to me. A few seconds later, I heard the ping from my own phone.

"Here's the bottom line," he said. "My paper might not have killed Thomas Mauro's bid. But we sure as hell didn't do very much to keep it alive."

He told me then that he was buying lunch. I told him that I'd let him, it was the very least a loyal *Globe* reader could do. Then he waved at the waiter and made a scribbling motion with his hand.

"One last thing," Cosgrove said. "When you talk to Vallone, you might want to ask him if what I've heard is true, that before Drummond became a floater the two of them were working on a top-secret book together."

"Is that so," I said.

Cosgrove nodded.

"Maybe my ex-reporter knows even more of Drummond's secrets than he let on," he said.

"Ones that might have gotten Drummond killed," I said.

"Yeah," Cosgrove said. "And not just him."

FORTY-NINE

I left a message for Matt Vallone.

I gave him my name and occupation and how I'd gotten his number and why I was calling and pretty much everything except what had been my rank and serial number what felt like a hundred years ago. And asked for him to call me back.

Then I texted him.

By midafternoon I had not heard back. I knew I might never hear from him. Maybe he didn't want to talk to me about Nick Drummond. Maybe mentioning the name of his former boss at *The Globe* made me about as welcome to him as a telemarketer.

Cosgrove had also given me Vallone's address, on Endicott Street in the North End. There were a couple Italian restaurants on Endicott that Susan and I liked: Mangia Mangia and Massimino's. But there were also a few we didn't like.

I decided to take a drive over there, parked in a lot on Cooper, and walked the rest of the way.

Vallone lived in a four-story red-brick apartment building that was actually situated between Mangia Mangia and Massimino's, good to know if he wasn't home and not coming home anytime soon and I suddenly became weak with hunger.

I walked up to the building and opened the front door and saw that there was a tiny entranceway with names and doorbells next to mailboxes, with a speaker above.

M. Vallone lived in 3F.

I could ring the bell and announce myself, but that didn't necessarily get me through the locked door in front of me if he wasn't interested in talking to me about Nick Drummond.

Or I could just assume he was upstairs and avoid rejection by getting inside the locked door in front of me and proceeding up to 3F.

It took half an hour for me to see someone I hoped fervently was a resident coming down the stairs. A tall young woman, hair as red as Rita's.

I pretended to be talking into my phone.

"I *am* downstairs," I said. "But your stupid bell must not be working."

I smiled at the redhead, as if embarrassed.

Then was back talking into my phone. "I'm sorry that you were in the shower, but you are aware that there's a winter going on outside, right?"

The redhead stopped. I smiled at her again. My big one. I hoped she wouldn't lose control.

Then I shrugged helplessly. "Apparently there are still problems in the world that technology can't solve," I said. "I didn't know getting up to the third floor was going to be like scaling Mount Everest today."

"Allow me," she said, and went back into the entranceway and opened the inside door with her key, holding it open for me.

"Random acts of kindness still fuel the world," I said.

"Not nearly often enough," she said, and then headed up Endicott.

I briefly felt guilty about misleading her, but the feeling quickly passed.

When I got to Vallone's apartment I banged on the door and said, "UPS."

I could hear music playing as I stepped away from the peephole.

I stepped back once more as the door opened.

"You're not UPS," Vallone said when he saw me, and started to close the door.

I held it open.

"I'm Spenser," I said. "We need to talk."

"You're the guy who left the messages?" he said.

"Same-day delivery," I said.

FIFTY

I t was a small apartment, the living room opening up into the kitchen, where Vallone's laptop sat on the table, surrounded by notebooks and various printouts. I saw a printer hooked up to the laptop from the counter.

"This is a little bit like forced entry," Vallone said. "Wouldn't you say?"

"Well, it's definitely an entry," I said.

He was small enough to have fought in Henry Cimoli's weight class. Maybe a lightweight, but no more than that. He was young, olive-skinned, and wore a long-sleeved gray T-shirt with jeans. His black hair was cut short, as was his neatly trimmed beard.

In the living room, there was a red-and-white box of Marlboro cigarettes on the coffee table that looked as if it belonged in a time capsule, and an old-school Zippo lighter to complete the picture.

He reached for the cigarettes. "Mind if I smoke, dude?"

"Yes," I said.

I liked secondary smoke, especially in a confined space, as much as I liked being called "dude."

"This place serve as your office now that you're not with *The Globe*?" I said.

"Only sometimes," he said. "I've also got this little no-distractions space in a storage building down the waterfront. Maybe a half-hour walk from here. Desk. Filing cabinet. I leave my phone here when I've got work to do. Traveler Street, number 33. Maybe you've seen it. It's right near that big old mural with the whales you used to be able to see from the expressway."

He made a show of pushing the box of Marlboros away from him, almost like a sign of good faith.

"You said you wanted to talk about Rita Fiore being shot," he said.

"Among other things."

He nodded. "Listen, I know Nick Drummond was hitting that before he died."

"Dude?" I said. "I might not have mentioned that Rita is a close friend of mine. But she is. So you should know that if you say one more thing about her that I find even mildly offensive, I will see how far I can drop-kick you across this room the way I would a jockey."

"Whoa," he said, making a calming gesture toward me, palms out. "Let's start all over again. Tell me exactly what you're working on."

"Wayne Cosgrove told me that you and Drummond might have been working on a book together."

"Where'd he get an idea like that?"

"I don't know," I said. "I'd hoped that maybe you could tell me."

He picked up the Zippo lighter and rolled it around in his hand. Cigarettes and a lighter. Maybe he'd grown up watching old newspaper movies, even if he looked young enough to be editing a school paper.

He was buying time. If I knew that, he probably knew that I did. I had bum-rushed my way in here, and now he was trying to regroup.

"Nick and I had *talked* about doing a book together," he said. "A quickie like those pro athletes do after they have their first big year." He opened the lighter and flicked it and produced a flame. "Then the guy up and died on me."

"Selfish bastard."

"Not my meaning."

"So did the book idea die with him?" I said. "Cosgrove said the two of you were pretty tight. You must have been stock-piling a lot of good information. Maybe even stuff about him only you knew."

Vallone frowned. "Why are you suddenly so interested in whether or not Nick Drummond wanted to do a book?"

"I'll tell you why," I said. "I think somebody murdered your friend Nick and made it look like an accident. I think it was because he either had information he wasn't supposed to have or information that somebody was afraid might come into the light. And I think it got him killed. On top of that, I think it got Rita Fiore shot. And I'm pretty sure it got Brian Tully killed once he started poking around Widett Circle."

"Sounds like you're working on a big story yourself," Vallone said. If any of what I'd said had rocked him, he wasn't showing it.

Or maybe he knew some of it already. "Listen, I am trying to put a book up on its feet, but I still can't figure out whether it's non-fiction or a novel."

"I thought Nick Drummond's life was like a novel," I said.

"You see my problem, then," Vallone said.

"Here's the deal," I said. "I'm working on who shot Rita Fiore. And I only care about the rest of it as it relates to her. So the real purpose of my visit is to find out what you know that might be useful to me."

"It sounds like you know a lot more about this shit than I do," Vallone said.

"There's one other thing," I said. "It appears that Nick Drummond's former chief of staff has disappeared."

"What the hell," he said. "Delores has disappeared?"

If I didn't have his full attention before, I seemed to have it now.

"She's been missing for a couple days," I said. "Right before that, she left a phone message for me, saying that she was in possession of information that she said might have gotten your friend Drummond killed. I'm just trying to figure out what it might be, and who saw it as a threat. And whether you might know what kind of intel we're talking about, having been as close to Drummond as you were."

"I swear I don't," Vallone said. "And, dude? If what you think happened to Nick happened because of that intel? I don't want to."

"Would be a big story," I said.

"That's what Brian Tully thought," he said.

FIFTY-ONE

I drove back to my office, made a few more calls to the State House about Delores Thompson, once again learned nothing of consequence. Before I left, I fixed myself a small Bushmills. It didn't help my disposition. But it didn't hurt, either.

By the time I was outside on Berkeley Street the snow had started to come down again, more than had been forecast for this evening, blowing from the direction of the Charles.

I pulled down my old Boston Braves cap tighter over my eyes. It helped with visibility, but not much, doing more to shield my forehead from the snow that made me feel as if my face were being slapped with icicles.

I crossed Newbury and then decided to take a right at Brooks Brothers and walk up toward the Public Garden, just to give myself cover from the buildings on that side of the street. I even considered going in The Newbury and having a drink inside the safe haven that The Street Bar had always been, and was still, no matter who owned the building.

But by the time I made the left onto Arlington, I just wanted to get to my apartment and settle in for the night, find out who still might be delivering now that another storm had blown in, the streets like a whiteout, even in the night.

There was hardly any traffic coming in my direction on Arlington. No one on the sidewalk. I stopped and looked into The Street Bar, seeing the people at the tables, feeling momentarily like a kid with his nose pressed against the window of a candy store.

Then I put my head down, pretending that I could somehow lean down under the snow blowing directly at me, and stuck my hands in the pockets of my peacoat. My phone was in the left-hand pocket. My .38 was in the right. Never leave home without both of them.

I wanted to tell myself there was a fierce beauty to storms like this, despite the frequency with which they'd come this winter, the relentlessness with which nature kept sending them our way. Maybe I would appreciate the beauty more deeply when I was back in my apartment, looking out the window with a fire going and a scotch and soda in my hand, not doggedly making my way past the Public Garden, being blanketed by more snow tonight.

My apartment was my finish line, and the Noodles in Ground Beef Sauce and Siamese Fried Rice that I was going to order from King and I on Charles. Maybe with extra steamed noodles as a side. As if I was getting the jump on carbing up for the Marathon.

I hunched down some more against the snow as I passed the

last of the public alleys on this part of Arlington, and tried to think about the case. But I could focus only on doggedly putting one foot ahead of the other.

Finally I made the left on Marlborough. No car traffic or foot traffic on Marlborough, either, at least not that I could see for as far as I could see.

I had taken great pleasure, and worn out those near and dear to me, with the notion of being able to walk home from work.

Not tonight.

Tonight, these few blocks had felt exactly like my own Boston Marathon, even as I now approached my finish line.

I thought about Susan and hoped that she wasn't driving in this weather, that she had canceled her dinner before the snow came.

Then headlights from a single car appeared ahead of me.

Through the snow, falling sideways now that I'd made the turn, I could see that it was a black SUV.

And though I could not see clearly, my brain was suddenly clear enough for me to remember that it had been a black SUV with Rita.

Then the car was skidding as it slowed, trying to come to a complete stop on road that had turned to ice, and in the next moment the window on the driver's side was being rolled down.

But the car continued to slide up Marlborough when I noticed the gun in the driver's hand.

And then it was Rita, all over again, as I saw the flash of the muzzle right before I heard the shot.

FIFTY-TWO

The car skidding as it had was just enough to throw the shooter off. I threw myself on the ground, and the next sound I heard was the bullet hitting the old gas streetlight in front of my building.

I dove toward the car instead of away from it, taking myself underneath the eyeline of the shooter and getting the .38 out of my pocket to fire wildly at the driver's-side window, not having time to aim, just letting the bastard know that somebody was shooting back this time, if it was indeed the same guy who'd shot Rita.

Not an unarmed lawyer on her way to the gym, a woman who'd never been shot at in her life.

Just him and me.

The car had finally come to a stop, but I pushed myself forward on my stomach, feeling as if I were hydroplaning on the icy surface, trying to get to cover from the snow piled high on the opposite side of Marlborough from my apartment.

I wasn't sure what kind of gun he had; I hadn't gotten a good enough look at it. But it likely had much better range than my own snub-nosed revolver. The .38 was one of my favorites and always had been. But Hawk liked to say it had about as much reach as I'd had inside a boxing ring.

Twenty-five yards on the outside.

I was good with it, but not in conditions like these.

I managed to get behind the snowbank just as another bullet ripped into it. When I allowed myself to look up, I could see that he'd raised himself over the roof of the car as he fired again. And then again.

Then I rose up to fire and had my head up long enough to see the front-seat window on the passenger side explode, the sound of it muffled by the weather. But maybe the weather wasn't completely hiding the sound of gunfire.

Maybe someone inside these buildings had heard and was calling 911.

Still, 911 wasn't going to help me right now. He had the cover of the car, and a bigger gun. We both had each other pinned down, but I liked his chances better.

I rose up and fired again, staying low this time, and knew I had hit the passenger door.

I looked down Marlborough.

Still no one on the sidewalks, no other cars coming in our direction.

The snow continued to blow in from the Charles.

He couldn't come around the car for fear of going down in the street and giving me, if only briefly, an unmoving target.

Then I fired again as I came out from behind the snowbank, flattening myself under my side of the SUV as he jumped down off the running board, perhaps having made the decision to come right at me, blasting away.

I fired at his legs and heard him scream with pain.

I kept going then, easily bodysurfing underneath the car, the surface of the road feeling as slick as an ice-skating rink, and heard the door slam again, the engine roaring to life.

This close, it sounded like a jet engine.

I pushed myself toward the rear tires as they started to spin in place on the ice the same as the two front tires were.

He was shot and wanted to get out of here.

But the car wouldn't cooperate.

Then I was all the way out from underneath the car, close to the rear fender on the driver's side. I got up on my knees.

Not much of an angle, but the best one I was going to get before he saw me back there.

The wheels finally gained traction then and slowly began to move.

Too late.

I had three rounds left.

I fired all of them in rapid succession through the driver's window, which he had not yet had time to close.

He slumped forward, his body causing the wheels to turn to the right, and prompting the car to head straight into another snowbank. The horn sounded then, like a car alarm that wouldn't stop, blaring ceaselessly into the night.

Only then did I hear the first sirens as I inched along the car to where the body lay motionless.

One more traffic fatality, I thought.

Weather-related.

FIFTY-THREE

Frank Belson had offered to drive me home from headquarters.

The snow finally stopped right before dawn, and the sun was trying to show itself in a still-heavy sky.

I had written out my statement for Belson, waited while it was typed out, read it, and signed it. I went through the motions of turning over my gun, but once they had tested it, Belson had slipped it back into the pocket of my coat.

"It's a dangerous world," he said. "More dangerous for you than most people."

I made a pot of coffee. We sat at the kitchen table and drank coffee.

"You think it's the same guy who shot Rita?" Belson asked. "The bullets we found in the snow aren't a match."

"Could be a different gun," I said. "Or could be a different player from the same team."

"Whose team?"

"Aye," I said. "There's the rub."

"He was trying to drive away?" Belson said.

"Or he was about to turn around and come back at me, guns blazing," I said. "At the end, I decided to be the one to shoot first and ask questions later."

We knew the shooter's name now. Richie Lowens. He was carrying an expired driver's license with an address in Everett. The cops went to his apartment. He hadn't lived there in years, according to the people who lived there now. Belson said they were quite pleased to have gotten a knock on the door in the middle of the night.

"Who wouldn't be?" I said.

They had run his name and his prints through the system. He had done time back in the nineties, nickel-and-dime stuff mostly, assault one time, petty larceny another. Belson said he'd wait until somebody was at Organized Crime in the morning to ask if anybody recognized the name.

"Why come after you at this point?" Belson said.

"They must think I know more than I do," I said.

"Frequently made mistake."

He went and poured himself another cup of coffee.

"Somebody's working hard to get something buried," Belson said. "Or keep it buried."

"Call me after you talk to Organized Crime about Lowens," I said.

He said he would and left. I watched from the window as the car pulled away, then tried to get a couple hours' sleep, despite the adrenaline and the caffeine. And somehow did.

It was past nine o'clock when I was awake again.

I called Vinnie Morris in Chicago.

"You're aware it's an hour earlier here, right?" he said. "So this better be important."

"It is," I said, and told him about what had happened in front of my building.

"You shot the guy dead?" he said.

"As luck would have it, yes."

Then I gave him Richie Lowens's name and asked if he might possibly recognize it.

"Yeah," he said without hesitation.

"You know who he might have worked for?" I asked.

"Yeah, as luck would have it," Vinnie said. "See what I did there?"

"Who'd he work for, Vinnie?"

"Joe," he said.

"Joe Broz," I said, not even trying to make it sound like a question.

"No," Vinnie Morris said. "Joe Biden."

FIFTY-FOUR

I called Susan then to tell her about the festivities from the previous night. She was silent as I took her through it, as if I were a patient.

When I finished she said, "I don't suppose you see this as a good time to think about early retirement."

"I don't have a 401(k)," I said.

"I'm willing to kick in."

"That would reduce me to being nothing more than your love slave," I said.

"Fine by me," she said.

Then she said, "I've got a client coming in five minutes. I love you. And please be careful, for fuck's sake."

"You know," I said, "there are times when you sound nothing at all like a nice girl from Swampscott."

"Where have *you* been?" she said. "I was never a nice girl from Swampscott."

MIKE LUPICA

She told me she loved me again, I told her the same, and then I called Hawk and told him about what had happened.

"In that case, I'm on my way over and you can cook me breakfast," he said, "then I'll walk you to school in case someone else tries to shoot you."

"That's quite generous of you," I said.

"No such thing as a free meal," Hawk said.

"For you?" I said. "Since when?"

An hour later, we were taking our time, walking to my office. The sun was out and so were the plows, and for the moment everything was right in the world. No one else had yet tried to do me harm this morning. But it was still early.

"So Mauro knew Joe Broz back in the day," Hawk said.

"Drummond had him on tape saying it was so, at least according to Wayne Cosgrove."

"Mauro know a tape like that exists?"

"I didn't ask."

Hawk snorted. It looked like steam coming out of his nose. "Some reporter you are."

We kept walking.

"And now one of Joe's old troopers tries to shoot you," Hawk said.

"Small world," I said.

"I assume you got a plan to take all this up with Mauro?" he said.

"More like a work in progress," I said.

"More things change," Hawk said.

232

FIFTY-FIVE

There was one theory of detecting to which I had clung fiercely since I had first started doing this kind of work for a living:

When in doubt, follow someone.

I had no proof that Thomas Mauro had sent Richie Lowens after me. I had no way of knowing just how tight Mauro had been with Joe Broz in the old days, other than a recording that only Wayne Cosgrove and his reporter had heard. All I knew for sure was that somebody who'd worked with Broz once *had* now come after me. I likewise knew that a lot of bad things had happened and have continued to happen since Nick Drummond died, now at an increasingly rapid clip.

So Thomas Mauro and I needed to have another conversation, and I wanted him to be far less comfortable than he had been on South Ocean Blvd., or at his office.

I drove over to 99 High now, parked across the street from the building, and waited.

I was asked to move only once. When the cop pointed out I was in a no-parking zone, I politely showed him my license.

When he handed it back to me, he said, "Nice. But nothing on it says you can park wherever you want to." I then said, "You didn't let me finish," and handed him Martin Quirk's very official-looking card, told him I was assisting Commander Quirk on a case, and said that if he wanted to confirm that, he could call headquarters.

It wasn't exactly like handing him a get-out-of-jail-free card, but in these circumstances, it did the job. I told the cop before he walked off that I didn't expect to be there much longer.

"Be still my heart," he said.

I had called Mauro's office and told his assistant I was with FedEx and had an envelope from the IRS that Mauro specifically needed to sign for, figuring that "IRS" with someone like Mauro was like talking about the bogeyman. I then explained that the reason I was calling was that I was running late, and wondered how long he was going to be at the office.

UPS one day, now FedEx. I played no favorites. Maybe DHL next.

"Wherever you are in town," the woman said, "you better hurry if you want him today—he's leaving around four for an out-of-office appointment."

It was three-thirty.

While I sat, motor running, Belson called. He said he'd been waiting on the guy from Organized Crime, but had now been informed that Richie Lowens had been off their radar for years, and that the most recent address they'd tracked down for him was in Florida.

"Where in Florida?" I asked.

"West Palm Beach," Belson said.

"Oh, ho," I said.

FIFTY-SIX

saw Mauro emerge out of 99 High a few minutes past four o'clock.

He wore a ball cap whose logo I couldn't identify, and a padded Bruins jacket. There was a black Mercedes waiting for him.

The driver came around and opened the door. He looked to be just as big and wide as the sideman I'd seen with McManus at the 21st Amendment. Maybe both Mauro and McManus hired only from the big boy shop.

After Mauro got in, the guy squeezed himself back inside the car and behind the wheel, pulling out into traffic before making a right on Congress. I was able to make a fast U-turn and stay a few cars behind them until they were on 93, heading south.

By now, I knew that Mauro had an estate in Lincoln but also kept an apartment at the Seaport. He had been divorced twice and was currently single, by all reports.

But wherever he was going right now, just slightly ahead of rush-hour traffic, he wasn't on his way to either of his residences. And he wasn't heading toward Hanscom Field and a private jet to whisk him away to Palm Beach.

The Mercedes finally took the Route 203 exit, and a few minutes later was pulling up to the Eire Pub.

It was a Boston landmark, with "BOSTON'S ORIGINAL" and GENTLEMEN'S PRESTIGE BAR on its green rooftop sign. The Eire wasn't the oldest bar in Boston, but I knew enough about the place to know that it had been right here on Adams Street for more than half a century, and it was more than just another neighborhood bar, one that had always been a required stop for campaigning politicians, all the way back to Ronald Reagan. I knew, from my own time drinking at the Eire Pub, that there was a photograph of candidate Bill Clinton actually sitting on the horseshoe-shaped bar, not far from hockey jerseys that belonged to the Hayes brothers, a couple Dorchester kids who had made it all the way to the NHL.

The Mercedes idled briefly before the driver was once again on the sidewalk, opening the door for Mauro, who walked inside.

I had stopped about a block away, on the opposite side of the street from the Mercedes, and shut off the engine. I hadn't decided how I wanted to play it now that I was here.

I could just walk inside, sit down next to him, and ask how he thought the Bruins were doing before I offered to buy him a drink.

I decided to wait instead. It was another one of Spenser's rules of ace detecting: Hang around and hope something interesting develops.

Mauro had to be meeting someone. If not, he'd certainly gone out of his way for a drink before heading home.

Was he the first to arrive, or was the person he was meeting already inside?

I continued to wait.

While I did, I went to the phone's playlist and selected "Ella Sings Gershwin," having finally figured out how to sync my phone with my car radio, and listened to her ease her way, smooth as silk, into "My One and Only" with the great Ellis Larkins accompanying her on the piano.

"My one and only . . . What am I gonna do if you turn me down . . ."

Sometimes, alone in the car like this, I would sing along with my music.

But not with Miss Ella's music. It would have been disrespectful. She was that special, and always had been and always would be.

I was about to get out of the car and walk up the block and into the Eire Pub when a Range Rover, also black, pulled up behind the Mercedes.

Even from the distance, I immediately recognized the oversized bruiser who got out to open the door for his passenger.

The passenger was Kevin McManus.

"Oh, ho," I said again.

FIFTY-SEVEN

After deciding not to confront them after a fair amount of internal debate, I was soon back on 93, heading home, and calling Hawk.

"Shit," he said, after I told him what I had just seen at the Eire Pub. "Guess it's true about politics making strange fuck partners."

I told him I hadn't ever heard it put exactly that way, but yes.

"You think they might be in this together?" Hawk said. "Can't lick 'em and join 'em and so on and whatnot?"

"But McManus already licked Mauro," I said. "So to speak."

"Maybe Mauro still got something McManus wants, on top of all that choice real estate," Hawk said. "Or maybe their interests be aligned because Drummond had bad shit on both of them, and they both been looking for the same thing."

"We think as one," I said.

"Damn," Hawk said, "I was afraid something like that was going to happen eventually."

"For now," I said, "I couldn't think of a good reason to let them know that I knew they were together today."

Hawk and I decided to meet at The Street Bar at The Newbury when I got back, since I'd passed on a golden opportunity to go inside the night before.

Then the hospital called.

It was good news for a change.

Rita was being released. Because it was late in the day, Dr. Harman had told Rita she could wait until morning. But, Dr. Harman had been told by Rita, in what was described as extremely colorful language, that the patient did not consider that a viable or even acceptable option.

Since Hawk was closer to the hospital, he waited for Rita and then drove both of them back to her place on Joy Street. By now, Rita had reluctantly agreed to let Hawk stay with her, as people *were* still being shot at.

"You and Hawk being roomies will be fun," I said when we were all seated in her living room. "You can make popcorn and watch Hallmark movies together."

"You're starting to sound as if you're the one who had a traumatic injury," she said. "To your brain."

"Is that a no on the popcorn or the movies?" I said.

"I don't make popcorn," she said.

I'd stopped on the way to Joy Street and picked up pizza at The Upper Crust, after Rita said she thought her stomach could handle a white one. By the time I arrived at the house, she had already showered, dried her hair, put on makeup, and was dressed in a green sweater and black jeans.

Once, both the sweater and jeans would have been much tighter on her than they were tonight. But she had lost a lot of weight in a very short amount of time. You didn't just see it in her clothes, but in her face. I knew it wouldn't last, that she would get back to her playing weight as soon as possible and back to the gym as soon as she was allowed. She was Rita. She was on the other side of this now.

"The other thing on the roommate situation," I said. "No funny stuff between the two of you."

Hawk smiled. "In the state she in now," he said, "even if she did something with me, I might not find out about it."

Even Rita laughed.

Then she wanted to talk about me being shot.

"Why you?" she asked.

"Somebody must think that I know whatever they thought you might know," I said. "And what Brian Tully might've found out. And what he might've told Shannon Miles. And what Delores Thompson wanted to tell me when she left that message."

"Enough people to form a damn conga line," Hawk said.

Rita had eaten just one slice of pizza. Now she was curled up at the end of her sofa, a blanket over her and her arms hooked around her knees.

"Maybe I didn't know Nick as well as I thought I did," she said.

"Or maybe you did, and there were just things from which he thought he needed to protect you," I said.

"Protect me from the kind of people who came after me?" she asked.

"Or from you finding out he might not be exactly who you thought he was," I said.

She closed her eyes, leaned her head back, and shook it slowly from side to side.

"I will never believe he was crooked," she said.

"Boy *was* a politician," Hawk said.

"He was different!" she snapped, her eyes suddenly on fire. All of her on fire in the moment.

"Sometimes people in positions like his feel as if they have to do bad things for the greater good," I said calmly, more for her than for me.

"And it's in your head that Thomas Mauro is somehow behind all of this?" she said.

"It was until I saw Mauro and Kevin McManus together," I said. "Now I'm not sure what I think. But I need to ask you something again: Did Drummond ever mention working on some kind of book?"

She shook her head again. "All he ever said about that was that the reporter from *The Globe* I thought he'd gotten way too close to . . ."

"Matt Vallone," I said.

"Right, the Vallone guy," she continued, "told him he ought to write one, just because of the hard-knocks life he led before he got famous around here and people started doing the young Kennedy thing with him, just from the wrong side of the tracks."

"He ever talk much about his childhood?" I asked.

"Very little," she said. "All he really ever said was that it was a little bit like sports. I asked him what he meant and he said, 'Survive and advance.'"

She looked at me and then at Hawk and then back at me, her eyes suddenly looking as red as her hair. "Of course, that was before he died young like a Kennedy," she said.

We all sat in silence, until I reached over and took her hand.

Still cold. "You know what you always tell me about being a defense attorney," I said. "Discovery is a bitch."

"He was such a good guy," Rita said in a soft voice, almost as if talking to herself. "He had overcome so much to get to where he was. But I just don't want you to find out he wasn't a good guy."

"We just a couple simple folk trying to find out who put the damn bullets in you," Hawk said.

I was supposed to spend the night in Cambridge with Susan and Pearl, but decided I was too tired to make the trip over there tonight, even to see the girl of my dreams, and a dog with whom I hadn't been spending nearly enough quality time.

So I walked to my car, patting my pockets as I did, comforted by the fact that I was carrying a Glock tonight, and not the .38, even though the .38 had done the job with Richie Lowens.

Once inside the apartment and in bed, I couldn't sleep, still picturing Kevin McManus getting out of the Range Rover and walking inside the Eire Pub to meet Thomas Mauro.

And thinking, before sleep finally came, that I might have to look at things in a different way.

Survive and advance.

FIFTY-EIGHT

Shannon Miles called the next morning from Paradise, saying she was just checking in.

I told her about what had happened in front of my building, and how I had shot and killed Richie Lowens, then filled her in about Lowens's history with Joe Broz.

"At least we know you're a better shot than I seemed to have been," she said.

"I've had more practice," I said, and then told her about the scene from the previous afternoon at the Eire Pub.

"It occurs to me that I know a lot more about Mr. Mauro at this point than I do Mr. McManus," I said. "Would you mind shifting your focus to him?"

"You think Kevin might not be the white knight of this tale?" she said.

"Every tale needs at least one villain and one hero," I told her. "But that doesn't preclude someone from being both."

sters.”Focus,” I stressed again, and then told her to call me if she
found out anything interesting about Kevin McManus.But then, as luck would have it, if I wanted to think of it as
luck, as I got to my office, I found out Mr. McManus had already
made himself at home.

“The boss is inside,” the super-sized bald guy standing outside my door told me.

“I hope he at least put the coffee on,” I said.

“And not for nothing?” the bald guy said. He was wearing the
same black leather jacket he’d worn at the 21st Amendment.
“You ought to think about a better lock.”

McManus was in one of the client chairs, his back to me,
checking his phone. He wore a sleeveless vest, navy turtleneck
underneath. When he heard the door open, he swiveled a little
in his chair and grinned.

“I knew you wouldn’t have wanted me to wait out in the
hall,” he said.

I walked around my desk and sat down.

“Anybody ever mention your bodyguard looks like the old
boxer Butterbean?” I said.

McManus was still grinning. “You’re pretty cool for someone
who just found somebody in your office.”

“I got shot at the other night,” I said. “Gives a man perspective. Gets him to not spend as much time sweating the little things."

"You know what, I remember Butterbean," McManus said. "He was in the ring with a guy one time and the guy actually started to cry. When they asked him about it later, Butterbean said, 'When they cry, you hit them harder.'"

"I know the line," I said. "Here's a better line: You know anything about somebody taking a shot at me?"

"Nope, first I'm hearing about it," he said. "They catch the guy who did it yet?"

"He's dead," I said. "I shot back."

"Don't know anything about that, either."

"I guess this would be a good moment to ask what you're doing here," I said.

"Or a good moment for me to ask why you were following me yesterday," McManus said.

"I wasn't," I said. "Following you."

"Max said he saw you parked just up the block from the Eire Pub," he said.

"Max is right. But I was following Mauro. You showing up was a bonus."

"Why were you following him, then, if you don't mind me asking?" McManus said.

"Don't mind at all. I was looking for a chance to ask *him* if he knew anything about someone taking shots at me. And sometimes, being a devil-may-care-type guy, I like to surprise people when I'm looking for answers," I said.

"Me, too," McManus said. "Now, how about we stop fucking around here?"

"Thought you'd never ask," I said.

He nodded at my Keurig machine. "How about some coffee?" he said pleasantly.

"Help yourself," I said. "You seem to know where everything is."

He chuckled. "You really are a pisser," he said.

Came out Boston-style. *Pissah.*

"You have no idea."

He made himself coffee, then sat back down. Did everything except put his feet up on my desk.

"For your information," he said, "we are, at long last, about to close on that land."

"It's this long?"

"It's Massachusetts," he said. "I don't know how closely you followed the original story, but even after I got awarded the bid, after jumping through more political hoops than anybody ever had before on a deal like this, some people in Southie sued the T, still thinking they ought to be building railyards there, because of how much it would have helped increase commuter rail frequency south and west of the city."

McManus sipped some of his coffee out of my David Ortiz mug.

"Basically," he continued, "I have finally arrived on the one-yard line. And at this point I need bad publicity like I need the clap. I don't need more publicity, I don't need any controversy, don't need to be back on the local news or on the front page of *The Globe*. I just want to break ground and start getting this thing built. It's like I already told you. I'm the good guy here. I'm going to develop land it looked like nobody was ever going to develop and build the best casino on the East Coast and a hotel to go with it. And now that gambling isn't a mortal sin in sports anymore,

I'm setting myself up to go after what's always been the big prize for me."

"What would that be?"

"The Red Sox," he said.

"I wasn't aware they were for sale."

"In Boston," he said, "everything is always for sale. I want the team, I want to build a new Fenway Park over by the water, on land there I've been quietly buying up for years."

"Happy for you," I said. "But why did I see you at the same bar with Mauro yesterday? It wasn't too long ago that the two of you were looking to rip each other's throats out, as I recall."

"Sometimes your enemies can become your friends," he said. "What can I tell you, Spenser? Maybe I reached the point in my life where I'm looking to reduce the number of enemies I've got, instead of adding to them. I was talking to Tommy about maybe letting him in and having a piece of this deal, like as a minority partner."

Tommy.

"Sort of like basketball players swapping jerseys after the big game."

"One way of putting it."

"So are the two of you going to be in business together?" I asked.

He shook his head.

"In the end, we couldn't see eye to eye," McManus said. "I thought he might not act like a pig, but he is who he is."

"Now that we've got that straight," I said, "how about we really stop fucking around?"

"We didn't already?" McManus asked.

"You act like I'd have something to do with any potential problems to your sweetheart deal finally going through," I said. "But I'm not the one who shot Rita Fiore. Or sent somebody after Shannon Miles. I didn't shoot Brian Tully when he started poking around your deal. I didn't make Nick Drummond's chief of staff disappear. And I certainly had nothing to do with Drummond ending up in the water, however he, ah, came to end up there."

"Listen," McManus said. "I'm sorry all those things happened. Another thing I told you already was how much Nick Drummond meant to me. But he's gone and he's not coming back. And he wanted this deal to go through more than anybody."

"So why are you here, really?" I said.

"I am asking you, in a gentlemanly way, to stay out of my business," he said. "Once and for all."

"And I'm asking you why either you or Mauro would see me as some kind of threat if one of you, or both of you, didn't have something to hide," I said. "And might have done something as monumentally stupid as trying to kill me."

"I can't speak for Tommy," he said. "But I know I'm not that stupid."

"You better hope not," I said.

He stood. "On that note," he said, "I think I should be going." He shook his head and said, "You've got me all wrong, Spenser."

"If I only had a nickel," I said.

"Yeah, well, the price of everything has gone up," McManus said.

When McManus opened the door, his man Max was standing there, trying to look menacing, something that frankly didn't require much effort on his part.

"Anything we left unsaid?" McManus said.

"Just this," I said. "Whoever is behind all of this is the one who's made an enemy."

"Meaning you," he said.

"Bingo," I said.

FIFTY-NINE

I was preparing dinner at the apartment for Susan and Hawk and me.

And Rita.

And now that the event was well under way, Susan and Rita seated across from each other at the same table, it was going as well between them as I could have hoped, and not just because wishing had made it so.

I had decided to cook a whole chicken in the air fryer Susan had recently purchased for me, an appliance I told her I now loved almost as much as I loved her. For sides, I made green beans with shallots, roasted potatoes, and garlic bread. The meal, as I expected, had elicited rave reviews from all concerned.

But the most positive part of the evening so far, even if I wasn't yet spiking the ball, was that Susan and Rita did seem to be genuinely enjoying each other's company. Susan had signed off on this particular dinner party in advance. But there had still been no way for me to really know how this would go, since in all the years I'd known them, I couldn't recall them ever being at the same table together, even if there had been charity occasions when they'd been at the same event.

By the time we had moved into the living room for after-dinner drinks, Rita still working on the one glass of chardonnay she'd allowed herself tonight, I could see her beginning to fade. It was at this point that Susan subtly shifted the conversation away from Nick Drummond to Rita, and how even a night out like this was such a big step for her toward normalcy, whether it felt like a small one to Rita or not.

"I even feel conflicted about my recovery, if that makes any sense," Rita said to Susan. "I mean, I know that barring any further stupid setbacks, I really am on my way back. But at the same time there's a part of me that realizes that I can never *go* back."

"Meaning to being the person you were before the shooting," Susan said.

"The person I was before the shooting?" Rita said to Susan. "God, I miss that old broad already."

Susan smiled. It was a haymaker of a smile, the kind she didn't fake.

"There's a clinical expression for this, one I didn't learn at Harvard," Susan said. "But it applies here: What doesn't kill you makes you stronger."

"I told you these shrinks are smart," I said.

Rita had eaten more during dinner than I thought she would. And if she was now beginning to tire, maybe it was because of all the energy she was expending in being whatever her best, and strongest, self was right now. I could see she had certainly worked hard to look as good as she possibly could. She knew Susan was coming. It was like everything else in life. Either you wanted to compete or you didn't.

For the moment, she and Susan were completely focused on each other. Hawk and I were focused on them.

"I left a lot of the old me on the street that day," Rita said. "Even without remembering very much of what happened, I keep experiencing some pretty serious bouts of PTSD."

"They're all pretty serious," Susan said.

"Tell me about it."

"I'd frankly be more worried about you if you weren't experiencing those symptoms," Susan said.

Rita took a small sip of wine. "What frightens me the most," she said, "is that in some important way I've left Nick behind, too. Because the more this thing goes on, the more I wonder if I really knew him at all."

"But you don't know that you *didn't*, at least not yet," Susan said. She turned and nodded at me. "Additionally, my boyfriend here hasn't yet finished a job we *all* know he's going to finish."

"Got a man crazy for me," I said. *"He's funny that way."* I grinned at Susan. "I could sing the rest of it."

"Please don't spoil a good meal," she said.

"Listen," I said to Rita. "You do know a lot of the big stuff about this guy already. Hell, everybody knows about what a shitty childhood he had, and how he not only survived it, but made something of himself, and his life. I wouldn't give up on him, and whatever your ideal about him is, just yet. It's like they still say in his world: Not all of the precincts have reported yet."

Rita got up then, saying it was time for her to get home and get to bed. Susan did, too.

Then they hugged each other.

Hawk whistled as they did.

"Whoopty-damn-doo," he said.

SUSAN WAS STILL in the bathroom for her nightly ministrations and I was watching the end of the Celtics game when Shannon Miles called.

"Is it too late to be calling?" she asked.

"I'm watching Jayson Tatum," I said. "And you wouldn't be calling at this hour if you don't have something interesting to tell me."

"I do."

"About McManus?"

She paused.

"No," she said. "About Nick Drummond."

"What did you find?"

"More like what I didn't find," she said, "about his childhood and adolescence."

"You're saying he made some of it up?" I said.

"More like most of it," she said.

SIXTY

Shannon and I met at a diner in Paradise called Daisy's. Rita had mentioned it once when she was still seeing Jesse Stone, telling me that it was owned by a famous local character named Daisy, who Rita said was anything but a sweet flower.

"In what way?" I'd asked.

"You'll see if you ever meet her," Rita said.

Now a woman who could only be Daisy was walking out of the kitchen when I arrived. She seemed to be of indeterminate age, looked as solid as a Paradise seawall, and had hair the color of a purple orchid.

I told her I was meeting a friend, and perhaps Molly Crane, too.

"They just called and said they're running a couple minutes late," she said. "You must be the private dick."

"We prefer to be known as private investigators."

"Oh, don't be a dick," she said, then went behind the counter and grabbed a coffeepot and mug, showed me to a window table, and poured coffee for me without being asked.

Shannon Miles and Molly Crane came through the door about five minutes later. They had clearly come from the gym or an exercise class, both wearing thick hoodies over black tights. They were rosy-cheeked, brimming with girl power.

And they did look like sisters.

"She refuses to let me go anywhere without her," Miles said. "She's even set up a desk for me at headquarters."

"The only person who's ever gotten shot on my watch is me," Molly said.

"Wait . . . Are you serious?" Miles asked.

Molly grinned. "You guys want to see my scar?"

"Maybe when we know each other better," I said.

Daisy brought mugs for them and poured them some coffee. "Anybody gonna eat something," she said, "or is this table gonna be like one of those time-shares?"

"Maybe in a little bit, my sweetheart," Molly said.

"Don't you wish," Daisy said.

Before we had ended our call the night before, Shannon Miles had told me the bare bones of what she'd found on Drummond— or hadn't found. But said she wasn't done yet, she was into it now, and fully expected to keep search-engine-ing through what she expected would be a long night.

"So you find out even more before your head finally hit the pillow?" I said to her now.

"Lots," she said.

She wasn't lying.

———

SHE SAID SHE had finally given up trying to find more skeletons in Thomas Mauro's closet, or Kevin McManus's, so had shifted her attention to Drummond at that point, reading back on all the early coverage of him that made his growing-up years sound like those of Pip in *Great Expectations*. Entering the foster-care system after the woman who said she was his grandmother—but whom he later found out was not—had died. Going from one group home to another. Finally attending high school at West Roxbury Academy, before leaving for college at what was known as the American Career Institute in Framingham. The next thing anybody knew, he had become a firebrand community organizer in South Boston, later working as an intern for the state senator he eventually succeeded.

"The rest, as they say, was history," Miles said. "Except the more I tried to check that history, the more I ran into a rather interesting series of coincidences, I guess you could call them. The group homes that he spoke about had all closed by the time he was working in politics. West Roxbury Academy also closed eventually. And then guess what went out of business? The American Career Institute, where he said he'd gone to college."

Molly said, "I keep asking Shannon the same question: How come nobody else in the media ever picked up on any of this?"

"We're talking about this handsome, charming, charismatic young guy," Miles said. "Then it just became a runaway train of a feel-good story: state senator to Senate president and then look out after that."

"And you can check me on this," I said to Miles, "but sometimes people don't want to let facts get in the way of a good story like that."

"Pretty sure I've heard that one myself," Molly said.

Shannon Miles frowned. "It's not always negligence, or even sloppiness," she said. "Sometimes it's like everybody is operating off the same set of facts, and these facts tugged at your heart-strings because of a childhood like his that didn't turn out to be a death sentence. Everybody just ran with the same story after that, like the wind."

"Until you finally didn't," Molly said.

"So what are we talking about here, really?" I said to Shannon Miles.

"I think maybe what we're talking about is a con man like that congressman from Long Island who basically made up his whole life story," Miles said.

"Like George Santos 2.0?" I said.

"Like that," Shannon Miles said.

SIXTY-ONE

stopped at Jesse Stone's office before returning to Boston, having left Shannon Miles to do more Internet sleuthing on Nick Drummond, or whoever the hell he was. I remembered reading all the jokes about George Santos after the world found out how much of his background he'd fabricated, people suggesting he'd done everything except dunk a basketball on LeBron James.

Stone had his feet up on his desk, tossing a baseball into a worn-out mitt that looked pretty damned wonderful to me.

"Pitchers and catchers reporting to spring training," I said.

"Ought to be a national holiday every year," he said.

"You still miss playing ball?" I asked.

"Only when I'm awake," he said.

He asked if I wanted coffee. I said I'd had more than my share at Daisy's. He asked how Daisy and I had gotten along. I explained that she'd finally bullied me into ordering pancakes.

"Heartless bitch," Stone said.

Then: "You making any progress?"

"Is a rat in a maze making progress?" I asked.

"Know the feeling," he said. "But I've always managed to find my way out. Bet you have, too."

"Yeah," I said. "But every time new information comes in, I feel like I move further away from finding out who shot Rita."

"I spoke with her last night," he said. "She said you got Hawk with her."

"I'm starting to feel like I'm running a placement service," I said.

Stone grinned. "You think Hawk will be safe with her?" he said. "Or should I say *from* her."

"Remember, she's still weak," I said.

Stone, still grinning, said, "I was always weaker."

He got up and refilled his mug and sat back down. I pointed at the glove and ball sitting there on his desk.

"Just looking at them never gets old," I said.

Stone reached for the ball and tossed it to me. "Keep it," he said. "I've got more."

I stuck it in the side pocket of my peacoat. "I won't ask you to sign it," I said.

"I'm gonna remind you that I will help you any way you want on this," Stone said. "Been a while since I had a crime wave around here, if you don't count kids throwing snowballs at school buses."

I told him about the gaps Shannon Miles had discovered in Drummond's bio, and how once she had more, I needed to figure where that fit with the rest of the goddamn knot I was trying to untangle.

"Do something for me," Stone said. "Tell me everything you got since she got shot."

I did. Telling it the way I'd tell it to Quirk or Belson. Like a shared language. When I finished he said, "I can make some calls. The state senator we got up here actually isn't an asshole."

"Have at it," I said.

He grinned again. Stone was cocky in a quiet way. Maybe it was the old jock in him. "Shannon Miles sounds like a good reporter," he said. "But I'm an even better cop."

"I believe you," I said. "First time I met you up here, that time when I was tracking Sonny Karnofsky's daughter, I figured out pretty fast that you weren't just another small-town shit-kicker."

"Don't make me blush," Stone said.

We sat in silence for a minute.

Finally Stone said, "You think anybody's better than you?"

"Nope."

"Let's do this," he said.

261

SIXTY-TWO

I called Matt Vallone on my way to the city, wanting to know if he knew any of what Shannon Miles had found out about Nick Drummond, and what else he might have been holding back from me.

I was sent straight to voicemail.

I didn't leave a message, deciding it wasn't a conversation I wanted to have with him on the phone, anyway. I needed to ask him in person if he'd also been someone who didn't want the facts to get in the way of Drummond's backstory. Or if he had simply missed them because he'd fallen in love with that backstory.

As a rule, I do not usually grade high on paranoia. But as I made my way south toward Boston, I found myself recalling a terrific line I'd read once from the old baseball manager Buck Showalter.

"I'm not paranoid," he said. "Just extremely alert."

So, too, was I these days.

I had been certain Vallone was holding back on me. Now I was wondering how much he knew about Drummond's background being a work of fiction, truly.

It was why, once I had crossed over the Tobin Bridge, I decided to head over to Vallone's apartment instead of the office. I could pop in unannounced again. Or, if Vallone wasn't home, I could wait outside until he was.

I PARKED IN front of Vallone's building on Endicott. This time I didn't have to bluff my way inside; I was able to hold the door for an old guy using one of those three-pronged canes, since he'd barely been able to push it open. He thanked me.

"Pay it forward, brother," I said.

I banged on Vallone's door when I got upstairs. No answer. I was pretty sure I could pick the lock if I wanted to. The small leather pouch with my lock-picking tools was in the glove compartment. But I wasn't sure what that would accomplish. So I went downstairs and back to the car and hoped he would be back soon.

I stayed until the late afternoon, listening first to Ella, then Carol Sloane, and then the greatest hits of Diana Krall. But there was no sign of Matt Vallone.

It was then that the detective—me—who'd told Jesse Stone a couple hours ago that he was the best at what he did remembered Vallone saying that he kept a tiny writing room down at a storage facility on Traveler Street. 33 Traveler. Larry Bird's number. At least I remembered the address. That had to count for something.

Maybe Vallone wasn't there, either. Maybe he wasn't anywhere. Maybe as I was driving down there, he would be on his way back up here. But I had already wasted this much time on him. I could waste a little more. Sometimes that's what master detectives did.

I put "33 Traveler" into my Waze and saw that it was only ten minutes away by car, Vallone having told me it took half an hour to walk.

Nothing ventured, nothing gained.

Unless that was something else about which I had been misled.

I tried not to take it personally.

SIXTY-THREE

I did remember the "Save the Whales" mural as soon as I saw it near 33 Traveler. Vallone had been right. There had been a time when you could see it from the expressway, before luxury high-rises had begun to sprout down at this end of the waterfront like wildflowers. *Yeah,* I thought. *And there used to be a ballpark.*

The day had already gone dark by the time I found a parking spot, the sky once again looking heavy with snow, even though none had been forecast for tonight.

I went through the front entrance to Prime Storage and found the management office on the first floor. There was a good-looking guy inside who introduced himself as Chris Richards. I told him I was looking for Matt Vallone.

"I think I saw him take the elevator up a few hours ago," Richards said. "Sixth floor. You can take the elevator, too, or the stairs."

I thanked him.

"His space is only ten by ten," Richards said. He smiled. "But you're going to love what he's done with the place."

"He showed you?" I asked.

Richards shrugged. "Writers," he said, as if that explained everything except how to save the whales.

I took the stairs. I had spent enough time in the car today, driving and sitting, so a little stair work was much needed.

I knocked on Vallone's door when I got up there.

"Hey, Vallone?" I said. "You in there?"

Maybe he was gone. Richards had told me there was an unsealed back entrance to the building. But if he was on the other side of the door, he had to have heard me.

I was about to knock again, getting even closer to the door, when I heard what sounded like some kind of muffled scream.

Or a cry for help.

I reached for my gun but never got the chance to clear it from my side pocket because suddenly the door flew open, and would have hit me smack in the face if I didn't get my hand up at the last second to protect myself.

But that was right before a giant in one of those crazy-colored wrestling masks was right in front of me, lowering his shoulder into me, swiftly putting me on the ground.

SIXTY-FOUR

Through the open door I got a fleeting glimpse of Matt Vallone tied to his chair, tape across his mouth, his face covered in blood, struggling to free himself.

I'd had plenty of practice gathering myself after getting knocked on my ass. I tried to collect myself, getting onto one knee, trying to get the Glock out of my pocket, but the giant kicked it away from me and then swung what looked like a blackjack at the side of my head.

I was still on my knees.

He was in some kind of black exercise outfit, and was ready to swing the blackjack at me in a round two. That was when I turned my head to the side and threw a right uppercut with as much force as I could manage into his groin.

I heard him grunt, and groan.

But he did not go down.

Instead, he turned and headed for the door to the stairwell, perhaps thinking he wanted to get out of here before I went for my gun.

I went after him.

I would get back to Vallone when I got back to him.

As the Masked Marvel was opening the door, still clutching at his groin, I dove for his legs and managed to get my arms around his knees. He still wouldn't go down, just shook his right leg loose from me before lurching through the now-open door.

By the time I was back on my feet I could see him taking the stairs a few at a time before jumping for the landing.

I reached for my gun then, more out of instinct than anything else, before realizing I had left it back down the hallway.

No time to go back for it now.

The only thing I felt in my pocket was the baseball Jesse Stone had given me.

I took it out as I got to the top of the stairwell.

The Masked Marvel had stopped at the landing.

The blackjack was in his left hand now.

There was a gun in his right.

Clear shot.

From there he couldn't miss.

As he raised the gun and pointed it up at me, I threw the baseball as hard as I could at him.

I was the one who didn't miss.

The ball glanced off the side of his head as he fired, two shots, one after the other, both of them missing because of Jesse's ball, the bullets exploding into the half-open door behind me.

I dove back through the doorway and ran down the hall to get the Glock, grabbed it off the floor, and ran back toward the stairs, gun out in front of me, ready if he came back through the door with his own.

But he did not.

I gently kicked the door all the way open and eased out, the Glock ahead of me.

From somewhere down below I heard a woman's voice yell, "Active shooter! Active shooter!"

Then a man was yelling the same thing.

"Active shooter!" someone else yelled from the fifth floor. "Stay inside!"

Chorus for the modern world.

When I looked down the stairs, the giant was gone.

But whose giant?

SIXTY-FIVE

Matt Vallone was in even worse shape than his office was, drawers pulled out of his desk, file cabinet on its side, papers everywhere.

Up close, I could see how much of a beating he'd taken, one eye closed completely.

I had gently removed the tape from his mouth before untying his hands, and found him to be less than overcome with gratitude.

"Thanks for nearly getting me killed, asshole," he said.

I let that go, telling him we weren't going to have much time before the police got here and wanted to talk to both of us. Vallone told me not to worry about that, he wasn't talking to the police on a goddamn bet.

"He must have been following you when you came to my apartment," Vallone said. "Then he started following me."

"Why did he wait to come after you?" I said.

"Ask him at your next shootout."

"What did he want?"

"He wanted to know what I'd told you," Vallone said. "About Drummond. I told him I hadn't told you anything you didn't already know. He said he didn't believe me and then produced some sap or whatever it was and swung it upside my head and the next thing I know I'm bound and gagged, and he's going through my shit."

"Looking for what?"

"That's what I asked him when he took the tape off my mouth," Vallone said. "Before he did, he pressed a gun between my eyes and said that if I screamed, he would pull the trigger."

There was a roll of paper towels on the ground. I ripped off a piece and handed it to him and he wiped some of the blood off his face.

"He made me give him my passwords and tell him the way I do two-factor authentication, and all that other computer voodoo mojo. Then he taped my mouth again and checked out if the passwords worked from his phone. I'm not an idiot, I knew what he was doing, making sure he could get into my Cloud. But at that point I didn't give a shit. I just didn't want him to kill me if I didn't do what he said."

"What else?" I said.

The cops would be making their way to the sixth floor any second. Probably working their way up, whomever was in the building probably not knowing where the shots had come from.

"He put the gun back between my eyes and said he was going to ask me again, and I better answer it honestly if I knew what was good for me. Told me to nod if I understood what he was saying to me. I nodded like a bobblehead doll. Then he took the tape off, kept the gun where it was, and said, 'This is your last chance to tell me what you told Spenser about the money.' I said, 'What money?' and he smacked me again. Then he said it was my last chance to tell him what I told you. I told him again that I hadn't told you shit, no matter how many times he hit me. That's when you showed up."

Vallone swallowed hard and said, "Who the fuck *are* these people?"

There was banging from outside then. Chris Richards, the manager, and a uniformed cop were standing in the hall when I opened the door.

"Everything okay here?" the cop asked.

"Yes and no," I said.

"From the looks of him, I'm guessing mostly no," the cop said.

The cop gave me a long look. "Who are you?"

"Spenser," I said. "Private license. That's in my wallet. There's a gun in my right pocket."

"Hand me the gun," he said. "Then the wallet."

I did.

"For what it's worth, I'm a friend of Martin Quirk and Frank Belson," I said.

"Whoopee," he said. "Let's go downstairs and have a quick chat and you can explain how Prime Storage turned into a shooting gallery just now."

"To be fair," I said, "I'm not sure two shots qualifies as a shooting gallery."

"I'll make sure to note that in my report," he said.

I told Vallone that we needed to talk about how much he

really knew about Drummond's background, because I knew a lot now, but it could wait until I came back upstairs.

I went downstairs to Richards's office and I told him all of it, including the part about the wrestling mask. When I finished, the cop gave me back my gun. Then the two of us walked upstairs so we could both ask Matt Vallone the questions we wanted to ask.

The office was still a mess.

Now Vallone was the one who was gone.

SIXTY-SIX

I was in Edward Oakes's office, one much bigger than Rita's at Cone, Oakes and far more lavishly furnished. As far as I could tell, the only similarity was that it seemed to have the same view of pretty much everything.

By then I'd left several messages for Matt Vallone, having no expectation that they would ever be returned. Or that I was ever going to see him again.

"I should point out that you seem to have gotten on the bad side of my client Mr. Mauro," Oakes said. "From what I know about you, it took even less time than normal."

"Just to be clear," I said, "is there a good side?"

When I'd reached out to Oakes, I'd told him I needed just a few minutes of his time, and his counsel. He told me to stop by his office before he needed to leave for a luncheon at the Harvard Club.

"How's it going?" Oakes asked once I was seated across from him at a desk the size of the outfield at Fenway. "Or not going?"

"If I tried to tell you that," I said, "you might miss lunch."

"You said you needed my advice," he said. He raised an eyebrow in a way I thought was quite patrician. "I assume you mean the kind of free legal advice Rita has been giving you for years."

"She's often gotten my own services in return," I said.

"Our services are far more expensive," he said.

"Well, Edward," I said, "you've got me there."

"What *do* you need?"

"If you were looking to fix a deal like the one for the casino and all that jazz," I said, "who would you need to pay off?"

The eyebrow went back up.

"Are you here to ask me to think like a criminal?" he asked.

Knowing I was incapable of raising an eyebrow myself, I tried to wink in what I considered a rakish way.

"Probably not even for the first time today," I said.

"You're aware that bribing a government official is a felony, correct?" Oakes said. "One punishable by real jail time."

"Actually, I am aware of that."

His jacket was off. He was wearing suspenders. I occasionally wondered how many men, even senior partners at a big-hitter law firm like this, still wore them. But these particular braces, in Harvard crimson, seemed to fit Edward Oakes, and not as some kind of affectation. He was who he was, without airs. I knew how much Rita liked him. And respected him.

"I hope you're not asking me about Thomas Mauro," Oakes said. "Because I'm not going too far down that road about a client, or risk getting on his bad side myself."

"Take him out of it," I said. "Let's look at the other guy. Say you're Kevin McManus. You want what you want and you're used to getting what you want. You even have delusions of grandeur about owning the Red Sox someday."

"He's serious about that?" Oakes asked.

"I think he basically wants to own Boston," I said. "But right now, the centerpiece of the dream becomes that piece of land. Not only did he want it, he didn't want Mauro to get it, because that's how it goes with guys like that. To really win, someone else has to lose. That's how men like this frequently keep score."

Oakes put his palms together and touched his chin with his fingertips.

"So you're asking me about the best way for McManus to fix the game?"

"Yeah."

"You'd need just a handful of players, if you selected them properly," Edward Oakes said. "It would start with the governor and mayor, but McManus wouldn't have needed to bribe them. It was such a sweetheart deal, just jobs-wise alone, for South Boston—the optics would have been terrible for him if they didn't finally get behind it."

"Plus, I heard that Drummond promised the mayor he wouldn't run against him, even though a lot of people were urging him to do it at the time."

"Young Mr. Drummond must've had far greater ambitions for himself," Oakes said.

"The guy fooled a lot of people," I said. "Including Rita."

The eyebrow went back up. I wondered if he practiced. "Fooled her how?"

I told him what Shannon Miles had told me about Drummond perhaps being the second coming of George Santos.

"Are you telling me that the prince of the city might have been some kind of con artist?" Oakes asked.

"Don't know how much of it I can prove, or how hard I'm going to even try, but yeah, that's exactly what I'm telling you," I said.

"So the State Senate president might have been up to his eyeballs in a massive for-profit grift?" Oakes said.

"Wasn't there a U.S. senator from New Jersey accused of pretty much the same thing?" I said.

"I met that Jersey guy a few times," he said. "I started to think of him as Senator Tony Soprano."

"Back to my original question," I said.

"As I recall, the City Council members were pretty split at the time," Oakes said. "You'd need a couple of them on board. Maybe the head of the Redevelopment Authority, even though one quit in the middle of the whole thing. And I'm pretty sure that Drummond, being the golden child of the Senate and being in the majority, probably had all the support he needed there, with perhaps a few exceptions. But I'd look hardest at the City Council, because if they'd voted it down, the deal might have been dead in the water before it ever got to the Senate, at least the way the governor had set things up in the interest of unbelievably full transparency."

Oakes stood then. His jacket was draped over the back of the chair next to me. He came around the desk and put it on.

"Bottom line?" he said. "If you knew what you were doing, you might only need a half-dozen or so fellow griftees, starting

277

with Drummond, if he really was the point guard for the thing from the start."

There was a mirror next to one of his bookcases. He used it to check the knot in his tie. When he turned back to me, he said, "How much proof do you have that any of what you're alleging went on behind the scenes? Or under various tables?"

"Hardly any."

"I'm assuming you understand what you'll be up against if you pursue this," Edward Oakes said.

"Yeah," I said. "What might turn out to be a vast criminal enterprise known as our city government."

"Man versus machine," he said.

"But what better man than me for a job like that?" I said.

SIXTY-SEVEN

Martin Quirk had decided to put a car in front of Rita's house. He didn't say it was to free up Hawk, but I knew it was. Quirk wasn't just a friend, he was a legendary cop, which meant he knew we needed all the help we could get right now.

"Consider it being in the public interest," he said. "The sooner you roll this thing up, the sooner people stop shooting up my city."

"What if somebody complains to the brass about Rita getting preferential treatment?" I said.

"You forget something," he said. "I am the fucking brass."

I was in my office, Hawk on his way there. While I waited for him, Shannon Miles called from Paradise.

"I think I know who Brian's source was," she said.

"Got a name?"

"Sure do," she said.

She told me.

"Do you know who that is?" she said.

"Sadly, I do not."

"Doug Haskins," she said, "is the city councilor for District Two, which happens to include South Boston."

"Have you spoken to him directly?"

"Been trying," she said. "But when I did finally get through to him, and told him what I was calling about, he hung up on me. I was thinking, though, that you might be able to persuade him to talk to you."

"Because of my charm?"

"Sure," she said. "Go with that."

SIXTY-EIGHT

The thirteen members of the Boston City Council met on Wednesdays, I had learned, in a fifth-floor room at 1 City Hall Square. I had further learned that today's meeting was taking place in the morning, and expected to be concluded by lunchtime.

All of the City Council members were expected to be present at the end of the week, along with a number of other local politicians, when there would be an official ribbon-cutting ceremony at Widett Circle, and Kevin McManus was scheduled to put the first shovel in the ground, even if it was covered by snow.

Hawk and I were waiting for Councilman Doug Haskins of District Two to come outside after his meeting.

"The girl sure Haskins was Tully's source?" Hawk said.

"She says he is," I said.

"But say she was, ah, rebuffed when she tried to talk to Haskins about that," Hawk said. "And now we got to do more un-rebuffing, like we do."

"I prefer to think we'll be asking him to listen to his better angels," I said.

"Provided he got some."

Doug Haskins, I knew from the images of him I'd found online, was white-haired, short and squat, a bit of a dandy who favored bow ties. He came walking across the plaza at one o'clock, carrying a well-worn leather briefcase with an old-school buckle on it, talking on his phone, not paying any attention to Hawk or me until we were walking on either side of him like oversized bookends.

We were in lockstep for only a few yards before he stopped.

"Call you back," he said into his phone, before stuffing it into a side pocket of his overcoat.

"May I help you gentlemen?" he said.

"My name is Spenser," I said. "My associate goes by Hawk. Now, our names might not mean anything to you. But we are working an investigation for Edward Oakes of Cone, Oakes, and would like a word."

"Then what you need to do is call a member of my staff and make an appointment," he said.

I smiled. "This is the appointment," I said. "So why don't the three of us do a walk-and-talk right now?"

"You can't just accost a member of the City Council on the street," he said.

But there wasn't much rope to him at this point, and he was beginning to flush slightly. I suspected it was more than just the cold.

"'Course we can," Hawk said amiably.

I saw Haskins take a closer look at Hawk.

"Okay, then, what's this about?" Haskins said.

"We want to talk to you about Brian Tully, and whatever it was you told him about Widett Circle," I said.

He was looking around, but there was no cavalry in sight.

"I will tell you what I told Shannon Miles," he said. "I don't know anything about that."

"No," I said. "What you told her was that you weren't going to talk to her about that."

"Did she send you?"

"It takes a village," I said.

"Why should I talk to you and not her?"

"Because whatever you did tell Tully probably got him killed," I said. "And you're going to help us make it right. Now, let's take that walk before you begin to test my patience. And my friend's."

Hawk patted him on the shoulder. Also amiably.

"Think of it as a meet-and-greet with a couple of your constituents," he said.

SIXTY-NINE

We only walked to where I'd parked my car at a hydrant, less than a block away.

By then I had done my best to convince Councilman Haskins that we meant him no harm, and that whatever he was about to tell us about Brian Tully would remain in the strictest confidence. Additionally, if he didn't believe us, he could call Edward Oakes. If we hadn't gotten his full attention by now, I suspected that Oakes's name would.

I left my car with Ray, a parking attendant at The Newbury whom I had known for years, and from there, we walked around the corner to my office.

Now Hawk was on the couch and I behind my desk. Haskins sat nervously in one of the client chairs. I had made coffee for all of us. For someone who had just abducted an elected official on the street, I was doing my best to be the perfect host.

"You're convinced that I might've had something to do with Brian's death?" he said.

"The thought never occurred to you?" I said.

"I just told him that it had come to my attention that the land was for sale in more ways than one," he said. "I'd frankly been waiting for someone to come along and ask me about all that. Tully finally did. But the last thing he told me was that he was going to look into it and get back to me. Of course he never did. So I had no way of knowing how far he'd taken things."

"Tell me exactly what you told him," I said.

He shot a quick glance at Hawk.

"How do I know for sure that I can trust you?" he said. He cleared his throat. "Either one of you. Or that my own life might not be in danger?"

"It's like a cop friend of mine told me the other day," I said. "It's a dangerous world."

"That's hardly reassuring," Haskins said.

"No one knows you're with us," I said. "If we were being followed, I'd know."

I was telling him the truth. I had been checking for tails since I had clearly been followed to Matt Vallone's apartment.

"I will have to trust you on that," Haskins said.

"You can trust us, period," I said. "Edward Oakes does. Brian Tully did. Rita Fiore, who's the reason Hawk and I are in this, literally is trusting us with her life. We're not looking to harm you, politically or otherwise. We just need to know precisely what you meant about the land being for sale in more ways than one."

Haskins had tiny hands. He clenched them and unclenched

them before taking a quick sip of his coffee. Then seemed to exhale all of the air he had in him.

"Drummond was the middleman," he said. "The money manager, so to speak. He said he'd basically been doing vote counting, and just needed a couple more votes on the Council. We were just one piece of the approval process, of course, but a significant piece. He knew I was still on the fence, but now he laid out how much money there was to be made if we got behind McManus."

"Weren't you surprised that the State Senate president would be offering bribe money?" I said. "He was the fair-haired boy of city politics at the time. Maybe the whole state."

"He said it was best for me, best for Boston, best for everybody," Haskins said. "If the deal with McManus fell through, the T was going to turn right around and bid out building railyards on that property. There were enough people all along who'd had cold feet on having a casino that close to downtown Boston. Drummond said we needed to get it done in whatever way was necessary, get it done now, and that he needed my help."

"What did you tell him?" I said.

"I told him that the land might be for sale, but that I wasn't," Haskins said.

He closed his eyes, shook his head. "But that night I got a call at home. Unknown caller. It was a short conversation. The guy just told me that I needed to reconsider my decision, the way others were being asked to reconsider theirs if they knew what was good for them. Then he added that actions had consequences."

"Go along to get along," Hawk said.

"You ended up voting no on McManus getting the land," I said.

"I did," he said. "Partly as a practical matter, because I was finally convinced by then that it was best for the city. But I'd be lying if I didn't say it was partly out of fear, too."

"But you never took the money?" I said.

"No," he said.

"Did you tell Tully that?"

"I did," he said. "I think he believed me. I had been a good source for him when I heard this kind of shit might have been going on with the other casino deal a few years ago. I told him about the offer of a kickback, told him I didn't know who on the Council might have taken the money, gave him the evidence I had, and said goodbye."

I looked over at Hawk. He looked at me.

"Back up a little," I said to Haskins. "What evidence?"

"The recording," he said.

He let that sink in. We all did.

"What recording?" I said.

"Listen," he said. "I only made it to protect myself, in case somebody tried to muscle me again. Or maybe give myself cover if the bribes Drummond was offering ever became public. But after I got the call at home, and the implied threat, I called Drummond the next morning, and told him I needed to know just how much money we were talking about. So we set up a meeting for that afternoon so he could lay it out for me."

"Did he show?" I said.

"He did," Haskins said. "When we finished that day, he asked if we had a deal."

"What did you say?"

"I'm not proud of this, as a Christian man," he said. "But I told him to go fuck himself."

SEVENTY

I was meeting Susan for drinks at the Russell House Tavern in Cambridge. It was located on John F. Kennedy Street, aptly named in any part of Boston. Good bar, good prices, good atmosphere, good food.

While I waited to head over there, I sat at my desk and made a list with one word at the top of the first page, a list growing by the day:

LIARS

Nick Drummond was at the top of the list.

He had apparently lied to Rita and to voters about almost everything except his name, and maybe even that. If it was all true about him, then he truly was a Dickens character in the end:

Jack Dawkins, from *Oliver Twist*.

AKA the Artful Dodger.

Liar and pickpocket and thief.

Poor Jack ended up being sent out to a penal colony at the end of the book. Nick Drummond? He'd ended up dead. I needed to find out if it was because he got too greedy. Or knew too much. Or all of the above. Still no way of knowing for sure. No shocker there. Every time I turned around lately, there was a new twist.

And not of the Oliver variety.

I did not know which lies Thomas Mauro and Kevin McManus had told me, but I felt confident that both of them, to some extent, had lied their asses off, if only to put themselves in a more favorable light with me. And maybe get me *off* their asses.

I would have to find out who was behind the killings and the shootings—even the beating of Matt Vallone, another guy I was sure had been less than forthcoming with me—to fully understand who was the biggest liar of them all.

Susan Silverman had once shared a Yiddish proverb about how half a truth is a whole lie.

"Oy vey," I said now, my voice sounding far too loud in the office.

Drummond's lies were what had started all of this. It was up to me now, with more than a little help from my friends, to finish it. Before I did, I was going to have to tell Rita inconvenient and painful truths about the man she had loved and lost. And gotten herself played by, along with just about everybody else in town.

I was about to leave for Cambridge, trying to time my arrival at Susan's place after her last patient of the day, when Jesse Stone called.

I told him what Haskins had told Hawk and me about Drummond.

"You need to tell Rita about this," he said.

"Working up to it," I said.

"I was gonna take a ride down tomorrow to see her," he said. "Maybe it would be easier if we told her together."

"You saying I'm afraid to do it alone?"

"Goddamn right."

Then he said, "For the time being, let me keep asking around at the State House, get some sense about how Drummond managed to fool as many people there as he did."

"Appreciate you," I said.

"Promise me you'll never say that again," Stone said.

I laughed. I hadn't run into a lot of laughs lately. I had to admit to myself, it felt pretty good.

"And while you're doing all that, what am I supposed to do, Chief Stone?" I asked him.

"Easy," he said. "Follow the money."

I told him I was pretty sure he'd stolen that.

SEVENTY-ONE

Neither Susan nor I were in any kind of big rush to eat once we got to the Russell House, so we lingered quite happily over drinks at the bar. Scotch and soda for me, martini for her.

When they had been set down in front of us I said, "So how did *my* day go, dear?"

"Clever," she said.

"Don't worry," I said. "I still got it."

"Define *it*?"

"A quality that fills the rest of the night with promise."

She sighed. "If I have to, I have to," she said. "Now go ahead and tell me about your day."

I did, all the way through Stone telling me to follow the money.

"And the councilman just handed over that recording to Brian Tully?" she asked.

"Tully told him that it was both of their careers on the line, and he would guard it with his life," I said. "And maybe that's exactly what he did."

"Could the Thompson woman have been in on this?" Susan said. "She was his chief of staff."

"She certainly fooled me if she was," I said.

"Joining a growing list of those who have done that."

"Nobody likes a smart-ass shrink."

"You do," she said.

She sipped some of her martini. At least I thought some vodka might have crossed her lips.

"So is Mauro the baddie here, or McManus?" she asked.

"Logic says McManus, because in the end he got what he wanted," I said. "But I still can't rule out Mauro."

"Why not?" she said.

"Let me present you with a what-if, Doctor," I said. "What if Drummond had been double-dipping, until it was time for him to pick a winner?"

"And Mauro found out he was being played," Susan said, "by someone even more deceitful than he was."

I drank some scotch.

"So what do you plan to do about it?" Susan asked, waving at the bartender for our check, catching his eye before I did.

"I need to make something happen," I said.

"Care to be more specific?"

"Perhaps I need to find a way to make both of them think I might be in possession of whatever one of them thinks is worth killing over," I said.

"Won't that make even more trouble for you?"

"Trouble is my business, sweetheart," I said.

She shook her head and looked sadder than if Pearl had run away.

292

"Yet another bad Bogie impression," she said. "But I walked right into it this time."

WE WERE ASLEEP later, Pearl snoring softly from the end of the bed, when I heard the sound of my phone from where I'd left it in the living room.

It did not wake Susan, who could sleep through a land war on Linnaean Street.

It was Quirk calling.

"You hear yet?" he said, skipping the preliminaries, as always.

"Hear what?" I said, knowing it couldn't be anything close to good news at this hour.

"Somebody took a shot at Kevin McManus a couple hours ago," Quirk said. "Drive-by."

"He get hit?"

"High in the shoulder," Quirk said.

"Where'd it happen?"

"He was walking out of the la-di-fucking-da Somerset Club," Quirk said. "One of his sidemen knocked him out of the way just enough that it wasn't a head shot."

You didn't ask to join the Somerset Club. They asked you. You couldn't even access their website unless you *were* a member. There was a well-known story about the place, about a fire in the forties when the fireman who'd arrived on the scene was asked to enter through the service entrance.

"You would have already told me if McManus was hurt badly," I said.

"Yeah, he's gonna live," Quirk said. "But I'm thinking that the scandal of it all may kill a Boston Brahmin or two."

SEVENTY-TWO

The *Globe* was able to get the story of the Somerset Club shooting on the front page of the late print edition, and of course it was splashed all over the paper's website. It even included a quote from Martin Quirk. I imagined what a thrill it must have been for the reporter to get Quirk on the phone, and on the record.

"A prominent member of this community was another victim of random gun violence tonight," Quirk said. "Our department is still gathering evidence related to this incident, and trying to determine whether there is a connection between this incident and the recent shootings involving Rita Fiore and Brian Tully. But I can assure the public, or reassure it, that what has been happening in this city cannot and will not stand."

I was back on *The Globe*'s website in the afternoon, checking to see if the reporters had been able to advance the story, when Jesse Stone arrived at my office. The two of us were going to make our way over to Rita's home and tell her what we had learned about Nick Drummond.

Stone told me he'd parked on Boylston with his police plates, and could drive us over to Joy Street.

"You got any thoughts on who might've taken the shot at Kevin McManus?" Stone said.

"I can't tell you how much I want McManus to be good for this whole thing," I said. "Only now he goes and gets shot. Which takes me back to Mauro, and him maybe being the worst loser in all of recorded history, in addition to being the most reckless one."

"Feel like you're spinning your wheels again?" Stone said.

"Sometimes I think I could teach an online course in it," I said.

Stone got up and made himself a cup using my Keurig, then spooned in as much sugar as I liked to use. Before long we'd be going to movies together.

When he sat back down, he said, "Almost forgot. I may have come up with something."

He told me about a guy named Leo Martin. Previously the head of the Redevelopment Authority. From the start, Martin had been the most vocal critic of selling the land to Mauro or McManus, believing Boston would be better served by new rail-yards rather than a new casino, even if the city ended up taking a haircut on money.

But about a month before the City Council even voted, Martin suddenly stepped down from his position, issued a statement that he was retiring and beginning a trip around the world almost immediately.

"Must have had money saved up for a rainy day," I said.

"Or came into some," Stone said.

"Some way you could ask Mr. Martin about his resignation?" I asked. "And if he in fact did come into some money?"

"Slight problem," Stone said. "No one's heard from him since he left town. Or if he even did leave town. Guy was in his sixties. Confirmed bachelor. No family. But now nobody knows where in the world the world traveler might be."

"Because you checked."

"I got this thing about loose ends," Stone said.

"Makes two of us," I said.

He got up and rinsed his cup the way Quirk rinsed his cups and glasses when he was here.

"Ready to go see Rita?" he said.

"No," I said.

"Makes two of us," Stone said.

SEVENTY-THREE

Stone sat next to Rita on the sofa. It was clear to me, as soon as I saw them in the same room, how much of a connection there still was between them. And how little it seemed to matter to either one of them that I happened to be in the room with them.

Once we were settled, Rita said, "I know you two. And you've both got that look."

"What look?" I said.

"The one where you're going to say something and I'm going to object," she said.

She then let me do the telling. And I did tell her everything we knew about Nick Drummond, right up to the minute, not making any attempt to sugarcoat any of it, or leave anything out. Stone came in at the end with what he had learned about Leo Martin of the Redevelopment Authority, and how he might have been on the take, too.

"A vast left-wing conspiracy?" Rita said.

"Right," I said.

When our presentation was over, she did not appear angry or sad or more wounded than she already was. And indicated no level of denial.

She just calmly said, "Men have cheated on me my whole life. Just never like this."

"Doesn't mean his feelings for you weren't genuine," Stone said.

Rita smiled. "Mary McCarthy once said that everything Lillian Hellman wrote in a book was a lie, including *and* and *the*," she said. "I'm kind of in the same place on Nick right now."

"He fooled a whole city, not just you," I said.

"And you're more convinced than ever that somehow all his double-dealing got him killed," she said.

"The more things come into focus," I said, "the more sense it makes."

"Can you really kill somebody and make it look like drowning?" she asked.

"There are ways," Stone said. "I had one like that in Paradise about ten years ago. Want to hear how?"

"No," Rita said.

I studied Rita now, and could almost hear her thinking, and not just about the guy who had been lying. The lawyer in her was reviewing the facts that had just been presented to her.

"But what specifically got him killed?" she then asked.

"Had to be the same thing that got you specifically shot," Jesse Stone said.

"And maybe got Delores Thompson killed, too?" Rita asked.

"She indicated to me in that last phone message that she had some kind of evidence," I said. "Could have been on McManus, could have been on Mauro. Or both."

"The M&M Boys," Stone said.

"Huh?" Rita said.

"Baseball thing," Jesse said. "Mantle and Maris."

"Aren't they old Yankees?" she asked.

"I don't blame them," I said.

"So it might have been simple greed all along," Rita said.

"You always hear how often murder comes down to love or money," Stone said. "But sometimes it can be both of those things. Love *of* money."

"I'm not going to try to justify what Drummond did," I said. "But this is a guy who came up from nothing. Maybe he never got over it. And found a way to make the public good and what was good for *him* coincide."

"He used to say that he didn't want to trade on his childhood trauma," Rita said, her voice soft. "But maybe that was more of an act." She gave a familiar and theatrical toss of her red hair. "All politicians are at least part actor. But maybe being an actor was all Nick was."

She stood. "I need a drink."

Then she quickly turned to Stone, the recovering alcoholic in the room. "You mind?"

He grinned. "I've told you plenty of times. I never minded anybody else's drinking. Just my own."

She came back with a glass of what I assumed, knowing her, was Tito's vodka over ice.

"Even if Nick did everything you're saying he did," she said, "he still didn't deserve to die."

"Neither did Brian Tully," I said. "You didn't deserve to get shot. And if Delores Thompson is dead, and all signs seem to point in that direction, she didn't deserve to go out that way, either. Somebody still needs to pay for all of that."

"I'll drink to that," Rita said, and threw back some of the vodka.

No one spoke for a few minutes. Stone got up and put another log on the fire. There was an economy of movement with him, even with a simple task like that. But he moved with a quiet grace. I could imagine him going to his left when he was a shortstop and gloving a ball with that mitt he kept in his desk, making a throw across the diamond and getting the guy who'd hit the ball by a step at first base.

"What if you can't prove who's behind all this?" Rita asked. She was looking directly at me. "At what point do even you walk away and do that thing you're always talking about, and letting God sort it all out?"

"I'll call Him when I need Him," I said.

"Her," Rita said.

"Either way," I said.

SEVENTY-FOUR

Kevin McManus showed up at my office again the next morning, once again with his man Max.

At least he called ahead this time.

Maybe our relationship was evolving.

Max waited outside in the hall, like a good soldier, and one big enough to have been the Masked Marvel. But then so was Thomas Mauro's driver. They couldn't possibly be the only body men in Boston who were that size. They were just the two I'd happened to lay eyes on recently.

McManus was wearing a blue vest that I thought matched nicely with the blue sling for his left arm.

"To what do I owe the pleasure?" I asked when he'd taken a seat.

"Let's dispense with the small talk," McManus said. "I've got work to do."

It would be useless to point out that he was the one who had come to me, and was sitting in my office.

"Sounds like you got lucky," I said, pointing at the sling.

"Tell my aching shoulder that," he said. "Max probably saved my life. He saw the gun before anybody else did, and moved me just enough that I didn't get it between the eyes."

He pointed at me then. "You ever been shot?" he said. "Not just shot at, I heard about that. I mean hit."

"On multiple occasions," I said. "But I thought we were going to dispense with small talk. So why are we here, not to get too existential?"

"Huh?" McManus said.

"Sometimes I say things just to amuse myself," I said. "You must want something. What is it?"

"I'm telling you for the last time I want you out of my life," he said. "For good."

"Kevin," I said, "are you breaking up with me?"

"Still amusing yourself," he said.

"Kind of," I said.

He said, "I don't know what you think happened with Drummond and all the rest of it. And at this point, I frankly don't give a shit. I'm just telling you, straight up, that it wasn't me. *Isn't* me. You want my opinion, it has to be Mauro who's gone off the rails. And then I managed to push him even further off when I didn't cut him in on the deal."

He shifted slightly in the chair and winced. "You want to go after him, nail his balls to the wall? Have at it. Just leave me out of it. The deal becomes official next week. Quit dicking around with me."

"You already tried to hire me," I said. "You need to stop order-ing me around like you actually did."

"I think I pointed out previously that I'm looking to reduce the number of enemies in my life," he said.

"I can see why," I said, "now that one of them tried to shoot you."

"My problem, not yours," he said. "Now just leave me the fuck alone."

"No," I said.

I could tell right away it wasn't a word he was used to hearing. In the moment, he seemed almost startled by it, as if I had sud-denly lapsed into speaking Mandarin.

"What?" McManus said.

"I just declined your offer to stop dicking around with you," I said, "at least not until I find out everything I still plan to find out, probably starting with how someone killed Nick Drum-mond and got away with it."

"Why aren't you worried about who might've killed me in front of the Somerset Club?" he said.

"You need to keep your story straight," I said. "You just told me a couple minutes ago that was your problem, not mine."

I stood up on my side of the desk then.

"Now get out of my office," I said. "I'm the one who's got work to do."

SEVENTY-FIVE

awk and I had finished our workout at Harbor Health. Henry Cimoli had watched for a while as we'd taken turns on the heavy bag, doing so much running commentary I finally asked if he were somehow live-streaming the whole thing.

"If you two pugs had gotten pointers from me when you were starting out," he said, "you coulda been contenders."

Hawk looked at me. "You think he's about to do Brando again?"

"Stella!" Henry yelled on his way out of the room, and I didn't have the heart to tell him it was from the wrong Brando movie.

"Been thinking," Hawk said.

"Never a bad thing."

"This all seem to be about what somebody thought Rita had, what somebody thought Tully had, what somebody must've even thought *you* had," he said. "And the reporter."

"Don't forget the esteemed Delores Thompson."

"Her, too," Hawk said. "Point being, whatever it is, it's not just something somebody wants, it's something they *think* is worth killing over."

"Something about money," I said. "That's what the head-banger was talking to the reporter about while he worked him over."

"So the question still is, what is it?" Hawk said. "And where is it?"

"That's two questions."

He fixed me with a baleful look.

"And if somebody still don't have it, it means it's still somewhere," Hawk said. "Maybe it was something Drummond had hid."

"Maybe somebody took it out of his safe-deposit box before Rita found out the box was empty," I said. "But I checked with the bank. The last person to access the box was Drummond himself."

"Maybe he had it there and moved it someplace else," Hawk said. "Re-hid it. Or maybe decided he don't trust banks."

"Do you?" I said.

Hawk smiled. "If they offshore."

"They thought Rita took something out, but she didn't," I said. "Which means she got shot for nothing. Who knows? Maybe it was Delores Thompson who found whatever it was."

"Let's ask her," Hawk said. "Oh, wait."

"Curiouser and curiouser," I said.

Hawk said, "You know Alice come up with that because she needed a new word to describe a whole bunch of confounding shit."

"You read *Alice's Adventures in Wonderland*?" I said.

"Pretended the White Rabbit was Black," Hawk said.

We planned to shower at Harbor and then go have breakfast at Pete's Dockside, on Channel Street, which had the best breakfast burritos in this part of town—perhaps the whole town.

"You think Drummond might have hid something in some place we haven't yet thought about?" Hawk said before we headed off to the locker room. "And then didn't get the chance to get at it 'fore they threw him in the water?"

"Rita said that Delores Thompson was the one who packed up Drummond's stuff from his apartment," I said. "Maybe she found something and kept it and only just now decided to do something with it. So maybe I'll call Rita later and ask her about that."

"Why not now?" Hawk said.

"She might still have company," I said. "That's why."

Now it was Hawk artfully raising an eyebrow.

"Chief Stone?" he asked.

"Uh-huh."

"Hope she don't pop no stitches," he said.

"Not sure that her physical state is the one we should be worried about," I said.

"Uh-huh," Hawk said.

SEVENTY-SIX

When I called Rita later in the day, she said that Delores Thompson had been the one to clean out Drummond's apartment before it was rented to the new tenants. After she'd done that, Delores had dropped off one box with Rita. Some of her clothes were in it, along with photographs of her and Drummond.

Rita said we could talk about all that later, she was on her way to a doctor's appointment for a new battery of tests and X-rays and an MRI, and would be unreachable at least until dinnertime.

"How are you getting to the hospital?" I asked.

There was the slightest hesitation on her end before she said, "Jesse."

Before I could respond to that she said, "Shut up." And hung up.

The snow that had been forecast for tonight had started to fall by then. I called Shannon Miles in Paradise for an update, and she explained to me how easy it could have been for Drummond to get away with being a fabulist the way George Santos had, after he got elected and before he got the boot from the House of Representatives.

"Maybe the school he really attended," I said, "was the University of Santos."

"He was smart enough, or maybe cunning enough, to know how little attention people pay to down-ballot races, especially in crowded fields like his was," she said. "And the fact is, not any of the people he was running against had the resources to do a whole lot of opposition research, even as they could see enough voters in Southie falling head over heels in love with him and would have been wasting their time."

Before she ended the call she said, "Any thoughts on when I can return to my so-called life?"

"Soon," I said.

"You feel like you're close?"

"I do," I said. "Though I'm not quite sure why."

She said, "When this is all over, I'd like to sit down with Rita, I've been meaning to mention that."

"I can make that happen," I said.

"How is she doing, by the way?" Miles asked.

"She's different," I said. "But in a good way."

I was about to make yet another trek to Marlborough Street when I had one more incoming call.

Unknown Caller

"Spenser here," I said. "Private investigations and snow removal."

No response.

"Hey," I said. "Anybody there."

I thought I could hear breathing, but nothing else.

Finally I heard this:

"It's Delores Thompson."

I realized I was standing.

"You have to come get me," she said.

I asked where she was.

"Nantucket," she said. "Rita Fiore's house."

SEVENTY-SEVEN

She said she was using a burner phone, and made me give her my word I wouldn't tell anybody that she was still alive, where she was, or even that she had called me, at least not yet. She said she would explain everything that needed explaining once I got to her.

But she said I needed to hurry, that there was a sleet storm blowing toward Nantucket and she was afraid they would stop running the car ferry from Hyannis before the last scheduled run for the boat at eight o'clock.

Then she told me again to hurry, and gave me the address, in a section of Nantucket on its south side, Tom Nevers Road. I'd always had a general idea of where Rita lived on the island, just not the exact location.

I gave her my word and planned to keep it. Despite the snow and the rush-hour traffic on 93 South, I finally managed to get one of the last spots on the seven-o'clock boat from Hyannis. I knew the ride generally took just over a couple hours, but there had been an announcement once we had pulled away from the terminal that it might take somewhat longer tonight.

While we made our way across the sound in heavy chop, I studied the map of Nantucket on my phone, and saw the route I would be taking on the way to Siasconset, taking the turn to Tom Nevers off Milestone.

To the place Drummond had called Neverland.

Maybe he was the kid who never grew up.

Or the street kid who grew up way too fast.

From the address, I could see that Rita's house would be close to the water but not directly on it, on one of the series of beach roads, like tributary roads.

The ride from the terminal to the south side ended up taking nearly an hour, because of the condition of the roads, especially once I got farther outside of town.

Even after I got off Milestone, I took at least three wrong turns on the beach roads, nearly losing control when the car went into a skid. The sleet was coming in sheets by then.

Eventually, despite the lack of visibility, I found 18 Tom Nevers. The high beams were like spotlights on what appeared to be a classic cedar-shingled Nantucket house, two stories, with a porch that stretched the length of the front.

There was a single light showing from the first level of the house. I nearly fell when I put my foot on the first step leading up to the porch, but maintained my balance.

I was about to use the knocker when the door opened, and Delores Thompson was standing in front of me, almost like a ghost.

"I didn't know who else to call," she said.

I told her I got that a lot, and followed her inside.

311

SEVENTY-EIGHT

She produced a bottle of Glenfiddich and poured a generous amount into a couple highball glasses.

She told me what Nick Drummond had told her when he and Rita were going around together about how Rita had no use for the place in the winter, or even after Labor Day most years. But that Drummond had often used the house when he needed to get away from his job and regroup.

Delores confirmed what Rita had already told me, that she had occasionally joined Drummond for working weekends in Nantucket, even in the winter, to basically hide from distractions and interruptions. Rita even had some kind of app on her phone that enabled her to remotely regulate the temperature, so that her pipes wouldn't freeze, and help her get by without having to pay a caretaker to look in on the place.

Delores Thompson spoke quickly, and earnestly, somehow acting as if these were absolute crucial facts.

I let her go on.

Neither one of us was going anywhere tonight. She had all the time she needed to explain to me how—and why—we'd ended up here, on this winter night.

"I had enough cash on hand when I ran," she said. "I used it to take a bus from South Station to Hyannis and then to get on the fast boat, the Hy-Line. Had enough money left for a taxi into town for supplies. I've been here ever since."

"Why did you run," I said, "and from whom?"

Then she was talking too fast again.

"I was sure he'd send someone to kill me," she said. "I have a nanny-cam in my apartment that you practically can't see even if you know it's there."

"Why a nanny-cam?"

She smiled sheepishly. "I used to have a dog. I wanted to make sure the woman I hired to walk him was actually doing it. Turned out she wasn't. And I never uninstalled it."

She shrugged. "Anyway, if someone is there, I get an alert. I saw him sitting there, waiting for me when I pulled into the lot. So I just got out, left the car where it was, and started walking until I got on the bus to South Station."

"Delores," I said. "Who sent somebody to kill you?"

"McManus," she said. "He had to have been tapping your phone. Or maybe mine. Because somebody knew I had found something, and the only one I told was you."

She went on for a long time then.

I tried not to interrupt her. The sleet and wind kept beating against the outside of the house. She told me that Drummond had told her that it was this side of the island that most got battered by storms, when storms would come off the ocean with this kind of sound and fury.

She admitted knowing that Nick Drummond was a fraud, almost from the beginning. But she had seen his potential, saw him as her ticket to the big time. Honestly thought he was going places. And was aware by then that some frauds could go almost as far as they wanted to in politics.

"Matt Vallone started to put things together after Nick won his Senate seat," she said. "Did Vallone tell you that?"

"There was a lot he didn't tell me," I said. "So what did Drummond do?"

"Bought him with access at first," she said. "But we both knew that wasn't going to last forever. And if Vallone wasn't figuring out how much lying Nick had done to get where he was, somebody else would eventually. And then somebody else after that. Like the dominoes that fell on George Santos. At that point, he decided to cash out."

"So you knew he wasn't just a fraud," I said. "He was basically a thief."

"What can I tell you? I was still blinded by the light," she said.

"And with whom did he cash out?" I said.

"With McManus," she said. "He was crazy for that land and willing to pay crazy money to make sure he got it, and not just to Nick."

"What changed?" I said. "Sounds to me like everything was working. For both of them."

"Nick got too greedy," she said. "Made up his mind that he was going to sell what he had on McManus for one final balloon payment. He called it principal balance at the end of a loan."

"He tell you exactly what he had?" I said.

She shook her head. "He said it was better I didn't know, but that it would be well worth it for McManus to pay, and that after then he was going to disappear. I told him it was too dangerous, as dangerous a game as he'd been playing all along. But he'd been getting away with stuff his whole life, and believed he would get away with this."

She started to cry then. "And then he died."

"Why didn't McManus come after you," I said, "as close as the two of you were?"

"Because I found out I could lie as well as Nick could when I had to," she said. "And I convinced McManus when he called me into his office that what Nick was doing, he'd done on his own."

"Did you ask if they'd completed their final transaction before Nick died?"

"It would have been like admitting I knew what Nick had planned," she said.

I drank. She drank.

"Why'd you call Mauro that day?"

"He'd told me that if I ever came up with something, he might be willing to pay for it," she said.

"I know," I said.

"Mauro told you?"

I nodded.

"Well, I was about to get greedy, too," she said. "And take him up on his offer. But I changed my mind."

Another gust of wind rattled Rita's house, shaking it enough that a piece of art on one of the walls came down, causing Delores to scream.

I had been patiently allowing her to tell it her way. At her speed. But decided it was now time for Delores Thompson to get to the main event.

"What did you find, Delores?" I said.

She reached into the side pocket of the oversized sweater she was wearing.

"This," she said.

She held up what looked like a flash drive.

"Where?"

"Nick's safe-deposit box," she said.

"Rita said the box was empty," I said.

"The other one," she said.

She smiled then, as if she were smiling at Nick Drummond.

"It turned out that the guy who said he didn't trust modern technology was lying through his teeth about that, along with so many other things," Delores Thompson said. "Because he kept more detailed financial records of the bribes than the Fed."

She said that the only reason she'd found out about the other box, at the Citizens Bank just up the street from 99 High, was because she'd gotten a bill asking if she wanted to renew it, since Drummond had put her name on the account along with his.

So she'd gone over there, accessed the box, and found the flash drive. Found a UPS store nearby that rented laptops and workstations. Opened up the file.

Saw what was on it.

"As soon as I did, I called you," she said. "But, as I said, Mc-Manus must have been tapping your phone, and heard my message, and sent one of his men to my apartment."

"Shit," I said. "Shit, shit, shit."

"What?"

"If they're still listening in on my phone, they had to hear you call me tonight and tell me where you were," I said. "It means that even if I did better getting here in this weather than they did, we need to get out of here. *Now.*"

But in the next moment, what could only have been a shotgun blew one hole in the front door, then another, and then the shooter was on his way through the door along with the storm.

SEVENTY-NINE

It was another big man, nearly as big as McManus's man Max. Or Mauro's driver. But not someone I recognized. He must have dropped the shotgun on the porch, because a Glock 9 was in his hand instead.

I realized then that I had never taken off my peacoat. My .38 was in my left-hand pocket. As I moved my hand in that direction the guy said, "Don't even think about it. Just take it out nicely, by the barrel, and toss it toward the door. If there's a single extra movement, I will shoot you now, and then her. And then maybe you again."

I took the gun out, gently and slowly, as told.

"Toss it over there," he said.

I did that, too, in the direction of the door in which he'd just blown a hole, before making his entrance.

"No mask tonight?" I asked.

"Shut up," he said.

He motioned for me to go sit next to Delores Thompson on the couch.

"For what it's worth," I said, "a lot of people know I'm here."

"Not unless you called them on another phone, hotshot," he said. "So let me explain how this is gonna play out from here. She hands over whatever it is she told you she has and then you two still get to be alive after she does."

"Or?" I said.

"Or I shoot you both and dump you in the snow and they find you sometime during the spring thaw," he said.

"Are you the one who shot Rita?" I asked. "Asking for a friend."

He kept the gun on me, ignoring my question.

"Where is it?" he said to Delores Thompson.

"In the bedroom," she said without hesitation.

"What is it?" the guy said.

"A flash drive."

Her eyes, very big, were on the gun, as if she were staring at the end of the big con that Nick Drummond had started a long time ago.

"I can go get it," she said.

"Yes, you can. But if you try anything, or even try to run in this weather, I *will* kill him and then do the same to you when I catch up with you. Which I will."

He grinned. "Unless you think you can swim for it," he added.

She put her hands up, as if in surrender.

"But if I hand over the flash drive, you'll really leave us alone," she asked.

"Yes," the guy said.

Maybe she knew he was lying to her the way she was lying to him. Lies on top of lies on top of more lies.

"Where's the bedroom?" he said.

"On the other side of the kitchen," she said, "facing the back of the house."

"Keep talking while you go get it," he said, "so I can hear you the whole time."

She did, talking about how she was walking through the kitchen and down a hall and into the bedroom. She said she was opening the drawer in the dresser, and that she was on her way back.

It was when she was walking back through the kitchen that the door blew wide open, and a combination of sleet and snow, with a howl, blew into the front room.

The long, hard winter finally doing me some good.

Startled by the noise, the guy turned his head just long enough for me to get my second gun, the one he obviously hadn't considered I might have on me—*my* Glock—out of my right-hand pocket.

I was firing then as I shifted onto my left side on the couch, putting the first bullet high into his chest as the big guy fired back, into the cushions behind me. Delores Thompson was screaming again.

I managed to steady my shooting hand and put a second bullet into him, nearly in the same spot where the first one had hit him, like I was grouping shots at the range.

He managed to somehow get off one last, wild shot.

But it caught Delores Thompson low in the chest before he fell forward and went still.

I was kneeling over Delores Thompson then, taking off my

coat and pressing it to the blood spreading through her sweater, telling her to hang on, trying to keep her alive, wondering how fast the paramedics on the small island could get here in weather like this, not even sure where they might be coming from.

"Perfect storm," I said to myself, barely able to hear my own words over the sound of the night.

EIGHTY

Delores Thompson survived being shot the way Rita had survived being shot, been transferred the next day to the Gun Violence Unit of the Critical Care Center. She was even being treated by Dr. Harman.

The time I hadn't spent with her at the Nantucket Cottage Hospital I had spent with the island police, and the detective from the local barracks of the State Police, a woman named Kilcullen. There had been no ID found on the shooter at Rita's house, or any record of his prints in the system. It turned out he had also taken a taxi from the boat terminal after arriving on the eight-o'clock boat. Maybe he had planned on taking my car back to town after he had finished off Delores Thompson and me, which he most certainly would have done.

One more ghost.

Kevin McManus had waited a couple days before calling me.

He had not been contacted by law enforcement since the shooting at Rita's house, or read about himself in *The Boston Globe*.

But had waited long enough.

Once he had me on the phone, he got right to it.

"Let's make a deal," he said.

"Your specialty," I said.

"What do you have?"

"A record, almost breathtaking in its detail, of every bribe you ever made through Nick Drummond," I said. "It's funny, if you think about it. A lot of people thought Drummond might be writing a book. Well, yeah, McManus. One filled with wire transactions."

He didn't say anything at first.

"Well, if you were going to do something with what you have, you would have done it already," he said finally. "Which means you must want something in return. And by the way? Don't even think about taping this conversation, I'll know if you try. I've got better phone people working for me than the government has."

"I bet."

"I'm going to need some proof," he said.

I was prepared for that. I put him on speaker, told him I was sending just one page of the file by text.

"Okay," he said about a minute later. "*Okay.*"

He paused.

"Tell me what you want," McManus said.

"To sell it to you the way Drummond was going to," I said.

"How much?" he said, without hesitation.

"One million, cash," I said. "Considering what I have on you, and how much the Feds would like to get their hands on it, it might be the deal of a lifetime, even for you."

"How will I know you didn't make a copy?" he said.

"Listen," I said. "I don't want to spend the rest of my life looking over my shoulder. And don't want to end up like Drummond. Or Brian Tully. Or nearly bleeding out the way Rita and Delores Thompson did. Just know that if anything ever does happen to me, someone *will* inherit the one copy I do plan to keep."

"And who might that be?"

"Hawk," I said. "Think of him as the beneficiary of this particular life insurance plan. But he won't just turn it over to the authorities. He will find you and kill you dead."

There was one more silence, as Kevin McManus, the dealmaker, considered the deal points he'd just been presented.

I waited.

"You got it," he said. "And we're going to do it old-school. A bag full of cash."

"All I need to know is where and when."

"Widett Circle tonight, nine o'clock," he said.

"Wouldn't you prefer somewhere a little more discreet?" I asked.

"Nah," he said. "It'll be a way of bringing the whole thing full circle." I heard him chuckle. "*Widett* Circle."

"Fine with me," I said.

"And if you try to get cute and bring somebody along, I'll know, smart guy," McManus said. "Just you and me in the ring, so to speak."

"Fine with me," I said again.

"Just like that?" he said.

"Just like that," I said, and ended the call.

Hawk was in my office with me, close enough that even before I put McManus on speaker, he'd heard both sides of the conversation.

"You know you're probably walking into a trap," he said.

I grinned.

"Not just probably," I said.

"But you just got to look the man in the eye," Hawk said. "Don't you?"

"Yeah," I said. "Yeah, I do."

"For you," Hawk said.

"For Rita," I said.

EIGHTY-ONE

What McManus did bring with him was one of those wireless wands you could use to make sure someone wasn't wearing some kind of listening device.

When the wand started to vibrate as he moved it down my coat, I told him it had merely picked up the flash drive in my pocket.

"Show me," he said.

I held it out for him to see. When he reached for it, I snatched it back and put it away,

"Patience," I said. "But I have to say, Kevin, that if you're doing that kind of sweep on me, trust really is gone from this relationship."

"It was never there to begin with," McManus said.

He was still wearing a sling, I could see it underneath his open topcoat.

He said, "You show me yours, I'll show you mine. Like I said: Old-school."

"A school we both attended," I said.

The night was actually mild, the sky clear and full of stars, the moon like a spotlight.

McManus made a gesture with his good arm that tried to take in all of Widett Circle. "Master of all I survey," he said.

"Not the first time you've felt that way," I said.

"And not the last," he said.

Then he said, "So let's have it."

I reached into my pocket and felt what was inside.

Then stopped.

"Not yet," I said.

"For fuck's sake."

"Patience," I said again.

"Have it your way," he said. "I've waited this long. I guess I can wait a little longer."

He reached down and touched the duffel bag, opening it enough so I could see the money inside.

"One time when I was coming up," he said, "guy told me that there were few problems in this world that couldn't be solved by a bag full of cash."

"Words to live by," I said. "Or die by, as the case may be."

"We are going to have to trust each other on something," he said. "You trust the money is all there. I trust that the only copy you made doesn't come into play until death do us part."

"Like I said," I told him. "I want you out of my life as much as you want me out of yours."

Now I looked around at what would officially be his land tomorrow morning.

"But before we conclude our business," I said, "I've got a few questions."

"That wasn't part of our deal," he said.

"Humor me," I said.

"Consider yourself humored."

"Why Rita?" I said.

He grinned.

"We're speaking hypothetically?"

"Of course."

"Well, say I knew a guy at the Longfellow Bank," he said. "And he called about a safe-deposit box I didn't even know Drummond had. And I'm thinking that maybe something like what's in your pocket might have been inside that box. But then my guy checked after she had left the bank that day, and he said the box was empty. And—still talking hypothetically—I figured maybe she had taken something that could kill *me*."

"But it was never there," I said. "Which means you had her shot for nothing."

"Somebody did," McManus said. "Now are we done?"

"Almost," I said. "Did you really have a sharpshooter shoot you to take suspicion away? And hire an old Broz guy to shoot me, so I'd think it was Mauro who hired him?"

"Wow," he said. "Those would be ballsy moves, wouldn't they? And pretty creative, if you ask me."

Still grinning at me by the light of the moon, cat–canary style.

"Come on, *now* are we done?"

"Just one more," I said. "How would somebody drown Nick Drummond and make it look like an accident?"

I knew how. But I wanted to hear him tell it, by the light of the moon.

"Still hypothetically?"

"Just the two of us, sitting here chopping it up."

"Let's say that hypothetically a guy who'd already been paid, and fucking handsomely, tried one last shakedown. And the person he was trying to shake down had had just about enough of his shit. So maybe that person would have a guy like that drowned in his bathtub, using some kind of velvet handcuffs like you read about so they wouldn't leave any marks, and then throw him in the drink after he was already dead. Hypothetically."

"Of course," I said.

Now he slid the duffel bag in my direction and stuck out his good hand again.

"The goods, please," he said.

I gave the man what he wanted.

"Now, then," he said. "That almost concludes our business."

"Almost?" I said.

He pointed to the middle of my chest then, and a red dot suddenly appeared on the outside of my peacoat.

"You were probably wondering why I was doing so much sharing," McManus said.

EIGHTY-TWO

S orry, schmuck," Kevin McManus said, grinning at me. "But now you're the one who's no longer of any use to me."

But then I was grinning at him. Like I was suddenly the master of all I surveyed.

"You sure about that, *schmuck*?" I said, stepping hard on the last word.

And pointed at his chest, where the red dot had shifted onto him.

Jesse Stone came walking out of the night then, toward the bleachers, the reflex light attached to the top of the automatic handgun in his hand.

"I love these laser deals, no shit," Stone said.

"Where's the guy who belonged to that gun?" I said.

"With Hawk," Stone said. "Turns out to be a Vegas guy. But suddenly chatty as hell."

"What the fuck!" McManus yelled, for lack of something

more clever. He was staring at Jesse Stone. "Who's this asshole?" McManus asked me.

"A cop," I said.

Then I took back the recorder I'd just handed over to him, one that wasn't a flash drive after all.

I held it up and showed it to Stone.

"You get all that?" I asked.

"Chapter and verse," Stone said.

McManus shifted his attention now from Jesse Stone to the recorder.

"Where's the flash drive?" he said.

"I assume with Shannon Miles," I said. "About to go on the air with it at her old station."

I shrugged.

"That's until she hands it over to one of her friends at the Department of Justice," I said.

Then I told Kevin McManus, the king rat, that he had to admit, the best liar of all had turned out to be me.

EIGHTY-THREE

Susan, Stone, Rita, and I were having dinner a few nights later at Grotto, a downstairs Italian restaurant on Bowdoin Street that was about a five-minute walk from Rita's home.

Rita had already announced, as soon as we were seated, that she and Jesse Stone were not back to being a couple. Just in case anybody was wondering.

"None of us were," I said.

"Liar," Rita said.

"I lied so well to McManus," I said, "now I can't help myself."

The scandal surrounding Kevin McManus, and the charges leveled against him and a handful of members of the City Council and State Senate—the chosen few—continued to play out in the media, now that *The Globe* had piggybacked on the story Shannon Miles had broken on Channel 7.

McManus had been released on a bond far more expensive than the cash that had been in that duffel bag, which had turned out to be a million, exactly. Rita had informed us that even be-fore McManus had been taken out of his home in Brookline in handcuffs—not velvet, in his case—he'd had the nerve to reach out to Edward Oakes and ask about possible representation from his firm.

"No, he did not," Susan said.

"Oh, yes, he did," Rita said.

"How did my friend Eddie Oakes respond?" Susan asked.

"He told him, with great delight, to go jump in the ocean," Rita said. "Preferably in South Boston."

By then I had distributed a big chunk of the money from the duffel to the Department of Children and Families, and smaller amounts to Doug Haskins's reelection campaign, Brian Tully's family, and to Hawk and Vinnie Morris.

Some of it had even gone to the Paradise Police Department.

"You like Robin Hood," Hawk had said, "'cept for the tights."

"Taking from the rich," I said.

"With both damn hands," Hawk said.

The MBTA had announced the day before that the Widett Circle land was going to be used for new railyards after all.

"So Mauro loses in the end, too," Susan said.

"Pity," I said.

Once drinks had been served, Diet Coke for Stone and wine for the rest of us, Rita announced that there would be no mention of Nick Drummond tonight. We all honored that re-quest.

When I had made the reservation, I had asked if we might ask Shannon Miles to join us.

"I told him no," Rita said after relaying my request to the group, "that I had enough friends. Male *and* female."

"Does that mean I made the cut?" Susan said.

"You got in just under the wire, Doc," Rita said.

Then she gave a familiar toss to all that red hair, and laughed a throaty laugh, and if she wasn't all the way back to being herself, this would have to do for now.

ACKNOWLEDGMENTS

I always must thank David and Daniel Parker, who have allowed me to continue their father's work, now with Spenser; Esther Newberg, the caretaker of the public trust that is the work of Robert B. Parker; my patient editor, Tarini Sipahimalani; and of course my boss at Putnam, Ivan Held.

Special thanks this time to Catherine Carlock and Kevin Cullen of *The Boston Globe*, and to former Connecticut State Senator Will Haskell.

I was helped mightily, as always, by Chief John Fisher of the Bedford (Mass.) Police, as much by his expertise as his generosity.

Finally, a shout-out to some friends who helped me land the plane: Ziggy and Nancy Alderman, Peter Gethers and—last but certainly not least—the great James Brendan Patterson.